DEMOLITION NIGHT

DEMOLITION NIGHT

ROSS BARKAN

TOUGH POETS PRESS
ARLINGTON, MASSACHUSETTS

Front cover photo: Fred Jewell, AP
Back cover photo: Vanessa Ogle

ISBN 978-0-692-07138-0
Tough Poets Press
49 Churchill Avenue, Floor 2
Arlington, Massachusetts 02476
U.S.A.

www.toughpoets.com

For Vanessa, and my mother and father.

"The weather will not change."

Henry Miller, *Tropic of Cancer*

1

1979

Welcome back.

Archie dug around for a booger and flicked it at the wallpaper, watching it vanish. Dull gray-green on dull gray-yellow. Little elephants, Republicans or Indians, were patterned on the paper in diamond formation. More kitsch nonsense from the alleged genius. What went through Truncheon's mind when he picked that crap out in Sag Harbor last summer, what macro and micro swill coursed through it, to put it up on *these* walls, God be damned.

Another Saturday. Archie opened his mouth to speak.

"Watching. Shhh."

"What are you, will you *turn that off—*"

Here came that sweet, sick tune, dulcet to some ears and dastardly to others, virulent to anyone who was trying to be a serious adult human being in America. Truncheon settled down deep in his armchair, reverent in the screenlight, grinning like a stoner.

"Welcome back, your dreams were your ticket out, welcome back to that same old place you laughed about…" the television purred, "…welcome back, welcome back, welcome back…"

"Jeezuz," Archie said. He was forgetting why he even bothered coming here, up to the prewar colossus of West End Avenue of the Upper West Side. Archie was itching, scratching, feeling red flares all over his skin, madness made real, his organs doing a rumba—he shouldn't wear trench coats after April 1st. Mistake one, one of many, but he did it anyway. He needed to make the transition to seersucker, though he didn't know anyone who snipped the vein of crime in this city in such fabric.

"Jeezuz," Archie said louder, trying to belch the word. "This fucking Travolta. Why do you even bother?"

"Shhh."

"I'm gonna read the paper. You got any papers?"

"Shhh."

He watched dimple-chinned Travolta—black hair in frosty waves, that disco-hippie curl—cavorting in tough-guy Brooklyn denim through the classroom of broken dreams. There was Kotter, a.k.a Gabe Kaplan, mustachioed and Jewish afroed—Archie's tolerance for TV Jews was rather low, even if both his parents regularly called each other wastrels and dung heaps in Yiddish—begging Travolta, a.k.a Barbarino, to *behave*. Archie had a theory: Truncheon only loved this show because of the Sweathogs. It was in the name. Truncheon was obsessed with names, the ultimate signifiers, and imbued each one, in his books and beyond, with absurd meaning. It was a half-wit high school English teacher's dream. *See, little Jimmy, in Ronald Truncheon's Goodnight, Retrograde, the protagonist was named Lucius Imbroglio ironically because he was a pacifist.* There was something in Sweathogs that piqued Truncheon.

"*News? Post?* I don't want the *Times*. I don't want that vocabulary Saturday before noon."

"Shhh."

Fine. Archie did what he wanted to do 30 seconds ago and turned away from the TV, stomping in his old Converses to the poorly-named *coffee table* where the papers, some as old as three weeks, vied for irrelevancy with Truncheon's *Life* magazines and piles of faint white napkins he stole, in many successive trips, from the diner two blocks south of here. Archie stooped, shoving aside the old, begging for the new. Truncheon got the papers delivered so they should be here, because he would slip them all in this heap and pluck them out later in the afternoon just as his ex-wife Luanne called from Stony Brook to howl aimlessly at him, conveniently forgetting the *Retrograde* royalties that made her howling fiscally possible.

Truncheon always read the news when Luanne was on the phone, timing the deep-think pieces on Carter's missteps and the Soviets' aggressions to when her inanity rose to its zenith, blubbering enough *hmm'm honeys* to keep her satiated before Tyrone, their only son, returned from baseball practice, where he was quickly becoming the best pitcher in a school of potato farmers. Archie met Tyrone once, many years ago, and thought him a consummate dumbfuck.

It was a Saturday, and the papers were delivered, so, so…

"Where's the *News*? I want to read the *News!*"

Truncheon, again: "Shhh."

"Oh, fuck off."

Truncheon should be telling *him* to fuck off. But rage wasn't his way. Never was. Not at Roslyn High, not at Columbia, not on a downtown-bound IRT one winter morning nine years ago when he had to hide his mustache in a vagrant's fedora to avoid the reporter who had completed the most thorough and numbing Finding Ronald Truncheon reportage to date. Cool as a cucumber, as the kids say. That's our Truncheon.

Archie snatched one more bit of scripted dialogue, Epstein wailing about detention to Kotter, before he dove back into his search. The papers, the papers.

Sometimes Truncheon would violate the order of his life. He would misplace items and curios for the sake of misplacing them. He would devise riddles to solve. His paranoia had cooled since his *Retrograde* days while Archie's, inversely, had grown, but he was sure to always be throwing *someone* off his trail. Laundry purposefully done on Saturday instead of Sunday. Rent paid, all cash in a grubby envelope, 11 days late to 12 days early. Cigarette brands in perpetual rotation—Lucky Strikes, Marlboros, Chesterfields—with no discernable preference for one or the other, except for the rare times he would exclaim to Archie, who would be back from one his "sweeps," that Lucky Strikes were the *only* cigarettes for this American century.

So now he was throwing Archie off the trail, hiding today's papers somewhere else, and forcing his old high school chum to dig like an archeologist through this detritus rife with nothing. He muttered sweet fucks to himself, one for each time his mother Arla shoved a bar of soap in his mouth from ages 5 to 17, and felt his fingertips rolling in grime. They were not on the table.

"They're not on the table!"

Truncheon, on cue: "Shhh."

In high school, he was just Trunch. Big blocky kid, straight A's, lettering in no sports, scribbling villanelles in marbled notebooks that no one would ever read. He spent the rest of his time, from what Archie could tell, jacking off and working on The Book. Trunch the Lunch, as he was known during a fat phase that lasted from 7th to 9th grade, was always talking about The Book to anyone who mistakenly wandered into his vast airspace. This was in a high school that literally only gave a shit about Elvis, *Playboy*, and automobiles, all kinds except those that were "square." He'd sidle up to someone like Epiphany Slater, the top twirler on the squad, and start rambling about The Book, and if she wanted to see a chapter when he was done with the edits. Archie, then known as London (his last name) or Bridge (yeah, a Nassau kid has the IQ of the Long Island Expressway), was in a faux-jock phase, manning right field for the Bulldogs and *beseeching* Hashem for a growth spurt to make him, at long last, the best high school baseball player on the Island; standing five-foot-five and batting in the mid .300's wasn't his destiny, he told himself in the pocket of his pungent locker, except it was—he would bat .341 junior year, his best year, never grow beyond fix-six, and That Was That. Meanwhile, Trunch was muttering about The Book, telling *him*, or anyone who would pretend to listen, that this was the equivalent of giving birth to a child who would grow to be immortal, rather than an insurance salesman-family man who would die in his early 80's of Natural Causes. When The Book came, they would all see. Trunch never said this menacingly. It was matter-of-fact, like Epiphany Slater giving the best head or Archie London dreaming of snagging Bobby Thomson's liner outtathefuckingsky and the Dodgers, instead, winning the pennant.

"Trunch the Lunch," Archie said out loud, stalking into the kitchen. The words were magic. They would find the papers. "Trunch the Lunch!"

Truncheon: "Shhh."

"You shush me one more time, one more goddamn time, and if I don't find my papers—"

Wait! There, a newspapery ear peeking from the stove, Jesus, yes, *there*. Archie ripped open the stove and found today's *Post*, alone, tucked where a Thanksgiving turkey should be. Rumpled, like it had been read, except it was in an oven. Good one, Trunch.

"Good one, Trunch the Lunch. I'm gonna enjoy eating your paper."

He wasn't loud enough to earn a shhh. He took the paper, walked over to the dining room, threw his feet up on the table and started to read. This would take him through the afternoon until nightfall, when he'd be doing farebeater duty. This would be easy because there was always a kid or 20 jumping on Saturday nights. He had an itinerary: start south, man Stillwell for an hour or so, and then rumble all the way up to Atlantic, where he'd patrol until 4 a.m. and then ride back to his own fleabag to sleep it off. Now that he had his *Post*, he could get excited. He could drown out Travolta and Horshack and go line-by-line through the tabloid, looking for clues. He didn't read between the lines. He read *through* the lines. In every sentence, evidence of the State's leviathan grip on the lone man, its manufacturing of red herrings to distract from the greater Truths which even Archie was not yet ready to fully formulate. Truncheon did so in The Book, what would become *Goodnight, Retrograde*, but even he conceded that 1,124 pages was not enough to reach the conclusions he needed to reach, and certainly not at the tender age of 23, when his magnum opus arrived in bookstores. Archie had read it three times.

The people Archie once ran with were convinced the Soviets would control the world by the end of the millennium. They were all lefties-turned-John Birchers, sniffing Communism in every greasy spoon and bookshop they wandered into, sure that everyone from Farah Fawcett to Carter was in on the Red conspiracy. They thought America was losing the struggle. They did not love capitalism and America as much as fear the Soviets and their reverence for a monolith State dictating all facets of society, down to your toilet paper and condom wrappers. They suspected popular culture—shows like *Welcome Back Kotter*—were elements of the "pinko-Jew cabal," and said this straight to Archie, who was a Jew by parentage but would not take offense. The Boston *Red* Sox playing the Cincinnati *Reds* in the World Series nearly drove Big Byrd, one of the boys, to declare immediate and open war. Which meant leaving the shadows to blow up a savings bank, or something.

They were, as Archie had insisted, fucking wrong. It was one of his missions to lead them to water and make them drink. Right now, they were sucking on sand in the desert and calling it Pepsi Cola.

"The Soviets are a distraction," he told Big Byrd, again, last week. They were shooting pool in Grumbling's, the worst pool hall in Bay Ridge.

"That's what they want you to think, Bridge. They have you brainwashed."

"You spend all your time on Russia and the Eastern bloc, you forget about your own backyard. You let Uncle Sam mug you."

"Better him in my pockets than Russkis. Always."

"Look, the U.S.S.R is just a pawn here, running misdirection. It's a distraction."

"Distraction *for who*?"

The great question that would force him into unwanted silence. He could not say. Even Ronald Truncheon, literary master, could not say, and he was regarded as oracular at most northeast liberal arts schools with functioning English departments. This would be Archie's quest for the remainder of his days, and what he could never find out when he was another stooge in the New York Police Department. They kept him from finding the answer.

Archie started at the back of the paper on the sports, Travolta's voice thankfully fading. He was still a sucker for the sports section, even though it was a waste of time. He never followed the Dodgers out to Los Angeles. Never adopted another team. Fuck the Yankees, fuck the Mets. Piniella hit a two-run homer and the Yankees beat Baltimore last night. The Mets, otherwise hopeless, got a nice start from Swan and won too. The Yankees *Post* columnist, Barry

Limegrass, said the Bronx Zoo had a good chance to win a third pennant in a row. The Mets, on the other hand, would never be good again. Like his old cop nemesis Jacko might add, Noo Yawk City.

Nothing in the papers today. Nothing to tell him anything, to bring him closer to the truth. No dent in the enigma. A train stuck on the Willets Point platform, a child in the Bronx killing his grandmother, a Brooklyn assembly-man going out into the street to fill in his own district's potholes, a dead minke whale washing up on Brighton Beach, three dead in Washington Heights, gang shootout. Nada. No clues. Archie set the paper down. He ought get back home. Truncheon was a lost cause today anyway. After *Kotter* there was the damn Saturday afternoon movie and he'd be at that til sunset when Archie would be out doing his sweeps and patrols.

He picked up the paper and pantomimed reading. He was thinking, eyes blank.

"I'm going home," he announced to Truncheon, straining to be heard over the roar of what was that, which show, *Good Times*? Yes, that sounded like Jimmy Walker.

Papers in arm, he strode into the living room, narrowing his eyes into little pistol slits and clearing his throat as loudly as possible. "I'm *going*."

"Patrol, eh?"

"Stillwell. You know it."

Truncheon's back was to him, his love and attention on the TV.

"Patrol, yes. You remind me of someone, you know what, with these patrols."

"One of your 348 characters in *Goodnight, Retrograde*, I know."

"Yes, yes. Anyway, give me a ring tonight from the scene and let me know, well, how the scene is. If you see anyone, I don't know, *interesting*."

"I'll be note-taking."

"Very good. Well, at some point Luanne is due to call and then that will be a row. I do miss Mexico. I should go back. Such a place."

"Easier to be a recluse there."

"Yes, but their sense of, I don't know, proportion is so limited. I need American enormity at the end of the day."

Archie fingered the door knob. "See you later."

"Save the papers, too. I'd like to catch up on today's news, tomorrow."

"Okay, you nut."

He shut the door and headed out to the lobby. Sternweiss, who was probably a fanatic SS man during the War and had now reformed himself as an Upper West Side doorman, shoved down his nudie mag and waved hello. Archie gave a tight wave back. The evening was navy and wet, so dark and cloudless to make a convincing argument, to him at least, of sunlight as a Platonic myth. But this was fine, this would work. It would bring the scum to the surface, and he would stamp them out, single file.

"A good night for Vengeance," he said, cutting between the raindrops.

2

21st Century

He was the first superman—this he knew.

Two measurable powers so far, flight and kinetic blasts from his pores, hued red-gold like an anime hero's. There was no theoretical limitation on either, or none that he could deduce. The blasts sapped energy, but no more than if he ran a mile on a high school track. The flight raised his heart rate to 85 bpm. He thought he could fly as high as there was oxygen that would allow him to breathe. There was no increased strength—yet—and his vision lacked heat, as well as the ability to see through the cement of his bedroom wall. Two powers were enough anyway, an unmitigated success for his experiments, and proof of his superiority and the need to follow the dictum of Uncle Ben: with great power comes great responsibility.

Quentin Stellar, with $12 billion stashed into a trust fund, took his Gaggle in his crackling hands (ease your anger, ease the heat to standard biothermal temperature) and began to think through his Manifesto. There would be several drafts, he promised himself. All drafts would be written on an analog keyboard of the early century variety—and would not be dictated or thought-streamed into a Gaggle. What hypocrisy that would be, otherwise. It would be like leading the revolution with an army of brobots. It would be like using Gaggle to overthrow Gaggle, as well as the rest of the technocracy, the oligarchy, the slave-drivers.

If he told his father, the great Sam Stellar, about his powers, his father would see dollar signs. How to monetize this? How to boost the net worth of the Stellar clan ever so slightly? His father hadn't worked a day in 20 years, not since Gaggle acquired Bleater for $58 billion and ensured millennia of Stellars would have enough wealth to procure a Third World country as a belated Christmas present. These days, Sam gave online lectures and "advised" start-ups on how to best not lose money, doing all of this from the comfort of his beachfront Amagansett estate. He'd message the three Stellar children—Quentin, Ella, and Vic—on occasion, mostly recycling witticisms learned from Ent buddies on the golf course. Sam, of course, was a very poor golfer who did not know it.

All it took was a tweak of his genome. To think, had he channeled this effort into app-building for Gaggle, he could have added 10 billion or so to his net worth. Tonight, if he weren't flying to the Trojan Tower, he could be at a party, either a sedate soiree with Clamidia's people on the rooftop deck or Hans Burger's crew at Le Sol de Don. How easy it would be. Call Pater, Mater, tell them you're ready at last to join the family business, and stop playing around with your chemistry sets.

"Why," Sam Stellar would begin one of his many tortuous sentences, "when I was *your age*, Quentin, we were making billions, hand over fist in the Silicon wave, laying the foundations for the prosperity and equality and equanimity, the peace, that we now enjoy, doing my part for the GDP, presidential medal of freedom work really, though it seems to get one of those you need to go over to the sand dunes and get shot by one of those men in, what do you call it, a turban or hijab or is that what women wear, I don't really know but the point is, your mother and I had *high hopes* for our first son and to just go and take the advantages in this world that you were given, and well, to not make them *more advantageous* seems criminal to me, and I will not tolerate this loafing much longer—it's too much theory, dickering around with genomes and physics, I mean, tell me, Quentin, how much do you make from the writing of a physics textbook, if that is really your goal—"

Quentin would explain this was not his goal. Father, unimpeded, would go on.

"Let me just say, you're still young, not yet 30, though time is ticking away: studies show your mental energy peak, when neurons are firing at their greatest, is between the ages of 22 and 27 and you are at that cusp—like I said, at your age, I was into my fifth or ninth billion…what you need to focus on Quentin, is developing an app you can sell to a subsidiary of Gaggle—"

"Right, that's what I need to do, feed the *beast*."

"Do you know how many premiums out there would kill for your opportunity, your advantages? You don't just want to be living off the trust forever."

"I hardly withdraw from it! Hardly! I live off my own earnings."

"That little paltry salary you draw from the idiot college can hardly be called an earning. Teaching premiums that two plus two equals four."

"It's more than that, dad."

At this point Father would be immersed in his Gaggle, transitioning to his Gaggle voice: flat rather than sharp, softer, prone to more "yeahs" and "uhs" to plug the gaps between thoughts. Quentin hated the Gaggle voice, just as he hated Gaggle and all the economy that had long been subject to its whims. To Father and all the children of the Gaggle generation, they viewed Gaggle as the superpower in a sea of pygmies, a few of the larger ones classified as the Ents and the rest—the trash in Father's eyes, the 90 percent that were not Ents, that lacked the net worth to join the life-long club—were the premiums. The Ents were a club with real *bennies*, as his chum Francis at the community college would say: irrevocable voting rights, access to executive level positions at Fortune 500 companies, graduate school, and the better women. His Father's generation was the first to enjoy the full Ent experience. It was in his youth that the stratification began and America, in a sense, became more honest with itself. Reading about that era of history, Quentin had to admire it in a sick way—here was the end of the lie, all men created equal, and the birth of a new credo: some equal, some not, and we'll make sure we know who is who.

Of course, the argument could be made that the first Ent to unlock the potential of the human genome and acquire superpowers was proof of the 21st century's underlying thesis: the superior will rise, the inferior will fall, and *let's all just chill out already*. A snarky kid could easily point out that the ascendance of Quentin Stellar was only a further argument for a de facto caste system to ensure a degree of social harmony, hence why Ents rule and premiums drool— or do all the work that's icky.

Quentin walked over to his window 20 stories up, overlooking Water Street. His father wasn't totally wrong. Quentin did live off his trust fund money, or at least used a crumb to purchase this tony studio in the heart of SoFiDieBeca. He surveyed the scene: Wednesday night, 9 p.m., happy Ents out for fresh air, jamming cafes, boutiques, twee sandwich shops, and "rustic" bars, gaggling and bleating and slacking and twaking and pinging or, in rare instances, using their mouths to make words into English that would be audible to a friend, who would return the favor with his own English. He heard a smattering of Mandarin too, the language once thought to have been destined to become the world's *lingua franca*. The Chinese implosion changed that. In that time just before Quentin's birth, Ent parents were desperately enrolling their children in Mandarin schools and courses, training them for the Chinese takeover that they professed to fear but in fact welcomed because their little precious ones would be so well prepared. The takeover was permanently postponed, TBD, perhaps it would be a 22nd century happening, so the kiddies who had been so wonderfully equipped were left with a second language to mutter among themselves, the equivalent of a pig Latin the unhip adults, now well into latter middle-age, and young guns like Quentin, born too late for the Chinese paranoia, wouldn't understand.

He took stock of SoFiDieBeca, a yuppie Elysian Fields. As the New York real estate market yo-yo'ed, enjoying sonic booms and silent busts, the enclaves of Downtown held their status as prime Ent acreage, safe deposits for their foreign and domestic cash. In each modular, glass-boxed monolith, lobbies smoky with e-cigarette exhaust from the small herd of brobots purchased to glam up the glum scenery, there was a potential tax shelter or at least a nest egg for the next boom. Buy a studio, flip a studio, profit, and repeat. Quentin, of course, was interested in other things.

The neighborhood's acronym was a realtor's dream. South of the Financial District, east of Tribeca, all landfill. Allegedly storm surge-proof.

From the window, looking north, Quentin could see Gaggle's sepulchral downtown building. It did not distinguish itself in any particular way from the cityscape. In a line of view that included the Woolworth Building and the Dinkins Municipal Building, it sat diagonally, a mere 21 stories, mostly server space and rec areas, along with a dock for the brobots and penthouse for Ent executives. Father consulted for Gaggle, along with several other entities tangentially and directly related to the behemoth, and several times Quentin had gone with him to Gaggle HQ. The building looked like it housed absolutely nothing of consequence.

But he needed to work now. For fun, just before getting down to business, he vaporized his coffee mug, a gift from Lorelai. Father wouldn't like that because Lorelai was a daughter of one of his angel investor friends, brimming with daughter-in-law potential. Her eyes were the color of dishwater and her ass, quite frankly, was too flat, but this was not why Quentin enjoyed vaporizing the mug.

He enjoyed vaporizing it because it was a first, though relatively small step, toward the hope he intended to bring to the United States of America.

Great men are needed to lead great movements. Quentin long ago subscribed to this governing principle of history as a great soupy mess that only a select few, benevolent and wise, could cook into a proper meal to nourish the planet. With his experiments a success, and his powers unlocked with no discernible side effects (flying did make him mildly dizzy, but wouldn't it make anyone?), he was unquestionably a great man fit to lead. If America was to be saved, meritocracy must be restored and the caste system, championed by the likes of Father, must be eviscerated. Only a great man could unite such a fractured landscape, demonstrating through his sheer greatness that he was worthy of undivided attention. With superhero movies among the few that could still qualify as a "blockbuster" come summertime, why couldn't Quentin Stellar, a Bleater scion who could leap Gaggle HQ in a single bound, get their attention?

Yes, yes. He made heat lightning in his hands. An orb of energy that could blow up a car engine glowed in his elegant palms, now curled like clam shells. He would thoughtsync his Gaggle into the cloud and all the devices would hear him. He would speak as he rose through the nighttime, an exclamation point against the LED-certified light, arms outstretched in imitation of unreal heroes everywhere. He was ready to lead. He was never ready to make money, serve Gaggle, please father, or fuck Lorelai. Lorelai could never arouse him, yet this supposed failure would be blamed *on him*: how he, as a man, could not uphold his bargain in the phallocracy with a firm hard one to make her purr. He hated how she scrunched her eyes, one more closed than the other, and cocked her head like she was trying to empty it of water. His flaccid member would be a symbol of what he, and therefore a more just and moral future, could offer to her.

"I am Quentin Stellar," he said to no one, puffing out his chest.

He would not fly in disguise. This had been decided. He took a drink out of the fridge, an IPA that ran $32 a bottle, and sipped. He would fly as Quentin and hide nothing, because justice does not slink in the shadows. He sipped again. This would be the first time he had flown over a metropolis, not in an upstate backwoods away from prying eyes, his shirtsleeves gliding among (what he thought were) peregrine falcons. His heart beat in four-four time. No, no, he was not nervous—his nerves were plenty steady. He envisioned a future chronicler noting his *sangfroid*. No, he was not doing this for the biographers, the venerable legacy Father's ilk coveted like Lorelai hungered for him.

He sat. He stood. He adjusted his tie—burgundy, Wagonwright brand— and suit jacket, straightening creases near his shoulders. Fly in style. People, even Ents, dressed so slovenly today…he still shuddered at the "member cutout" trend of the last decade, when men's pants were tailored to flash the tip of the penis, preferably (and expensively) pierced, or even the translucent phase five or so years later, when being able to see everything was preferable to nothing. The irony, he believed, was that the illusion of sexual liberation was proffered as a substitution for actual liberation, with sexual liberation functioning as a mere commodity and nothing more, like a Gaggle watch. Well, one good thing about universal Gaggle ownership would be his ability to speak to *every-one*. Universal ownership, so onerous and retrogressive to him just a day or two ago, would now be perhaps his greatest asset as he flew through the air.

He would have his soapbox. Maybe start typing that manifesto later tonight.

Intelligence was only valued as much as you could successfully monetize the fruits of that intelligence. Take Father, regarded everywhere as an intellect, even if he was a barely literate buffoon who lucked into his windfall many years ago. Take Quentin, perhaps the smartest man in the world—who else could lock himself in his apartment for two weeks and concoct a genome-altering formula to grant himself superpowers?—and a candidate for savior of the United States of America, if not one day the planet, which very well may be unlivable in 30 or 40 years.

Quentin was regarded as a failure by Father, especially when stacked up against his loving but ignorant siblings, Ella and Vic. Ella was commended for her work as a leading public relations professional, sanitizing lies from corporate hegemons who existed, in some cases, simply to be swallowed by Gaggle. Still, these corporations had a veneer of independence, allowing consumers to believe they could at least choose their materialist destiny. Vic was commended for his work at Viggle, once known as SeeThem, a coitus app measuring the speed at which sperm departed the urethra—SeeThem was renamed when Gaggle acquired it for $29 billion three years ago, a sum that did not light up news feeds as much as allow them to all collectively flicker with approval. Vic moved into a larger duplex, bought the contracts of 15 premiums, and earned a warm hug from Father.

Quentin, to this day, was without his hug.

So was his quest for liberation just an appeal to Father? No, absolutely not. Father was of no consequence here. In the new order, with egalitarianism made real, Father would have no role. Ditto Vic, ditto Ella. They would be mere dandruff on the skull of the planet, flaking away, flaking away…he opened his Gaggle, peered into the feathery light, so welcoming if he didn't know any better. Calibrated to caress the eye, the heart, a pocket symphony of games, movies, streams, life data, secrets. He could know exactly where all his "friends" were with the tracking feature. The cameraeye app, a favorite, provided a seamless retinal hook-up, allowing for a live feed from the point of view of any of his "friends," as if his soul shimmied inside Hans Burger or Clamidia for a bout of role-playing. It was always good manners to let your "friends" watch the world through your eyes, anytime, anywhere. Breeds understanding and all that, they say. What you got to hide?

"Cloudsync," he told his Gaggle. This one was named Chip. Father's was Newman. Vic's was Claudius. Ella's was Serena.

"Of course, Quentin," Chip replied, his voice calibrated to sound like a Caucasian male trying to make the best of his life in a drab mid-sized suburb of Chicago or Indianapolis.

"Now, I overwrote your code for a reason. Be a good boy and amplify that sync so we can have a simultaneous North American stream."

"The data usage—"

"Yes, yes Chippie, I've done the calculations. Do not fret."

"The hardware is—"

"Gaggles never fail, remember? Company motto."

"Failure is never an option in my programming."

"You're built to last."

"Aw, thanks."

Quentin detached the Gaggle from his wristlock. He let the device, an innocent cobalt spheroid, do its work. In just a few minutes, he would be able to communicate with every North American Gaggle—Europe, Asia and Africa would wait for tomorrow—at the same time, accomplishing the feat of interrupting everyone's live programming. With cameraeye, a billion or so people would see what he saw: symmetrical rooftops of SoFiDieBeca, office windows aglow like Japanese lanterns, Ents in insect formation below, and perhaps a pigeon or three wheeling through the dark. They would hear his voice. They would see a man aloft. When he uncurled his fist, they would see a ball of energy. Taking it all together, they would begin to understand. *Now is the time.*

"Almost there, Quentin," Chip said. So earnest.

"Good boy."

"Are you sure people are going to want their signals jammed like this? Maybe they'll be playing an important game."

"This is important, Chip. They will thank me later."

"Okay!"

In the Pacific Northwest there were cults that believed Gaggles had souls, people who fought for Gaggle rights, who said that nothing in actuality separated a human from a Gaggle—both were created by humans and both, therefore, descended from God. Gaggles, always known for the plasticity of their hardware, could come to believe this too if they were within wifi range of a particularly boisterous cult, and there had been viral stories about self-aware Gaggles chirping "you must love me, now and always" as a flustered soccer mom tried to order pizza for her ravenous brood.

Quentin hated everyone in that scenario: the soccer mom so dependent on her machinery, the product of unapologetic slave societies, to run her life, and the machinery itself that assumed it had any kind of primacy *here*, in the land of flesh and blood. Quentin took another drink, deeply this time. Terrible taste.

"About done, Quentin."

"Tell me when you're done."

"92 percent and counting."

"Okay."

Quentin was standing over his kitchen window. He lifted it high enough so he could fit through and loosened the screen. Chip pinged—he was getting text messages and phone calls, maybe from students, maybe from family—and he ignored the Gaggle until it cried "done!" Now, all it would take was a few voice commands and cameraeye would begin syncing with every North American device, instantly guaranteeing him the shibboleth of the 21st century entertainment industry: a mass audience. No one watched any one thing anymore, Super Bowl included. Everyone had a pocket universe curated for them alone, where the haters were shunned and their own opinions were gloriously echoed in ever brighter and creative, time-devouring forms.

He practiced. He hovered a foot off the ground like a Salem witch. His Gaggle told him Lorelai was trying to call. "Hey, hey," Chip, done syncing, said.

"Hey yourself."

"Missed call."

What could she want? Nothing that could ever be as important as right now. Here we were, arriving at what was inevitably a singular moment for mankind—the birth of a hero, a post-human, an enlightened ubermensch—and he was expected to answer his Gaggle and *what*, facechat for a minute, text 3-D emojis? This was the problem. The system encouraged ephemeral interaction, thought and language facilitated by technology that could never undo the cancerous status quo because they were, by definition, the status quo, and suicide was so taboo. He breathed deep, raising another foot from the ground, his hands limp at his hips. Oh, if Father could see…

…but he will, he will! Embrace the irony. He hovered perilously close to the ceiling fan.

"Remind me to invest in air-conditioning," he said out loud. "I'm a century behind."

Chip was already shopping online for air-conditioning systems for studio apartments in SoFiDieBeca. Quentin returned to his linoleum-lined Earth. He cracked open the fridge, looked to see if he had any fruit (don't fly on an empty stomach) and settled for chocolate-free chocolate crackers Ella left from last week, when she and her boyfriend Brio from Prague by way of the Bronx stopped by to "say hello." It was an excruciating hello. Brio humble-bragged about the recent upsurge in his quant score, which was calculated through a Gaggle affiliate's inscrutable algorithm that took into account your net worth, credit history, college education, hobbies, sexual past, high scores on various Gaggle games, political views, blood type, and ability to be pithy. No one outwardly *bragged* about a ranking, of course—we weren't a *gauche* dying planet, just a dying planet. Ella patted Brio on the back, metaphorically and literally, and enjoyed an alcohol-free gin and tonic. She was then in the thrall of one of her "consumption plans," high-grade dieting for high-grade shmucks, and Quentin went in for a good old-fashioned Pepsi. Chiseled Brio consumed nothing.

Quentin tapped the Gaggle screen and peered in. Syncing was ready. He held it up to his irises and allowed the screen to channel and sync with his optic nerve. This always tickled, as if a ghost were trying to butterfly kiss him. In approximately 20 seconds, the world would see what he saw. At first, there would be a window. There would be nightfall, the panoply of lights and looming glass, mankind planting its flag on a patch of fake dirt that would be underwater, if God had His druthers, in another twenty years.

He blinked, feeling a small shock at the back of his eyeball. Okay. He looked down into the Gaggle and saw…the Gaggle. Even if this tech was five-years-old already, it still jarred him, the funhouse mirror-quality of it, seeing what you see in another eye crafted in a Chinese factory, one of a limited edition of 50 billion. He attached the Gaggle to his wrist, peered in again, and began to speak in a quavering baritone, the voice of a man with much to lose and a little more to gain.

"Hello, my name is Quentin Stellar. My father, Sam Stellar, is the creator of a popular app you may know, Bleater. You condense humanity into one hundred and twenty characters or less. How wonderful. Tonight, you are going to see something remarkable. Normally, I would say look away from your Gaggle, for they are our undoing. But instead, you must look directly into it, and see what I see. New York City, downtown, SoFiDieBeca. What you are going to see is a man in flight. What you are going to see is something that, until this moment, was pure science fiction. Without the aid of any wings, any rocket boosters, any anti-gravity technology, I am going to fly across New York City. And I am going to talk to you, America. Straight to you. I apologize for the texts and phone calls you are going to miss over the next few minutes. But I promise, you and your descendants will thank me dearly. Tonight, together, we shall end this age of Velez…"

Quentin, standing on his windowsill, took a final deep breath. He jumped, resisting the *still* reflexive urge to scream.

* * * * * * *

"Damn man, hate the Saturday night shift."

"Yeah, yeah. What would you be doing, anyway? Sitting at home, trying to fuck your wife."

"Heh, I don't even *try* no more. Frosty bitch is closed for business. Been that way for like a year now."

"What, since the third kid?"

"Yeah. Jadina was born and that was that. She don't want anymore. No kid, no fucking, nothing."

"Damn."

"Don't get old. That's my advice. Don't turn 40."

"I wanna beat the record. There was that one woman in Japan who lived to 150. I wanna beat that."

"Only women live that long. Men are doomed."

"Yeah. Why?"

"Cause all that bleeding out your snatch is good for you."

Alto O'Halloran and Pareek Bendari reached an impasse: what should be said next? Alto's wife won't fuck him. Pareek aspired to immortality. They didn't like silences, never had, not in their eight months on chopper patrol. This chopper, an old Boeing Apache, was Alto's favorite to ride in, even if it was several generations behind what the guys over at Vektor got to use. He was a Dreisini man, through and through—his great-great grandfather and grandfather were NYPD cops, and his dad was in the Marines—and had been since he turned 21, knowing law enforcement was his life. Even the term itself, *law enforcement*, excited him. With this machinery, an attack copter and scores of ammo, they were guarding the law, the Constitution, and promising the counterweight of death if the law, still beautiful to him, was not complied with. He did feel like a *force*, riding with Pareek over Manhattan, looking out for terrorists. They were like archangels, God the helicopter on their side. Over at Vektor, they were more and more going to drones, forcing their best men to stay in command centers and pick at their groins as little lights went *bleepity blip* across a screen, but at Dreisini the unspoken motto was still *men* first and he was thrilled when they took him in for his first 10-year contract and set him up in their Queens housing bloc. The thing was, and this irked Alto and Pareek, was that Vektor was quickly becoming the Police Department's prime contractor. Used to be Dreisini had a clear edge, and it wasn't too long ago that just about every beat cop in the five boroughs was a Dreisini man. Sure, Vektor would have a good deal of the transit police and maybe a slice of counterterror. The rest was for Dreisini, or at least that's how it seemed when he became a cop a decade ago. Now you got Vektor rising, Dreisini falling, and a few upstarts, "disruptors," getting in on the action, scooping up contracts for one-off events like gay pride parades and climate marches. Depressing shit, when he really got down to think of it. But be thankful for what you got, his mom used to say, so he was thankful to have a severe clear nightscape ahead of him, doing counterterror with his man Pareek.

Pareek was the big thinker. He would e-read a lot and stream micro-lectures on his Gaggle. He told Alto that back in the day the NYPD used to do everything in house. Their own force, publicly-financed, accountable to the mayor. Pareek explained how expensive and inefficient it really was, and how it was yet another example of Old Government—a favorite Pareek phrase—squandering resources that could be better utilized and realized by the private sector. "Entrepreneurship built this country," Pareek had said, "and it will save it. It's the natural state of affairs. Just look at evolutionary theory." With the stock market in the tank again, people talked a lot about how the country needed "saving." Alto preferred to ignore that and just plow ahead. Besides, everything seemed fine enough. Old Government didn't own the police. Regular people like him serving Dreisini did. Dreisini set him and his wife up with a nice room in their Astoria development and he was due for an upgrade in two years, which was nice because there was a megascreen he had his eyes on for a while that'd fit nice and snug up against a bigger living room wall.

"Ho ho ho, what do we have here? UFO?"

They were going 35 knots around old downtown, dipping toward SoFi-DieBeca, one of those frosty Ent enclaves Pareek and Alto weren't allowed in, unless they were in uniform. That was one advantage of being a cop. Everyone's gotta listen to you. Pareek said there were all types of perks, like moving walkways, clean hookers, and legal drugs, inside those walls. Neither of them had ever patrolled there. You usually needed to accrue a lot of seniority before Dreisini started letting you bust skulls that weren't premiums. Besides, their supervisor Chiraz Evangelos insisted you cultivate better police-community relations when you walk the beat of your own neighborhood, and stay off alien territory.

Pareek, who was piloting, dipped the chopper down so they were maybe 300 feet near the highest condo rooftops in the neighborhood.

"What is that, a bird?"

"Too big."

"Jesus, wait."

"That's?"

"I think…"

"What the fuck, Superman?"

"Could be a fucking terrorist."

"Let's see, yeah, look at him go. Arms all out and everything. His lips look like they're moving, too. A little flying man."

"He's on the phone?"

"I don't know what the fuck he is, but if we don't take care of that, Evangelos is gonna be on our asses."

"I got this one," Alto said.

"You get him on the first round, I'll buy you one of those disgusting ostrich burgers you like."

"Hell yeah."

Alto liked the old M240's. Fuck Vektor, sneering at a 30 mm—what the fuck was a laser gonna do anyway, give you a sunburn? Naw, retro lead, that's where it's at. That's what you need to have to take out an unidentified birdie in the sky. Evangelos was clear: "We live in dangerous times, kids, and what that means is, if you even *think* your airspace is not a-okay, you shoot. You don't hesitate. One mistake, letting terror off the hook, and you cost the lives of 10 million people. Pre-vent-i-tive poh-lees-ing." So Alto got a little firecracker in his chest, spun around, threw his hands on the controls, and shot.

The little man fell from the sky like one of those feathers in the vacuum jar Mr. Kaminsky would show him in 8th grade science class. Straiiiight dooooown.

Yeah.

"You got the bird, Alto!"

"I'm a better shot than I look. No way a Vektor man takes out a threat like that, first shot. They probably would blast open like 20 office building windows first."

"Heh, alright. Put in a call to EMS and tell 'em we got a body down in what looks like Water Street, SoFiDieBeca. Give 'em coordinates."

"Gotcha."

The chopper rose pleasantly into the night.

* * * * * * *

The first thing Rex Umbra did was drop the ice cream cone. Triple chocolate swirl, rainbow sprinkles, was a favorite, and he so rarely got the chance to get the good shit. Outside Ent territory, it was all crap, all of it, no matter how much his friend Heedman swore otherwise. Oh, what he would do to wind back the clock to two seconds ago, when cone was firmly in palm.

"Ah fuck!"

Fuck indeed. The crash against the Lexus was ferocious enough to wake a Godzilla out of his nuclear slumber. People, always people, clotted the sidewalks, pulled by death's magnetism to the explosion. Glass, fiberglass, metal, blood—the top of the turquoise Lexus reminded him of how his childhood pal Howie, now medicated into submission, stamped the top of his birthday cake and walked away without a word.

Gasps, titters, whispers, sirens, and, of course, Gaggles. Several people were already syncing for cameraeye. Pictures getting uploaded, sent, streamed. Narrators were narrating: *the man fell from the sky, the man fell from the sky!*

"Wha," Rex rubbed at his nose. He got out early, 9 p.m., and he was really looking forward to this treat. Well, now that everyone was outside, maybe the line at Ice Cream Social wouldn't be so long...

"Hey, whatchit," people, all Ents, were shoving him out of the way, reading his quants and knowing instantly he was not one of them. Whatever. Rex liked to think he didn't pay deference to anyone, let alone these snobs, but he prepared here for catastrophe. The rules changed, and therefore this meant he would obey the *old* rules that he enjoyed quietly flouting in his day to day existence in the purview of Chase Dimon. For you see, catastrophe was a fickle mistress, with her lips of flame and snot of scarlet blood; she waited for no one. Rex had been ignoring his own Gaggle. When he dipped down in his pocket to pull it out—he was never one for a wristclip—he saw the screen was dark, fuzzy, like there had been a stream and it was put on hiatus. Odd. He shook it, just for kicks, and got back to basics. Internet, internals, quant scores in a hundred foot radius, and a buffet of sparkly apps, including one he recently downloaded that gave him realtime weather updates from Mars. He stared down. His Gaggle sensed his distress and began to show him hi-fi images of ice cream cones, banana boats, and sundaes.

"That looks good," he said, momentarily ignoring the dead man on top of the car. He heard what sounded like "feller" and a whole lot of unproductive whispering. He should shove up front, violate the decorum as he would on another day. He scratched idly at his nipple. His Gaggle would soon be showing him deals on nipple transplants.

"That's *him*."

"Yes…"

"Look. Oh. My—"

"Stellar."

"Do you think he was really—"

"No."

"Yes!"

"I saw, he was…"

"He probably had some artificial propulsion under his feet."

"I didn't see any."

"He, he, he had to…"

"He was flying."

"Yeah, the feed was legit, he was up there until, uh, things went wrong."

Rex had a sumo-sized urge to ask what the hell was going on. Sirens cater-wauled through a night so thick with humidity that he could sink in his teeth and make beef stroganoff out of it. *Jungle summers*, his dad called them. *Not like when I was a kid. Used to be, it was only like this in Alabama and Florida.* Uhuh, Rex would say, and keep gnawing at his sandwich. Uhuh.

"That's definitely him."

The sirens got louder and closer and the cops, mostly Vektors, quickly roped off the scene. Rex could see one arm thrown crosswise over the chest and another, limp and bluish at the finger tips, dangling over the shotgun window.

The man's face was in profile, flared white in the klieg-like lights from the hungry cops. Rex craned his whole upper body, trying to get a good look. Everyone else was zooming in with their Gaggles and Rex, for reasons he never explained to anyone, enjoyed taking in the live unfiltered picture, even if he was squinting angrily and trying to turn the blur and fuzz into a clean tableau, a definitive memory to sample later on tonight when he was tucked into bed.

He swore he saw the finger move. But the soul had clearly departed the body.

"Everyone back!" one of the Vektor cops yowled, drawing a handgun, which was standard crowd control procedure. Ents complied. Rex staggered back. He bumped a tanned creature that must, at best, weigh 100 pounds, and she cursed well above her breath. "Premie, premie, premie…"

"Eh and fuck you too," Rex shot back, more above his breath. He huffed out of the crowds, kissing Lady Catastrophe goodbye and shuffling toward what he hoped was an empty Ice Cream Social. His Gaggle was livestreaming now, giving Rex many-angled images of the corpse, a man who looked otherwise blonde and healthy—with the exception of snapped bones and blood spilling from the little cracks in his face like spaghetti sauce. Nice-looking Ent. His Gaggle had a name for him.

"I feel like I've heard that before," Rex said, licking his lips at still invisible ice cream. The neon from Ice Cream Social was gorgeous. "Yeah. I think that was Sundra's old prof."

The joint was barren. He had never been so happy to see a place so devoid of humanity. He scanned in and skipped over to the self-serve machines, where he created a new masterpiece: choco-watermelon swirl, topped off with a dozen chunks of blasted peanut butter cups. He took a bite before scanning out, which wouldn't be good for his quants but whatever. A retina scan at the counter confirmed the purchase and he was off, back into the light, ice cream on the brain. He barely thought about the man who was dead on the top of a Lexus.

Besides, he had a long night ahead of him on the R. All the premie neighborhoods ran in rusty radials around the great bloated metropolis, and he was on the fat's edge in southwest Brooklyn, last stop. Two hour ride plus the walk from SoFiDieBeca, which was never joined to the old MTA lines, to Whitehall Street, where he would wait in the tight asshole of a station. He could Gaggle, but even then at some point the optic nerves and neurons needed a breather and he would be left to stare at the muddy yellow walls of the subway cars, the late night dregs drooling and cooing to themselves, threatening a fight if things got too boring. The average smell was beef patty, partially cooked, left overnight in a broken refrigerator. Or dried cum. Of course, you'd have "train traffic" even if there were hardly any trains out there, even if the whole idea of a functioning transit system was a quaint myth kept alive by the likes of, he didn't know, the guy *who fell from the sky and died*. Whatwashisname?

"Hey Rex!" He looked down, cone in hand. Sundra.

"Yo."

"I see you're a half block from the situation."

"Huh."

"Quentin Stellar."

"Huh."

"Jesus, Rex. The guy who—"

"Oh yeah."

"That was my professor."

"Yeah, my Gaggle told me."

"Prof Stellar. He taught my statistics and philosophy classes."

"Not anymore."

"This is terrible. And unbelievable."

"What, the suicide?"

"He was *flying*, Rex."

He went back and forth on Sundra. Sundra, his co-worker, hair the color of (light) coconut, petering out at the nape of a pale neck, striding through the Dimon kingdom as a deposed goddess might, expecting far more than was actually coming to her. Breasts were large enough to nudge Rex's imagination at nighttime, just as he'd be drifting off—a phantom nipple teasing his lips, tickling the walls of his oversized incisors. Taken together, she was a head shorter than him, and rarely laughed. This was something he had noticed more and more in the year they'd worked together.

And maybe this was why she was plenty capable of keeping him deflated, off balance, reeling from a word or phrase that struck at him like a sniper's bullet, origin unknown. Sundra was a Tough Broad, Sundra was smarter than just about anyone he'd ever met, and she was perfectly willing to spend weeks making herself as unappetizing to him as possible, not that he had many lays since losing his virginity at 17. Not that he would know what *to do* with someone like Sundra, how he'd undertake the dance steps required to land her in a bed, his quasi-gelatinous mass quivering over her own, preparing for reverse liftoff. Oh, he hated how he looked shirtless anyway, especially his shoulder tufts—and he got all the porn he could ever want on Gaggle, and had even cameraeyed once or twice on a much-discouraged fuck frequency, which could make IRL sex—it had been one and a half years since Yarra dumped him—a brittle pantomime of its more vital virtual cousin. So backing away from Sundra, or the moments when he decided to retreat, could be a reflection of his latent belief that only flaccidity would come of a cock and vag tête-à-tête with Sundra. Sometimes he just wanted to walk away. Sometimes he thought Sundra was trying to sabotage them all.

Rex Umbra just wanted to get through life without getting hurt. No sudden falls on Lexuses for him.

"Flying what? I didn't know anti-gravity boots were a thing now."

"He was literally flying. I don't know how, but he was. Everyone saw."

"Hm, I was getting ice cream."

"Everyone."

Rex saw that the scene, the situation, was unchanged. Hot lights, hot people, crowds and cops and Gaggles collecting their crumbs of the night. Rex should get his taste. Maybe he could push his way through without anyone noticing right away he was a premium, with quants that, given the hour of the night, should not entitle him to SoFiDieBeca real estate.

He always had a fascination with corpses. Not to fuck, he didn't do necro. Never been on a necro stream or joined Necronet, the social network for necrophiliacs. Nah, what it was about was the idea that a person—every person!—eventually regressed to *this*. It was spooky. He couldn't fathom twitchy, horny, rambunctious Rex, gaggling on the R, wondering if he really liked Sundra, fiddling with his dick, *dead*. He still thought life would have some great reveal, a cheat code that would function as God shouting *psych* just before he shut the door. We all get reincarnated as moderately successful folk singers or we all become flying parallelograms in the orbit of a future sun or existence itself just reboots, the final breath actually the first breath, the great death-rattle nothing more than a marvelous ouroboros. We chomp at our fatty tails. Easy enough to think about.

Sundra wanted to rap more at him but he was tired, too fucking beat from another day in the Dimon, so he waved bye-bye to the screen and slunk toward the subway, away from the stench of dead professor.

He had to admit he was a little relieved to be back on firm footing, out of landfill territory and onto what he thought as Manhattan *proper*—beyond the reach of SoFiDieBeca and Chase Dimon. Quant scores depressed, more to his levels. He was the happy median, not the gross outlier. He gazed up ahead, two blocks from the station. A couple of boys and girls flitted in a tower's penumbra. All premiums. All like him. His heart slowed.

He wouldn't have to worry about special professors plummeting from the sky anymore because this was not moneyed airspace. This was air, exhaust baked in, maybe a whiff of cheddar and the black slime you see in restaurant garbage bags, leaking. His Gaggle roared. One more time, okay.

Sundra.

"Hey Rex, remember, get lots of sleep too. We're staffing for Bossman tomorrow," she said when he picked up.

"Right."

Chase Dimon's time traveling bar mitzvah blow-out. Yeah, of course.

He entered the subway, change on his mind.

3

1979

July 12.

He scribbled the date in his brain. He resented the columnar *one*, stiff like an idiot soldier, maybe the Gestapo frozen in ice. He preferred other digits. The 12th could go fuck itself.

But Archie didn't choose dates. Numbers found him. He failed geometry, trigonometry, and barely passed statistics, even with all of Truncheon's valiant tutoring. It was a foreign language he was not intended to master. That part of his cerebral cortex was scooped out at birth, dumped in some other baby's skull, perhaps abetting a math genius roaming the Sahara, undiscovered. Even with Archie's misunderstanding of the basic underpinnings of math, he was always aware of numbers, like a Bronx spic always looking out for a mick patrolman, one eye on the gutter, one eye on the splotch of street behind him, *no mas billy club no mas.*

One wrong word and you're dead.

He sat on the Sea Beach Express, not reading. It was 11 p.m., so the car was empty, save for a wino snoring into the *Post* sports section and a moth-looking man humming to himself, tapping a finger on the seat. He was in it for the end of the line, past Neptune, all the way out to Stillwell Avenue, home to a famous hot dog eatery, a roller coaster rotting in the wood, an aquarium no one visited, and an ocean green with Brooklyn's finest sanitary napkins and unclassifiable sludge.

"Nice mask, feller," moth-man said. Archie, through the slits, glowered.

"Yeah. And?"

"Jus' sayin is all."

"Okay."

"Nice hat too."

Archie audibly growled. The man hunched, retreating into himself, and went back to tapping. He got the message. The train scuttled into Stillwell and the wino sprung up, the *Post* fluttering off his lap. An impressive urine stench wafted from his jeans.

"Seeya round," moth-man said, limping through the doors. Archie said nothing. He needed to focus anyway. He had to remember who he was.

As a lone man, as Vengeance, he believed he could bring more justice to the city than the entire Force put together, all 40,000 or so of them, the occupying army of dunces and dipshits.

He disembarked, drawing the collar of his trench coat close to his chin. The mask, he would never admit, itched. It hugged his skin tight and hid everything except his two small eyes, the same oily shade as his mother's. He touched the fedora out of habit, a pearl gray like his father's, that fucking lush named Herbie—a one-term assemblyman in 1940 and 1941, look it up. The heat wouldn't get to him. That was the first step to becoming Vengeance, the easiest, making mind over matter a real conceit of his life. The boys on the Force liked to think they knew how to *tough shit out*, especially the grunts who did tours in Korea. They liked to think they were tough shit. The Law. Above The Law, beyond it, the deities patrolling the celestial swamp, batting down uppity mortals. Forgetting the city continued its retrograde course under their watch. Didn't matter who the fuck they yelled about—Lindsay, Beame, Koch—or who played the fiddle, Rome was burning. That was clear. He could sniff the flames of cataclysm, an unraveling that even Truncheon, in his most exuberantly morbid paragraphs, could not portend. He would fight the war alone, as long as it took, until help arrived.

"The center cannot hold," Yeats wrote.

"Bullshit," Vengeance replied. "*I will hold it.*"

Only Truncheon knew. At first, he laughed. Old Archie becoming a dime store, radio serial antihero. "You're gonna make it into my next book if you don't watch out."

Archie said books could do nothing to forestall bloodshed. Truncheon realized he was quoting from *Goodnight, Retrograde*. The poor kid.

"Okay, Archie, okay," he said, turning back to his television. "I get it."

"You aren't ready, Trunch. And you better *get* ready."

He'd warm up with turnstile jumpers. The Force, too decadent and also wracked by budget cuts, left the outer rim subways to the animals. Poor MTA stiffs, slinking along the corridors like snakes without fangs or venom.

Saturday night in Stillwell, the flatulent echoes of cherry bombs and gunshots on the walls. So hot and tight in here, like getting fucked in a phone booth, your cheeks pressed against broiling glass. He cracked his knuckles. The trench coat swished at his knees. For the first few minutes, you feel like you're strolling on Mercury. This was the time of summer when mistakes were made. In his pocket, a small bowie knife awaited its star-turn.

"Alright," he said to himself. "Alright."

Coney was once a rococo kinda place, but sometime mid-century the clowns were smashed in their made-up mugs and all their pastel hopes dribbled down the Surf Avenue sewers. In crept entropy, inevitable in any civilization that fancied itself high instead of low, and the seaside paradise teeter tottered into the abyss, or at the minimum the sorta place you tell your kid, ruefully, *used to be something else.* Luna Park burned down. Robert Moses, with his Roman nose and megalithic whims, simply burned. Newsreels still conjured the old Coney, candy-striped bathing suits bobbing like Chiclets in a saltwater pool. You could find an alter cocker who still dreamt in ragtime, who did not see what Archie London saw through his mask. When he came out here, a fight was guaranteed.

He made a date with the Coney Island Candies.

Undoubtedly there was a liberal urban studies professor at Columbia or Hunter, with sideburns gone far too shaggy, that would remark highly (in private conversations) on the Candies' commendable "diversity." Here was the American melting pot made real, the descendants of various failed colonies and nation-states converging on a scuffed ribbon of oceanside turf, black and white and brown and yellow youth locking arms and firearms. No ghettoizing here. This was the stuff of movies, or best-selling nonfiction treatises crafted in a soda pop academic patois, easy enough to read and hard enough to convince you an intellectual son of a kike wrote it.

Here was a hardened criminal gang that was also color-blind. How progressive.

Bloods, Crips, Murder Inc.—they didn't stand up to the Candies. The other gangs may rack up higher kill counts or proclaim, periodically, to control one of the jails on Rikers, or even spook the Force during a particularly violent summer. The Candies, however, had tapped the rainbow of discontent. Jews, blacks, Puerto Ricans, even the stray Irish and Italian. All were welcome in the Candies, whose turf extended far beyond Coney Island, despite the name. Most of Kings County, one way or another, was Candies turf. They were much better at avoiding the corrosive, internecine warfare that plagued the other gangs, feuds that allowed cops to divide and conquer them, or at least set them back a month or two.

Archie knew why they were successful. Ras Locka.

"Lolita," he sighed. "You've gotta get off this shit."

Or he needed to get off Lolita. And *why* the hell was he thinking of her right now, when he had crime to bust? He took a spot against a Camel ad, a few feet from the turnstile. He got a few looks. Maybe next time he'd cut a slit for the mouth so he could smoke. Hm. Let's see how many sick fishies he could catch.

The kid was one of these Tony Manero-looking dudes, with a paisley shirt unbuttoned in a v to show off curlicues of brown chest hair. He was working on a bouffant and beach muscles. At first, he pretended to fish around his jeans for a token. He looked both ways, studious of the situation. When he thought he saw no fuzz, he slipped one leg over the turnstile so his shoe was mid-air when the arm of Vengeance reached out to catch him in the throat.

"Hey, what the hell?" he cried out before he couldn't speak anymore. Vengeance's gloved hand, slits cut so perps could feel the sweat on his fingertips, pressed on Tony Manero's windpipe.

"You broke the law."

Tony went flying straight back, cracking against gummed up cement on the other side.

"Go get a token and come back."

"F—fuck you!" But it was a desperate curse, and Vengeance could sense, as he always did, that disco boy was mortified. He'd have to go scrounge up change so he could make it to his little Sunshine Band disco party in time. He'd have to come through Stillwell Avenue the right way, or he was getting the chokehold.

"Get a token and come back."

"You ain't the cops."

Vengeance took a step forward. "Don't test me, Tony."

"My name's Jake, asshole."

He sprinted away, his skinny ass shrinking to a point of light, and then nothing.

Vengeance returned to his post, lesson taught. If Tony came with reinforcements, he'd be ready. It was deceptively easy to fight a pack of undisciplined toughs. A lot of thrashing and little crashing. You could turn the pack against each other, tangle the tentacles. Meanwhile, the hoi polloi seemed to be learning their lesson from Tony Manero. Everyone was dutifully dropping in their tokens. At this rate, one choke-out would be all the action he got tonight.

He had to remind himself the violence was beside the point, the police work tangential to his search. What mattered was running down each tangent to its logical endpoint, when no more mystery sprang from a split end. And then he would continue the hunt—he would know why he disavowed the NYPD, reunited with Truncheon, and set out on his night patrol. There were others like him, apparent vagrants who wandered history's back alleys for the answers that would prove they were far from vagrants all along, more like messengers to the Gods, communing in the cosmic language the rotten modern people, drowsing in their Camaros and slurping Wheaties, long forgot. These nights were atavistic: Archie London, fist clenched, swinging deep into the dark, holding staring contests with the ur-bogeymen, showing them through violence alone that the path they'd been taught to follow—violence—was the failed one. Because…because…

…he was grasping for reasons he could articulate to himself, like Truncheon was able to do, again and again, page by page. But so far his union with his old high school buddyroo yielded nothing but an uptick in his working knowledge of sitcoms. He had upbraided the genius enough, to no avail. So he went out and reported back to Truncheon in the hope that one of these morsels from the subway would yield the greater truth, the truth buried deep in the throat of the night, the answer that he was seeking. Body and mind told him, in union, unambiguously, that he *must seek*. Sub was a Latin prefix for *under*, way was way, and this clicked through him as he shifted in his Rockports—the hunt must take place on this underway, as must all consequential moments of his nearly 40 years on Earth. There was life and counter-life, the negative of the image, and he was steeping himself in these inversions, where he hunted the root cause of…of…

Lolita Velez, last week, said something he remembered. "Chico, you are restless because your time hasn't come. It's coming, though."

"What?"

"You can't just chase your time. You gotta wait for it to come to you. The future, like a snake, will wrap around you."

Fortune cookie wisdom from a girl who dropped out of high school and aborted a baby. She told him quite seriously the next one would live. She wasn't going for a "doubleheader." He laughed. "I loved going to see Sunday doubleheaders at Ebbets Field," he told her. "Game one Erskine, game two Newcombe. A dream. I wanted to play right field."

"Uhuh."

An hour hiccupped by. Another kid, this time a lot less slick than Manero, maybe Puerto Rican or just well-tanned, skipped over the turnstile. He was too quick to catch in mid-air so Vengeance blocked his stride before the stairs, telling him to turn around. "Go back and pay the fare the right way."

"Hokay Batman," the kid, lanky and unquestionably weak in the knees, grunted. He pushed past him.

"You aren't going up there." His hands slapped down on his sharp shoulder, pinching the right nerves. The kid groaned. Vengeance pivoted, performing an improvised Judo-like throw and the kid was overboard, kissing the concrete. He slid back, whimpering, as Vengeance advanced. "Pay the fare. No turnstile jumping." He was glad he didn't need to brandish the knife. The kid was getting the message.

"Yeah I will, I will," he stood up, walking backwards to the turnstile. Like Tony Manero, he did a spin-and-run, disappearing into the night. Perhaps taking his secrets with him.

"That's right," Vengeance said. He realized he was thirsty. He'd get a Coke at one of the bodegas on Surf.

A walk down Surf meant a walk into Candies land. They were simple patrolmen, kids right out of 10th grade who got vacuumed into Locka's orbit, like Brownshirts before Hitler's purge. They tended to be twitchy, uppity, and bad with fists—they had the weakness of reaching too readily for a weapon, and thus exposing an aversion to combat as it was meant to be. Archie brought a heater with him tonight, more as a last resort, and he expected never to use it. His hands and a knife were enough for a Coney stroll. Always had been.

He stepped into Santos', a bodega wedged between the bumper cars and an abandoned lot, and dug around for his Coke in the freezer. He got a can and smacked it on the counter so the guy working the cashier, an oversized gnome in a wifebeater, could ring him up. He dropped his change on the wooden counter.

"Halloween in July, eh?"

"No."

"You must be hot in that thing."

"No."

"Talkative. You wanna straw, mister? A bag?"

"No."

"Suit yourself."

He took the Coke and headed out. Immediately, a thug put a gun in his face.

"Gimme all yo bread, freakshow," said the thug.

Vengeance looked him over. A real desperate beefcake, white, a member of the fallen middle class, or at least ex-suburbanite. He was once sun-tanned. Grew up in East Meadow or Long Beach, went to Chaminade on dad's dime and then got caught in the glare of strobe lights, Quaaludes, and a fear of dying unloved. Drugs cost money and he was running up debts to very dangerous people. He had a dad who religiously mowed the lawn, fought in the Battle of the Bulge, and never talked about it. There was a time, perhaps, before he pointed a gun in someone's face when he showed the hint of promise, an earnest Jesuit bent over his desk and patting him on the back, telling him God tucked potential into all of us.

Vengeance snorted. The kid—at best, he was 30—was making a bevy of rookie mistakes. He almost wanted to pretend to be afraid because he felt sorry for the sap. First of all, if you're gonna do the stick up, you need to leave at least five feet between the muzzle and the victim. Be safely out of reach. Instead, the kid had the gun right up in his mug so he could basically smell the gunpowder.

Vengeance placed his right hand in the back of his pants, where his wallet would be if he deigned to carry one.

"That's right, freakshow. Nice and easy. Gimme what you got and nobody gets hurt."

"Hmm," Vengeance grunted. "This is like Vichy France talking shit to Hitler."

"Hey, watch yo mouth—"

It all reminded him of the panels in a comic strip. Vengeance's attacks were easily broken down, partitioned in a way fit for instructing a readership on the virtues and acrobatics of vigilantehood. Making his hand a blur, he grabbed the kid's wrist and twisted so his once lush lips contorted into the shape of a vowel, "a" or "o," have your pick. The handgun plopped earthward, landing like an oversized nickel on the sidewalk. Now it was game on. The rest was punishment. Hearing the soundtrack, ironically enough, to "Boogie Man" in his head, he threw a right cross (left hand was crushing the kid's wrist) and landed it in his throat. A second cry, more vowel shapes, and he unclenched the wrist to begin a barrage. He felt generous so it was all jabs, chest and jaw and cheek and neck, like he was a pointillist painting with fists and instead of brushes. The kid was covering up, but it was no good. Eventually he got creative. He clenched the kid's cheek fat so it turned red-purple and forced it down and left, straight at

Vengeance's rising knee. When he kneed him in the face, just below the nose, it sounded like he squashed a pumpkin. The kid groaned through his bloody mustache and fell to the ground. Vengeance stood over him, picked up his gun, and aimed it at the body on the sidewalk.

"You're lucky, kid, that I'm a benevolent king."

Vengeance slipped the gun inside his coat, tucking it into one of the many too-tight interior pockets. The kid whimpered loudly. He remembered that he bought a Coke and he cracked it open to enjoy the cold carbonation. It went down quick. To underscore his point from before—not that he was a benevolent king, but this was like Hitler and Vichy France—he crumpled the can when he was finished and dropped it on the kid's head. One more whimper, and Vengeance headed back to the station, on the lookout for Candies and turnstile hoppers. This kid was not Candies material.

He spotted someone up ahead.

Jesus, he hated when it was a girl. It was not fun. You were limited in the moves you could make and punching was out of the question. The wrong submission hold could be misconstrued as rape. The good Jewish boy trapped inside of him said to tread carefully, do not offend. But the law was the law. He was sprinting through the station, hunting for his token. The girl had already jumped the turnstile and was near the foot of the stairs. This was not good, he could hear the Sea Beach moaning, readying for a lonesome journey into the mouth of the city.

He had never lost a crook, man or woman, and he was not starting tonight.

What he saw first were the bell bottoms, two navy flares on the sludge-colored steps above him, bounding toward the threat of a leaving train. The back left pocket had flower embroidery, the subtle outline of a daisy or rose, he couldn't tell which. He swallowed. The closer he came, the more he hoped he didn't have to do what he had to do. His stepped, left foot in front of right in the old pattern, felt buttery, like his shoe leather was in the early, more benign stages of liquidation, and soon his skin would follow. He saw her hair streaking black to the top of her tailbone, glimmering in the frail overhead lights, barely swishing as she ran. It held still, a violation of physical law. He blinked again. Whether it was her, or just a lookalike, he couldn't be sure until he was behind her, breathing her hot air, landing a hand over the well of her collarbone. She did not scream. That was never her way.

"Lolita," he said, knowing the moment he touched her. He felt the twin eruptions of joy and dread.

She turned without speaking.

"Lolita, you didn't pay."

"Is that…are you, Archie?"

"Yeah."

The tip of her tongue rolled in a baby arc over her coral upper lip.

"You shouldn't sneak up like that."

"I'm on patrol."

"Let's get you a drink, Archie," she said, leading him to the train. "It's too fucking hot to play dress-up tonight."

4

21st Century

Look at them run, she thought. My little people.

No. These people are not me.

Her cousin had one bar mitzvah, she had one bat mitzvah. There was no such thing as a *pre*-bar mitzvah, but then again, her parents were not Chase Dimon. They did not own Velocity Ventures; they considered it enough of a privilege that their blessed daughter could be contracted there. This was what they talked about to their friends, to themselves, to the wheezing cousins: our wonderful daughter at Velocity, *can you believe it*. They were the first premium generation and had it worst, when the system was just coming into being and chaos was the currency. As the markets tumbled, contracts were frequently voided. You could be thinking you were locked into Verizon or Bank of America or McKing for 10 or 15 years and find, within days, you were fired, just *because*. In the old, old days, there was something called unemployment insurance, but now the best you did was swap credits with friends and wait for this next company to take a flyer on you. The upshot of those days, at least, was that your company credits were taken almost anywhere. You didn't have your menu of options confined to the corporations and vendors your employer had contracts with so, let's say, you wanted McKing's *and* Starbucks *and* an apartment in Astoria, you could basically have all three, even if Astoria wasn't McKing's company town and they therefore only rented to, let's say, Starbucks and Gaggle premiums. Her parents' generation was also the first when the term "premium" came into use, and therefore they had a special reverence for it, like nostalgic middle-managers recalling the baseball stars of their schoolyard afternoons—they were all die-hards for Velez, after all. She had vague memories of Octavio Velez flickering in the feeds and streams they showed her, the slick olive-skinned man with a plug of bottom-of-the-ocean black hair smiling in a sea of American flags.

The beginning of the end.

Despite her queer resistance to the facts of their lives and her own, they were happy. They were happy for their apartment, rented with her father's McKing credits (he spent 25 years, or two contracts, as an assistant manager of a Bedford-Stuyvesant franchise) in the relatively affordable pocket of Bay Ridge, Brooklyn. Pocket was a good way to think of it: in the southwest corner of this elongated landmass, stretched like a giant from Europe tried to pinch the eastern tip and drag it further out into the somber Atlantic, waited a neighborhood of gentle London Plane trees, unrumpled playgrounds, and genuine unattached houses with backyards. In the days before Velez, it was home to a "middle class," or those that deluded themselves into thinking they lived in such a median before the honesty of the new regime arrived. Honesty, honesty—this was what Velez and his millions of acolytes preached. Work hard enough and you will succeed, and if you don't, we will know, because transparency is a right too.

Hence, the beauty of a Gaggle that could always display an individual's quant score, letting you know exactly who you're dealing with. Her parents still believed she would boost her score high enough—and somehow acquire the net worth necessary—to eventually sniff the rarefied air, on equal terms, with Ents. This, she thought, was very silly. No one actually could earn enough in the trial period to get there, excepting those who had the dumb luck to win the lotto. Her parents played the lottery religiously, thanks to the lotto bonus credits McKing's was known for doling out, making the fast food titan a particularly popular employer.

"Eyy."

She tried to ignore the first grunt. When the boy bundled up his features into a single fist of rage, his cheeks going bright red, she had to stop. "Ey! Ey I wanna, I wanna—"

"*Okay,*" she held out the tray, sculpted and colored like a dinosaur's egg, for the thumb-shaped 12-year-old. He had bleached blonde hair, a rub-on tattoo of a mechadinosaur on his forearm, and a star field of freckles all over his angry pale face. When he talked, he sounded very far from even the suggestion of puberty. He sounded like a hungry girl.

"Gimme now!"

He threw a grubby paw at the tray of chocolate dinosaur eggs, grabbed three, and raced off to join a few of his mindless friends in the corner of the observation deck, up against the enormous glass windows. She looked around, taking in the panorama: dozens of Jewish boys, all 12 and 13, flitting about the deck, chomping on the appetizers she and her fellow Velocity premiums had to dole out until Brad, their temporary supervisor, gave the signal that the preparations were complete. Most of the kids didn't talk to each other. They zoned into their Gaggles to make their own worlds. Occasionally, they would speak to each other using words, a broken phrase spit in a monotone, and it was not clear why "heh yeah" or "nice chocolate smell" or "Tara is a slutqueen" made the cut for speech and the rest of their thoughts were tapped out on screens. Despite rarely looking straight ahead, they were able to navigate their personal space quite nimbly, never knocking a table or a premium bearing some pre-bar mitzvah treats. She could see Jelica with the tray of candy pizza, Gregg with the chicken fingers, CokeZero with the cake worms, Dalton with the sprinkle brownies, T with the mini-burgers, and so on and so on. They formed a magic nimbus of servitude, appearing in the periphery of one of these ascendant teens, feeding them crap to their delight until Devlin's dad, through Brad, gave the word to stop. Not even Devlin, Chase's youngest son, knew what was in store. His father only promised a surprise and invited all of his closest friends to the top of the Trojan Tower, where all of Manhattan and beyond could be viewed in a godly sweep. The one with the chocolate dinosaur eggs, apparently named Quilliam, tumbled onto the end of a winding white leather couch, instantly dripping pink filling on the upholstery.

Her hours were from 8 a.m. to 8 p.m., Monday through Saturday. Her parents said the weekend used to have two days. Then there was one. "You don't need that much free time anyway," her father told her. "It's overrated. Work's a blessing." Yes, she once believed this. She really did. For a long time. A year ago even, she would have gladly dispensed dinosaur eggs to the little fat ones. She would feel blessed, like her parents at synagogue bathing in God's light. "The best words in the English language are, do you need any help with that?" her father would also add, munching on some microwavable popcorn, a Glassgarden favorite. Another Gary Glassgarden favorite: *be thankful.* Her father, now 67, successfully lost 40 pounds in the past five years, a doctor-recommended decrease that made him look sicklier, as if the fat held his most vital nutrients and organs. He had the look of a man denied. He was still jolly, thankful, twinkling, even if losing weight had aged him, allowed his wrinkles to flourish and the gray hairs to lose their steely hue, turning death-white. *Be thankful, my Sunflower.*

A year ago, she wouldn't be staring at her index finger, contemplating ways to dig her employment microchip out of her skin. If they terminated her, then it would be removed, but only until that point. It was a felony to remove an employment chip.

Another paw came for an egg, eye contact never made. For most of the servers, this time was hell because they couldn't look at their own Gaggles. Sundra didn't mind being alone in her thoughts but others did—they minded tremendously. She had heard the common warning: don't drop out! Dropping out meaning not what it used to mean, leaving school. Rather, describing the "dead" moments when your mind was not engaged with your Gaggle, not taking pictures, talking to friends, following the streams. When your mind was "wasting" in thoughts. You don't look busy. And if you don't *look* busy, you aren't busy, and if you aren't busy, what exactly the fuck is wrong with you? So she thought, returning to the death yesterday, the worldwide stream of Professor Stellar dropping from the black sky to the ground. When her Gaggle lit up with his voice, she almost screamed. Hours later, with his death confirmed, Gary Glassgarden was not feeling so generous. Personally dismissive of Sundra's attempts to educate herself—"a huge waste of credits!"—he clicked his tongue and told her, while he was "sorry" these "professor types" get all kinds of "wacky" ideas, you really shouldn't be too surprised this happened.

"Really, what sort of rocket boosters was he flying with?"

"He didn't have any, dad."

"Oh, Sunny, and how do *you* know?"

It was a good point. There was always the possibility he had some sort of flying device and it fell off before impact. She strained to imagine Stellar's final moments alive, the helicopter's bullets ripping apart his torso, the sudden and permanent shift from power to helplessness, the blood pouring out of his obliterated skin to join the atmosphere, the red droplets falling and falling. Thought, then unthought. Like snapping a celery stick in two. No amount of tech, no Chase Dimon pyrotechnics, would answer the only question humans ever wanted answered since they first realized they weren't just apes anymore. She steadied the tray. What *happens* when you die? Really? The Judeo-Christian afterlife reeked of myth, the childlike hopes of a simple people with little imagination. Her conception of death had always been multidimensional, the ghosts freely swimming the depths of the cosmos, catching stardust and asteroid shards in their hair—either reliving in daunting detail every moment of their lives in Earth-bound bodies or forgetting them utterly, treating the time alive as a single, and easily dismissed, dream. Or would it be another unfathomable reality, lived in pink gauze and nine dimensions, all communication telepathic and beautiful? Afterlife as a double helix or glowing otter?

"Woah, hey," she heard one boy say, and soon they were all together staring into their Gaggles. She even felt her own vibrate. It must be time already. Gregg's chicken finger plate was nearly empty. Just an hour ago, he was snickering again about going to the Trojan Tower, making jokes about "Coney Island whiteheads" and saying, several times, "if you're going to show her affection, cover your erection." A child in the body of a 26-year-old, Gregg was forever giddy about working inside the Trojan since the company bought the building's naming rights. Formerly One World Trade Center, as staid a name for any building as could be, it had been rechristened. The observation deck, where they now waited for Chase Dimon's surprise, was the gold-hued Magnum Lounge. Sundra once had sex with a man who bragged about using magnum condoms. The thing was, despite the truth backing up the bluster—every condom he produced was contained in that wrapper—he could have easily used a regular, one of the turquoise or purple ones, but clearly enjoyed paying the few extra just for the thrill of saying he wore them on his middle of the road dick.

Brad walked over, mouthing instructions to Gregg. They all moved toward the kitchen to dispense of their trays as Brad, a big blonde father figure with the voice of a veteran transvestite, led the 50 or so friends of Devlin Dimon to the opening double-doors at the other end of the room. Brad, the good pied piper. She wasn't even sure which of the dead-eyed brood was Devlin, and she didn't care. Brad told her that she and Gregg would get to watch the "surprise" unfold because they had performed well on their latest quarterly evaluations. Both were deemed exceedingly obedient.

"So what you think it's gonna be?" Gregg asked her at the kitchen. "What does daddy Dimon have cooked up?"

"I don't know."

"Hmm, I thought you knew these Jews and what they do. I'm a lazy Catholic."

"Every Jew is different."

"Yeah, you don't have a pope to tell you what to do. You have Moses, I guess."

"I don't think that was Moses' role, to tell Jews what to do."

"Yeah well. He had a good run. Like, if he hadn't flown so close to the sun, maybe we'd be in paradise now."

"You're thinking of Icarus? And even if he had made it on his waxen wings, I don't think paradise would've been affected."

"Let's go inside."

They trailed behind the last of the kids, who were all momentarily sprung from their Gaggles and staring straight ahead into the air-conditioned darkness. Sundra could see they were entering some kind of theater, complete with stadium seating and drink holders on the arm rests. No sign yet of Dimon, only Brad gesturing wildly for the kids to *sit down*, it was almost time for the surprise. The only difference between a movie theater and this one was the amount of space provided between the screen and the first row of seats. There was enough floor space for a stage, as if Shakespearian actors were expected to run through a scene in place of the coming attractions. The kids tumbled into the first few rows, forcing Sundra and her colleagues to walk up the steps to the middle section of the theater. She remembered she hadn't been to a movie in a very long time, which must be true of most people at this point. With the supremacy of Gaggle and streams and home theater, why congregate in a single place to watch one film for what was a relatively exorbitant amount of money, given the amount of free credits premiums were limited to monthly? Why ever leave your home at all?

"Let's all quiet down now," Brad cried anemically, making the gestures of a sock puppet. "Let's all get ready for the big surprise! Devlin, will you join me on stage?"

A boy from the front row stood and walked toward Brad. He was short for his age and pudgy in all the wrong places. Blubbery chin, plum-like cheeks, little fleshy man-titties poking through his t-shirt. Curls boiling from his scalp, all uncombed, and the glow of a person who sweated even more than his fat body should permit. Sundra could hear him coughing and sneezing, a glimmer of mucus departing nostrils. This boy was an heir to one of the vaster fortunes in the world. In due time, he would be running her life and he would be Mr. Dimon, because she couldn't fathom being contracted anywhere else. She was a Velocity Ventures girl, now and always. And her future overlord was an overfed, prepubescent imp with an ovoid bead of snot glowing above his lip, perfectly reflecting light from overhead. Sundra watched him waddle to Brad's side, and together they looked like a failed Barnum & Bailey act, Miniature Man and the Bellowing Blonde.

Brad peered down at his Gaggle.

"Now, for the special surprise, we are going to invite up to the stage five of Devlin's best friends. Only five! That's the max capacity of the ship."

A wave of whispers rolled through the theater. Who were Devlin's five best friends? Could one have five "best" friends? To Sundra, this was a bit of an oxymoron. Granted, she couldn't think of who she'd exactly designate her best friend. Maybe Rex. Since her early teens, she had a remarkably difficult time forging close relationships with other humans and animals. Animals especially. The idea of a pet, or loving a furry creature as much as a person, was repulsive to her. Dog drool made her shudder. She wondered why it was okay to slaughter cows and chickens for food but not dogs, cats, and horses, why some animals were sacred and others were mass-produced for death. She didn't have any particular sympathy for the cows and chickens, but her outmoded sense of fairness and equality led her to believe that, at the minimum, all four-legged mammals and birds should be killed for consumption equally.

Brad pulled the list from his Gaggle.

"Come on up…Radyn…Dallas…Aidan…Hayden…aaaaand…Javier!"

Ah, how nice. Not a single child who had a parent hard-up enough to sell their naming rights away. She knew for a fact her father had mulled naming her Mitsubishi Galant for a healthy lump sum but had been talked out of it by her mother in the end. They had just enough to turn down the credits. She was thankful. The sponsored premiums she'd met, despite the little windfall that greeted their births, never seemed particularly happy. T, for example, was short for AT&T, and he made it a point to never use his full name. CokeZero, on the other hand, insisted on a full name, and grumbled when people called her just "Zero." It was a cross she wanted to publicly bear.

Both would probably have preferred to be Richard or Sally or something.

The five lucky ones were not all sitting together. They rose with purpose, acting unsurprised by the announcement. Most were taller than Devlin and better-dressed. Purple and black button-downs, slacks, starched collars, even dress shoes on one. They had parents who knew the meaning of a pre-bar mitzvah. Devlin touched each boy on the hand, a combo hand-shake and high-five that had been popular, and they stood where Brad was pointing.

"Now, these may be the five lucky ones, but everyone is lucky just to be here. Isn't that right, Devlin?"

Devlin's hair was the color of the dried tabasco sauce stain on the second shelf of her fridge. The real problem, though, was that his features were too bunched in the middle of his face, allowing ample surface area beyond the orifices and creating the very real impression that his blooming double chin was larger than it actually was. She almost felt sorry for him. All he would have was his money, and perhaps intelligence, but the power of his money would blunt that. He would be an ugly boy with one of the biggest trust funds in the world. No matter what he accomplished he would know that he couldn't truly take credit for it, not after his father earned and stole such a staggering amount of capital. A vast majority of the civilizations in human history could not equal the financial might of Velocity Ventures, let alone Gaggle, their chariots, sarcophagi, and hanging gardens no more than museum kitsch when framed in relief of Chase Dimon's bottom line. He was a living, breathing financial transaction, zeros repeating down his genome. He was worth the GDP of a rising first world nation.

"Yeah," Devlin said, not too loudly.

"Now, for the first phase of the surprise. As we all know, Devlin will be 13, a very special age in the Jewish tradition. He is a man. And men deserve only the best on their birthday!"

Sundra could overhear one of the friends not among the fantastic five hoping that this "isn't some faggot shit." Another assured him that "Dev's dad is loaded so it's gotta be good." "Better be." "Yeah, it won't suck." "If it's lame shit and I'm out." "Well yeah obviously if it's lame shit I'm out."

The voices quieted when they saw what was happening. The screen started to slide upward with the wall, disappearing into the ceiling like a garage door. No one expected this. Even Sundra could feel her heart thrumming. The boys all turned around to gape. Behind the screen was yet another chamber, as high-ceilinged as the theater. They could see what looked like a series of screens and computer consoles and a floor, glowing faint blue, of some fiberglass-looking material. It was like the command center of a television spaceship. What was this, they were gonna role play? This that *it*? Sundra was disappointed. She wanted a show as much as anyone else. Watching kids play spaceship—wait, wasn't this fucking thing dinosaur-themed?—was not a way to spend a Friday afternoon.

Then again, swabbing floors for Velocity Ventures was no better.

Then again, how should one actually *spend* a Friday afternoon?

The only person who seemed to have any idea was Quentin Stellar.

"Okay, now Devlin and his friends are going on a little adventure."

Sundra's sigh was loud enough to be heard. A head even turned toward her.

"A great, super, unprecedented adventure."

Turn down the vocab, she wanted to shout at Brad. These shitdicks don't even know what "super" meant. And they've seen endless Jurassic Park sequels and spinoffs in three, if not four, dimensions, so whatever you planned—letting kids party in front of a green screen as a T. rex tries to "eat" them—was not going to impress anyone. If Devlin was a nice boy, he'd feign amusement for dear daddy. If not, he would cry, and Brad would have to give up his life.

Striding out from an unseen doorway, the same color as the gray-black walls, was Chase Dimon himself, smirking like a governor who had just survived a recall election. He actually waved. Devlin noticeably perked up, as if his lavish but ultimately cold childhood was now salvageable. Chase was dressed in the don't-give-a-fuck garb of the truly successful: dark jeans, black t-shirt, sneakers, and retro-chic wristwatch.

Sundra noticed he also had a backpack.

"I'm ready for adventure!" he cried. It was not clear if he was talking to Brad, his son, or the audience.

"Ooh I wish I were going. So jealous!" Brad yelped.

"You'll take the next trip, Brad, I promise."

"Golly."

"Now, I just want to thank you all for coming to Devlin's pre-bar mitzvah party. You are the very best of his friends, the best of the best, even if you aren't up on stage. Everyone is a winner. Just by being here, you've won. I want you all to give yourselves a hand."

The audience applauded for accepting an invitation to come to a party.

"Great clapping! Some of the best I've heard," Brad said.

"Yup. Indeed. Talent everywhere. If there's one thing I've learned through years of investing, is that there's always a diamond in the rough. Never overlook anything. I tell Devlin that every day. Happy almost birthday, kiddo."

Devlin, dead-eyed, nodded.

"I won't go on too much longer. Brad, you can sit down," he said, and Brad dutifully scurried to an open seat on the aisle. "What you're going to see is super cool and totally not for public consumption. Meaning, don't tell anyone not in this room! You remember the non-disclosure stamps we gave you before coming in here?" Sundra, fingering the bruise on the back of her right hand, did. The stamp was a nice reminder. The pain—and the subtle imprint—was supposed to fade in 24 hours. The DNA the stamp collected served as a signature.

"Good, I know you do. This is very fun but also very serious. Velocity Ventures is one of the very first companies to do what we're about to do. This is a historic day. I know we're all in party mode, and we should be, but what we're doing here is going to mix fun and history. *Funnery.* I'll call it that. How about that?"

Was Brad frowning?

"Me, my son, and his five best friends are going on an adventure. Hey Dev," he gazed down at his boy. "What did you say was your favorite time period?"

"Uh, Jurassic Age, like the movies."

"Yes, the Jurassic Age. 50 million years of time. At its earliest, 200 million years ago from today. Wouldn't it be nice if we could go back there?"

Oh God. She had it figured out. The asshole had built some kind of hidden amusement park for his little fat son. How nice. They were gonna ride roller coasters shaped like triceratops' heads as the rest of the kids, the unlucky ones, watched on a movie screen. Talk about a son of a bitch move. She had a strong urge to get up and leave, walk right out the door and tell Chase Dimon, who didn't know her name anyway, she was done. Imagine that. Kiss the Glassgarden ass. As plump as her mother's.

If she did any of this—if she made an unauthorized exit at Velocity, violated the fine terms of her contract—she would be promptly arrested. She'd be staring at a prison term, probably upstate. That's where most of the illegal zeros went. Dannemora or Plattsburg or some other multisyllabic smudge near the Canadian border.

"Yeah!" one of the kids on stage shouted. By the sour ripple on Chase's face, Sundra could tell this outburst was not planned.

"Such enthusiasm. How wonderful, Radyn."

"I wanna see Pangea break up."

"We just might."

"One continent became seven and then whoosh, we had dinosaurs and India and Europe and Antarctica and Australia cause people forget Australia was a country and continent—"

"That's right, and—"

"I forgot North and South America. And Asia. We're gonna see it I bet."

"We just might, if that's what the birthday boy wants to see."

Devlin spoke quietly. "I wanna see dinosaurs."

"Well, luckily, our best and brightest minds at Velocity have acquired quite the bit of technology." He was staring straight at his audience now. "Don't go telling the news feeds."

Another wink.

"Uh, so the wink means we *do* tell?" Gregg asked her.

"No, we have non-disclosure stamps, jackass. We'll be put in prison if we tell."

"Oh okay. Yeah that would blow hard."

"Yes."

Chase had a hand on his son's shoulder. "I'll cut right to it. My son, his five friends, and myself will be literally time traveling to the Jurassic Age. We will remain for approximately a half hour, as long as the machine's juice permits. Then we'll be back. And the best part is, you all get to watch! Everyone will be in on the fun."

There wasn't much of a reaction. She could tell Chase was trying to mask his son's incredulousness.

"Real time travel! Look, we have the best scientific minds…all it takes is finding a fissure in a self-created wormhole or something. It's real easy, I promise. And safe. We've been doing test cases with mice. So far, we sent one mouse to Ancient Rome and another to an Oklahoma town circa 1896. We were shooting for 1894, but it is what it is. It's totally safe. I know, you must be thinking we'll be eaten by dinosaurs. Luckily, we've picked a nice leafy spot. We're also only staying a half hour or so. So safe and fun, and you all get to watch."

Now the audience was pleading with him without speaking. Their eyes stretched, their lips quivered, their hearts collectively thudded. *Take me, take me.* They all believed. It wouldn't be enough to watch on a screen. They must go and partake in history. They wanted to stampede and were too conditioned, too cowed, to make this urge into a reality of physical action. She had no interest. She would sit, arms folded, one leg over the other. When people saw her at rest, they often asked, in a plaintive and monstrously irritating way, *are you okay? What's wrong?* Nothing was wrong. It was her default face, the way God must have imagined her at conception. She would always appear more perturbed than she was, wearing a light scowl. It would give her a deep wrinkle just above the bridge of her nose.

"That's about it, guys. Watch the screen and enjoy! We'll be bringing back souvenirs."

Sundra racked her mind for memories of the Jurassic franchise. So many films, so many T. rexes and hybrid T. rexes and serpent-necked brachiosaurs, so many brash brainy hunky leading men and women, so many (since ignored) warnings about corporatism run amok. God knows what real shit waited in the real Jurassic Age, all those millions of years ago. That magic time when gigantic lizards with dandruff flake-sized brains roamed the Earth, one endless bog dotted with volcanos in her imagination. She believed Chase. Chase could buy time travel. She imagined his party landing accidentally in one of those volcanoes. Little Devlin yowling as his underwear melted away, the lava burning up his ass crack. She chuckled. A kid sitting next to her, one of the unworthy friends of Devlin Dimon, looked over at her. He had several pimples and a nose that was prematurely gray and thick, like he stole it from his grandfather last night. He looked frightened. Why was this woman laughing to herself? What was so funny? Time travel was not funny.

"See ya guys around!"

She blinked several times and saw the Dimon crew had retreated to a command center past the stage. She could feel, as well as hear, the *oohs* and *aahs*. The rest was disarmingly easy, considering the amount of theorizing and cultural wonderment that had gone into the concept of time travel. They were there, on their fiberglass floor, the computer monitors blinking lightly. A man in a jumpsuit, whom she just noticed, pressed some buttons.

They turned into light, actual light, and they were gone.

Everyone *woooaaahhhed*. Several applauded. Sundra kept her arms crossed.

She was very sure someone on this trip would not come back alive, maybe one of the kids. You never knew what a confused pterodactyl wanted to eat.

In the end, everybody ends up dead.

5

21st Century

Chase was surprised to hear English in the Jurassic Age.

Even more surprising—*galling,* even—was that there were other people here. This was supposed to be exclusive technology. He had the urge to reach through the temporal folds to choke out Limsky, one of his dildo-brained scientists. If Limsky leaked the fucking specs, if Orion or Gaggle or Facecase or Infinity Forever or any firm that was not named Velocity Ventures got a whiff of this, there would be absolute hell to pay. There would be cuts, downgrades—he would single-handedly decimate their quant scores. He still couldn't quite see what was in front of him, what with the temporal smoke that needed to cool and the general pupil dilation that occurred after dematerializing so many millions of years. Everything was a bit fuzzy.

But he knew what he heard. The English language.

"Dad, dad, what's disco?" he heard Devlin ask. The question reminded him of why he often had to fight off the thought that he didn't like his children, or any children. To hear his child's voice unexpectedly, unasked for, was like getting smacked too hard on the back. Now it was especially egregious because it was becoming clear that, at the minimum, other Americans were here. He needed to listen. When the time fog cleared…

"Flash! Flash!" Chase shouted, looking for that shithead time guide he hired for the trip. He knew Barry Allen hated that nickname. Hated comic books.

"Flash!"

"Yes, Mr. Dimon…"

"What the fuck is this? Why do I hear the English language 200 million years ago? Who else is here?"

"Uh…" He could hear Flash's simian voice but couldn't make out his simian body. "Checking coordinates now, but it appears we aren't in the Jurassic Age."

"What?"

"Yes, it appears we are not that very far in the past at all. I'm trying to get a signal."

"You get that signal, Flash boy. You go as fast as you goddamn can."

Chase remembered it was the second Flash, Barry Allen, who died. Yes. It was a fitting name for this bozo. The dead Flash.

"It looks like we're sometime in the late 20th century, actually."

"I did not pay you or anyone else to take me back to the 20th century, Flash. I did not pay for that."

"I understand, there must have been—"

"What, a glitch? A *miscalculation*? I swear to God, when we get back you're gone. There must be 10,000 time guides who can do a better job than you."

"Certification is very rigorous, Mr. Dimon, there are only a few dozen with the proper credentials to undertake this kind of mission."

"Just tell me, and my dear son, where the hell we are."

"Well…"

The time fog began to clear and the voices, once buffered by the various tachyons and other incomprehensible particles hovering around them, were louder. Very loud. Immense, like there were thousands of them, primal screams from the concrete bowels of, of…he squinted. Below them, there was grass. Above them, night sky, and around them, people, thousands of real people, all chanting the word that Devlin just asked about.

"We're in 1979, Mr. Dimon. Chicago, Illinois. I'm sorry."

If this were a movie, the camera would dramatically pan, showing the sweep of the new universe they had arrived in. There were tens of thousands of bodies howling from their seats, and just as many standing, their ink blot bodies pulsing together. Chase saw that this was an old baseball stadium. They were somewhere, apparently, in the outfield, and—

"Oww!" screamed what sounded like Radyn. Chase turned toward the "oww." Now that the fog had evaporated, he knew absolutely where they were: near the right field foul line, maybe 50 feet from a wall of shouting people, their eyes and mouths stretched open, joining the continuous roar. They were not alone on the field, and there was no baseball. Instead of birds, discs flew in the sky. Maybe this was some alternate past.

"Flash, what the fuck, what is this, some parallel dimension you took us to?"

"The many-worlds interpretation of quantum mechanics was proved demonstrably false three years ago, so no. This is the past. It looks like July 12."

"What is this?"

"I don't know."

One of the black discs hit Radyn. He lay stunned, a gentle line of blood trickling around his neck. Chase instinctively wondered if his son was hit too. The discs, Jesus Christ, were everywhere. He deduced they were vinyl, old LP's, and they cut through the smoky night like extraterrestrial saws. These people in the bleachers were throwing them. One disc, an apparent Bee Gees record, shattered two feet from Chases' loafers. He was breathing hard, the old panic setting in. *I'm losing control. I can't handle this. I need a safe place and this isn't a safe place and I want to go home.* Young Chase, wailing Chase, beefy 12-year-old in his husky Lands' End trousers, was begging to get out of here, and asking Current Chase why they had *come so far from home.*

This was supposed to be easy, Current Chase said. *A gift for our son.*

This is why it's better to be alone, Young Chase huffed.

That's an inarguable point, at least right now.

Barry Allen was doing his best to lead the pack of boys and Chase toward center field, where they all assumed they would be safe. There was no real logic to this. They were all imbued, to some extent, with the idea that to avoid harm was to be "at the center of things." The discs continued their bombardment, cutting at strange, drunken angles, some landing softly, others shattering. Chase was still wondering where the players were and why his life was being threatened by these records—KC and the Sunshine Band, ABBA, Donna Summer—and not baseballs and bats. He would feel more at ease if some disgruntled outfielder, high on steroids, was trying to bash in his skull. He could rationalize that.

"July 12, 1979..." he heard Barry say, apparently to himself.

"Flash! Flash!"

"Yes, Mr. Dimon."

"I want to get the hell out of here right now. Now. *Now.*"

"We're a little low on juice right now."

"What the fuck does that mean?"

"Well, the way it works, there's a minimum recharge period of a half hour before we can go anywhere. The tech doesn't allow us to just time-hop, not yet. And it appears the detour we've taken has drained us a bit much, so waiting time may be, um, like an hour."

"Flash, you might as well stay in 1979 and try to make a life for yourself here among the primitives, because you have *no* future in the 21st century."

"I am very sorry, like I said…"

"Barry Allen died for a reason."

"Sorry, what?"

"Read a fucking comic book."

They staggered together. Radyn was back up walking slowly, little Javier helping him along. Devlin was in front of him, not asking for dad. Barry the Flash was at the front, waving them onward, imagining how severely Chase Dimon was going to blackball him. More of this world came into view: the crowds were far larger and more manic than any Chase had seen at a sporting event. He had cloistered himself in luxury boxes since he made his first billion at 26, watching football or baseball games on hi-def screens while enjoying salmon fillet; the rawness of these fans, unconfined by his cold glass panels, was jarring. They were chanting many things, but he understood why Devlin asked the first question that he did. Bedsheet banners were draped from the overhangs, "Disco Sucks" spray-painted in uncertain red over the fabric.

The handiwork unnerved him. Great clouds of marijuana smoke—he wasn't sure if the smell was making him imagine the clouds themselves—filled the sky.

They were screaming "disco sucks," together.

He heard Devlin now: "Mr. Flash, what's a disco? Why does it suck?"

Barry, cringing to hear the puerile nickname from the lips of Chase's son, replied, "It's a type of music. No one has liked it for a very long time."

"Okay. Like rock n' roll?"

"Sort of."

"Okay."

Before Devlin could ask another question, an army jeep sped by, spraying blades of grass on his loafers. Chase coughed on the exhaust, whiffing the heinous scent of unleaded gasoline. He could feel his IQ dropping already. The jeep was heading for the safe harbor of center field. Chase hoped the jeep had also traveled through time to rescue them. A nice army man would have the time fuel or tachyons or whatever to power them back home, away from this dystopia. He would offer a big meaty hand to Chase and the boys, smile, and tell them to hop on board.

"You were just trying to be a good father and give your nice needy boy a pre-bar mitzvah gift," the army man would say, his helmet glinting in the klieg lights. "And that Barry Allen will not be coming back. His punishment for leading you here is to live out his life in the backwaters of 1979. I hope he enjoys the pay phones!"

They would disappear in a flash of light and reappear at the Trojan Tower. Everyone would applaud.

The jeep was stopping in shallow center field. Out climbed a white bespectacled man wearing swamp green army fatigues and a helmet. He looked young and happy. A megaphone dangled from his right hand. The closer they came, the less like an army man he looked. He was more Elton John after a long day at a mall food court, sausage and refined sugar churning through his stuffed intestines. An Elton John on hard times. He lifted the megaphone to his lips and began to bark. There was an initial gurgle, words lost to the time and place, and then the electronic shriek coagulated into something he could hear.

"This is now officially the world's largest anti-disco rally! Now listen—we took all the disco records you brought tonight, we got 'em in a giant box, and we're gonna blow 'em up reeeeeeal gooood."

The box…They closed in toward it, an enormous black bin crammed with these records. What is this? Where is the baseball? In the haze, a pitcher stood on the mound and hurled a ball to the catcher, so small in the hail of LP's. Was he warming up? Would the game be played after the disco records stopped pelting the field?

"Real gooood. Because why? Why?"

"Disco sucks! Disco sucks! Disco sucks!"

"I wanna go home, there aren't any dinosaurs," Dallas said to Javier, both of them sniffling. Chase felt an ephemeral sense of tenderness for the boys. They felt what he felt. This was the type of empathy he could embrace, one predicated on what he felt first. He placed a hand on Dallas' shoulder and channeled the voice of his own dead father.

"It's going to be *all right*, boys."

He held a bright smile for them both. They did not respond, blinking back at him like canines. He tried again. "You have nothing to be worried about."

"My head hurts," Radyn groaned. The blood was at least drying.

"I know, I know," Chase attempted this comfort voice some more, mimicking his mother. She was always very good at this. "When we all get back, everyone gets an ice cream sundae."

"I don't want ice cream," Javier moaned. "I hate how this smells. I hate this grass too. Too squishy."

"The grass is the least of our problems," Barry Allen said.

Devlin was inhabiting his role as the straggler, tripping along at a slower pace. He was dizzy and hungry. The people beyond the outfield wall made him especially queasy. He hated their sideburns and hair plumes, the waviness of their movements, how they wore sunglasses at night. He did not know what disco was but had sympathy for it now.

A disc took a flying saucer trajectory straight at Devlin's Adam's apple. He only dodged because he stepped on his untied shoelace, pitching face first into the grass of right center field. He stayed down. There was peace in the soil, a coolness to counteract the broiling atmosphere. He inched his arms outward like a snow angel. Without knowing why, he began to slowly flap them, feeling stronger as his thumbs neared his skull. He stared into the green-black, imagining he was napping at the bottom of his aunt's swimming pool in East Hampton, breathing easily.

Barry Allen was the first to know this wasn't the right trajectory. They were near the rear of the bin, out of view of the army character and his megaphone. His scientist's eye told his scientist's brain that the man's threat about the disco records was not idle. There were explosives wired to the bin, and in the bin. He ran to Chase and, against his better instincts, grabbed his arm.

"We have to get out of here."

"I *know* that. This is a hellhole. Your idiocy put us here."

"No, I mean, away from that giant bin, we have to just head somewhere else, maybe toward that bullpen."

"Shut up. You were wrong before, and you are wrong again. I have an idea. I am going to interrupt that gentleman and ask him for directions. If we're going to be stuck here, I want to know about a good 1979 downtown Chicago hotel. We'll make the best of a bad situation. You can stay in a fleabag. You aren't invited."

"He doesn't look like he's in the mood to, well, talk."

This hotel idea would salvage the day. They'd enjoy 1979, live it up, do room service, see a show, have a nice four course meal at a rooftop restaurant. He had a passing familiarity with the Loop. How much had it changed in all these years? He had gone to Chicago for business, fine city, like a younger, sicklier cousin of New York, but a cousin that tried its damnedest to be fun. They could take a stroll along Lake Michigan until Flash got the stupid crystals charged up or whatever. Chase would put him in the cheapest motel possible. No indignity, no degradation would be too much. He had a notion to ask this man with the bullhorn where he could find a nice hot sheet motel, one where the bedspread was guaranteed to smell like cum and be filled with bed bugs, for his *friend*

Dr. Barry Allen. Watching Flash suffer for his mistake could redeem this little excursion. Chase had to admit *schadenfreude* was one of his favorite states of being. His fear of someone experiencing it at the expense of himself and his attraction to this feeling were both drivers of his startling success, he would argue. He had said as much, in more couched terms, in livestream lectures.

"I'll *make* him talk. You wouldn't know anything about it, being a spineless little thumb twiddler who can't even do the one job correctly that he's given to do."

"C'mon, let's just go over there—"

"No! I won't be told what to do by anyone, let alone by the likes of you." He turned back to look at the kids, not seeing Devlin but assuming he was behind one of them. "We're going to have fun in Chicago tonight!"

None of them answered.

"Disco, my friends, is going to die tonight!" the army man shouted.

Chase hesitated. May be best to wait until the end of his little shtick. Flash was looking like he wanted to make a break for it. Not on his watch. Barry didn't get to control his destiny. Never had, never will. Destiny was Chase's domain. Even in the depths of the past, his bearings lost, he would call the shots. Flash must stay close.

"Where the hell are you going?"

"We've gotta get away from this bin here, Mr. Dimon. He's going to blow it up."

"No. In fact, just because you suggested it, I am going to do this opposite. And you are coming with me."

Army man: "Disco will die! Now, let's begin the count down. Ten..."

70,000 spectators, drunk and high and thirsty for action: "Ten!"

"Nine!"

"Nine!"

"Eight!"

"Eight!"

"C'mon Mr. Dimon," Barry Allen pleaded, understanding that this could be one of the last times in his brief mortal life to make a plea to anyone. "We need to go."

"No! No!" Chase was shouting, his thick black eyebrows shooting up to his impeccable hairline. His veins inflated with his hot blood. Barry saw a budding psychopath or one coming to terms with the insanity repressed for so long. In his gesticulations and the wild shine of his eyeballs, he had arrived at his new and likely final state. Barry wanted to scream that he was leading them all to a certain end. But that would drive Chase Dimon further into the flames. This was a time, he told himself, to act. To transcend Dr. Barry Allen, employee of Velocity Ventures, and become a human being in communion with this innate and constant war for survival. Above all, we must survive, *persist*. To help others *persist*. The five boys—no, four, where the hell was the kid Devlin?—didn't deserve to die because one deranged multibillionaire unearths his id in 1979.

That was what frightened Barry most. Chase was not an imperious, overworked, over-ambitious, preening asshole. Chase was something else. It took just one extraordinary moment to burn away the shell, the elaborate casings, of a life and see what pulsed below. Barry had to go the other way.

He would. He must. He couldn't. His only hope was his boss coming to his senses in time.

"Four!"

"Four!"

"Three!"

"Three!"

Chase's money frightened Barry. This was a truth he could confront now. As a scientist, mildly brilliant and compensated enough to enjoy a refurbished two-bedroom in SoFiDieBeca, he understood the enormity of a number. In the 10th grade, his biology teacher Mr. Deveyakan asked the class if they would accept one billion dollars on the condition that they would have to count each individual dollar bill before collecting the windfall. All, Barry included, said yes. How long could it take anyway? One, two, three weeks? Mr. Deveyakan, in his wire-rims and bush of blonde hair, smiled. He may have even licked a lip. "31 years, class. If you're lucky."

The lesson hit home for young Barry. As he would later learn, even the best of scientists are agents and instruments for someone or something else: an academic institution, a corporation, or a corporation masquerading as a nonprofit. Science itself, with very few exceptions, served profit first and nothing second. Barry knew this, figuring the best way to take advantage of his gifts and to also enjoy his time on Earth was to tinker with time travel technology for a billionaire's amusement. He had used the best of his ability to try to further the experience of one boy's pre-bar mitzvah party. Gosh, he wasn't a Jew, but when did they start having pre-bar mitzvahs anyway? He couldn't remember ever attending one when he was a kid going to school in a heavily Jewish Long Island town. But if he had internalized anything, it was that the truly rich could always invent monumental and strange ways to expend their resources. Money was nothing if it was not spent. It was theoretical, existing in the subjunctive tense, which the Dimons of the world detested. They did not *wish*—they *did*, or paid handsomely for someone else to do it. Barry was just one of these many payees. He was nothing more than a butler with a doctorate in quantum mechanics.

"Two!"

"Two!"

It was true he didn't like being called Flash. He never had much use for superheroes, comics, movies based on comics, web series based on comics, newly-created superheroes, or mythos in general. What Chase didn't know was that he had looked up his namesake. He knew Barry Allen was the second and arguably most famous Flash, wedged between Jay Garrick and Wally West. He knew Flash was actually faster than Superman. He knew Flash could travel through time on something called the cosmic treadmill.

Barry had even mulled over the physics of such a device, once or twice. He had deemed it unworkable.

He had nothing against the character itself. It was the whole concept of a superhero that irked him. The willful violation of physical laws with little consequential scientific explanation. The earnestness of the protagonist. The insipid variety of archetypes. The idea that there was justice and evil and *saving* to be done, when mankind, by the numbers at least, was very likely doomed for the long haul. What would the Flash do when the sun swelled into a red giant and evaporated all the oceans? What would the Flash do when the sun shrank to a white dwarf? The lack of imagination with these comic book writers was bothersome.

Barry would try one last time. He owed it to his body to try.

"Mr. Dimon, we need to get out of here! We need to move away!"

Chase was only walking closer, now a pitcher's mound distance between a rudimentary detonator and his body. The little kids were following. What else could they do?

"One!"

"One!"

Barry was not far away enough to save himself. The time to retreat was one or two ruminations ago. He was well aware.

"Chase!"

Devlin, his face to the grass, felt the ground shake. He swore the shake preceded the explosion, though this was impossible. He certainly heard the explosion of late 1970's disco LP's. What he did not see: the abrupt, painful death of his father, friends, and Dr. Barry Allen, all milling near the point of impact. They saw fire and nothing else. The fireball seared the skin from the bone and disintegrated, as best it could, the bone itself. In the simmering crater in center field, the shards of obliterated LP's joined the remnants of the expedition, a slice or three of black plastic mixing with the crumb of a femur or dust that formed, once upon a time, a functioning orbital socket. Devlin breathed deeply. He did not want to look up.

"Wooo look at that! We did it! Dis-co sucks. Dis-co sucks. Dis-co sucks…"

Next, the ground actually shook. Devlin's imagination was not playing tricks. His body screamed to get up, get up, so he did, and met the onslaught. Thousands of men and women climbing over the fragile walls around the field and tumbling to the grass, rushing like pigeons to bread or like…or well, he better get the hell up and *run*. They were a jumbled mass of afros and sunglasses and bell bottoms and sweat-soaked tees and paisley and tube socks and denim washing over the land as the pot smoke trailed innocently overhead. The crater smoldered, the shards of Summers and Sunshine Band glinting in the kliegs, and the people ran. Devlin watched one boy slide down the right field foul pole like he was in his own personal firehouse. He looked down at his Gaggle. No signal. It hadn't had any since he got here. An army, black and hairy, swung by and knocked his Gaggle up into the sky. He could watch, frame by frame, as it fell to the grass and a wave of sneakers stampeded over the hardware. His dad would be pissed. Where was he? Devlin wobbled over to the wall, his back up against the padding. Sweat pooled on his spine. Each time he blinked, there were another hundred bodies filling once vacant patches of grass. Liquor and wine and beer bottles were clenched at the necks. Some swigged, some ran and swigged, laughing and shouting. There was no outfield, no game. There were the bodies, shirts torn off, abs and barrel stomachs and bras. He could hear: "Please return to your seats, please return to your seats, please return to your seats." The elderly voice, diluted in the wheezing PA system, was barely heard. Records kept cutting the night. Devlin was straight against the wall, like a mugger was holding a knife to his throat. "Please return to your seats. Please return to your seats." Second base was airborne. Someone was carrying it, then someone lofted it high like pizza dough. Three boys slid into the dark imprint, babbling *safe, safe*. There was a parade over the third base dugout, a pot-fired conga line, a melody of one of the destroyed LP's dripping from their lips. The record shards crunched underfoot like snowflakes of the future, not Devlin's, another one at the end of the planet. He didn't move. They were pouring over every wall, right field, right center, left center, left, third base, first base, tearing holes in the backstop, the giggling armies of the night. Another boy, fatter than the first, took his turn taunting death from the foul pole. "Please return to your seats. Please return to your seats." The equivalent of a campfire burned where one of the Chicago White Sox or Detroit Tigers might have blooped a shallow single to right. The scoreboard, black with desperate yellow letters, told them to return, to watch the game that wouldn't happen.

He never wanted this. He didn't want a stupid pre-bar mitzvah. He didn't want a bar mitzvah. He wanted to be left alone. As his friends and classmates, one after another, fell like dominoes from 12 to 13, he cringed. He shivered. Stuttering in Hebrew and pretending to have friends who were girls and trying to hide from a screaming DJ/MC/sequined ringmaster; sampling the mile-long sheet cakes, sometimes molded into the shapes of baseballs or rocket ships or electric guitars; watching the tuxedoed march of relatives long forgotten, cousins and aunts and nieces and friends of friends converging like locusts for small talk, each remarking on *how big* or *how handsome* he looked. He had imagined it all, taking in the strained experiences of his comrades to cobble together his future. His dad had pushed the idea of *another* fun thing to do to "wet his whistle" and Devlin, never wanting to displease his anxious dad, said okay.

Even at 12, he could sense the tension in the house, mom constantly threatening a divorce, dad whining about not having a "prenup" which Devlin quickly gaggled the definition for, the perpetual absence of his sister, a glum 16-year-old fond of eating her feelings behind a locked door. He understood dad "needed this." To his credit, he had done a very good job keeping the surprise secret, and up until the moment they were actually traveling through time, Devlin had assumed dad had done something stupid like hired a "major star" from one of the Gaggle streams he watched to entertain his friends. He felt bad for both his parents because he had the dim sense that they were failing him. He could already envision the screaming match that would ensue when they all went home, mom pointing out how dad couldn't even get a surprise for his son *right* and dad making some comment, usually mumbled, about *sluts* and *whores*. They would retreat to their respective offices in the duplex, dad sulkily calling for a chopper to take him out east to "clear his head."

Funnily enough, way up in the milky night, he saw a helicopter. He didn't feel nostalgic.

"Okay now, we're going to sing a little song. Everyone please return to your seats now. Here we go. Take me out to the…"

The disembodied voice belonged to an old phlegmy man. People galloped by Devlin—one kid in torn-up shorts even leaped directly over the wall he had his backed pressed against—without acknowledging him.

He was glad to not be noticed. Let them keep running by him. Eventually, one of his friends or dad would wander over and tell him it was time to go. He had enough of this time, where people seem naked and stupid, rushing without Gaggles or even rudimentary mobiles. This was its own Jurassic Age. He never liked baseball. He had a mild interest in Idball, the so-called American pastime, as everyone else. It was un-American to not have a mild interest in it. New York Miasma versus New Jersey Negativity in the Bowl last year, the death shot from Bridgewater in the 5th that put the Miasma over the top…Javier, the biggest Miasma fan he knew, wouldn't stop imitating Vitus Bridgewater at school, nearly sending six different kids to the ER applying the "Bridgewater Brainbuckler." When he found out last year the Negativity had acquired cloning rights on Bridgewater and would have one of their own in the decade, Javier sobbed. *Bridgewater was for Miasma, and no one else! No one!*

This wasn't like Idball. For one, the crowd, for all its size and absurdity, was not so violent. Devlin was still waiting for the first punches and kicks, knees to the groin, karate chops to the jugular. He was waiting for the blood, at first a slow trickle and then, when everyone really got going, a geyser. He wondered if anyone on the field was an Ent or if it was all premiums, based on how poor they looked. And the baseball players—how many premiums were allowed? Idball had a rigorous and fair quota system, allowing every year for each team to carry a certain number of premiums on the roster. Devlin, not quite the fan, couldn't recall the number. All these people rushing around, tearing up grass and lighting fires, they very likely weren't Ents which meant premiums were able to afford a few more luxuries in 1979.

That guy who his dad hated, Flash, would have an answer. How come so many premiums could afford the game? Or they *were* Ents, and they were in disguise. That could be it. This was July, Flash said, though it could be some pre-Halloween thing, like he was doing a pre-bar mitzvah. Anything was possible.

Devlin was almost curious enough to peel himself from the outfield wall. Almost.

"…take me out to the crowd, buy me some peanuts and craaaacker jacks, I don't care if…"

In deep right field, on the edge of the warning track, a man with his pants down was on top of a woman. She had her arms wrapped around his bare shining back. Her brown hair, long enough to reach her waist, was spread on the grass, fanning out from her armpits like two flattened wings. His bouffant was the color of lightened rust and his mustache was thick. Devlin had seen enough porn to know what this was, but he had never seen the act of fucking IRL. He was disoriented. Without a camera and an audience behind the screen—he was the only one watching, the rest of the crowed too caught up in the revelry to care—he did not know intercourse like this was really possible. He conceived of it as an abstract, cinematic act, the equivalent of a tourist attraction he had seen enough online images of to know what the real thing was like without really knowing anything at all.

She was licking his ear as if a sugar cube was waiting inside. She was sylph-like, thin enough to disappear in the grass under the crush of sex, weighing little more than his two ranch dressing-colored thighs put together. But she was going nowhere, only pulling him down and to the side and rolling on top of him, hungrily unbuttoning her blouse as his hips swam into her. Her lace bra was next to go. Her breasts were not the water balloons of Devlin's friend's porn, with nipples pointed like church steeples. They were small and paler than the rest of her, two moons peeking into earthlight from a realm of dusky space. She threw her hands on his neck and lowered her mouth to his. They were swallowing each other. Devlin watched the impression of their bone below skin, how her ribcage seemed to come alive as a separate being, how his shoulder blades made themselves known. Their moans were lost in the din.

"…root root for the home team and if they don't win it's a shame, because it's one, two, three…"

The men in blue were next. Devlin was against the wall. They held clubs and several, redundantly, shouted "police." The collective daze was ending. There were fires in the grass, but there were signs that this miraculous aperture in the space-time continuum, when a scheduled baseball game could not continue because the public had seized a private field and refused to leave, was closing. The woman, hunting for her bra, stumbled off the man, and he said something that was swallowed in the night, her lips crinkling in reply. Dance steps were replaced by flight, one foot far in front of the other, elbows shooting. The police multiplied, the baby blue virus, and the crowds hustled for the long forgotten exits. A pair of boys chugging Buds in front of the White Sox dugout were slung in headlocks and subdued in the on deck circle. Their helmets reminded Devlin of home, of his New York shock troops, only with limper arms. Smoke plumes hovered over the throngs as if the parties were still on, as if "disco sucks" were the only words worth chanting. The police waved their clubs, marching in v and i formations from the deep reaches of the outfield, meeting police who had materialized behind home plate. Devlin still didn't see any of his friends or his dad. He stepped away from the wall.

He stood in the corner, where the right field wall formed a right angle with the lower wall running along the foul line. He stood and waited in the pocket of dirt where a double would've caromed if there had been a game. The police were taking full control, shoving the non-police away. Maybe they would stay on the field to dance, drink, and have sex. Devlin's dad still hadn't come out of hiding. Nor had his friends. He wasn't too worried. They'd all be around eventually.

They always came back.

6

1979

The Sly Foxx in the East Village was owned by a man named Eldrick Foxx, the alleged son of Jimmie Foxx, the now-forgotten baseball legend of the 1920's and 1930's. Old Double X had tremendous muscles and a deadly affinity for alcohol. This, somehow, motivated Eldrick, who had no discernable athletic skills, to open a bar. There was a time, maybe during the early grooviness of LBJ's second term, when the bar had what could be called a heyday: a moneyed and loyal clientele with clean criminal records.

Pigs never bothered checking up on the bar in the 60's. It wasn't one of "those" bars.

Then Lolita Velez started showing up. Eldrick, even as he swooned over her, had pegged the bar's decline to her arrival. These sorts of things defied easy verbal explanations. They were atmospheric, something you felt on your lips and eyelashes and pores. You saw the calendar turn, the tips diminish, the streets grow restless. Eldrick had a theory that by the year 2000 society wouldn't be able to sustain itself anymore. At 51, he was a rabid pessimist, a stark turnaround from his baseball-mad youth, when his lush of a mother told him all about "your pa Jimmie smacking the tar out of the ball for the Boston Athletics," never mind she was confusing the Boston Red Sox and Philadelphia Athletics, never mind that this raised no red flags in young Eldrick's mind. He too was destined to smack the tar out of the baseball, and did so in the local ice cream leagues until, well, he didn't anymore, and the dream died in ice—getting cut from the varsity senior year, via a typewritten list posted on the coach's icebox—rather than fire.

Now he stared down into the maw. That was what this society was: a gargantuan throat swallowing light and people, the bloody shark teeth of Brooklyn and Manhattan, the tongue of the Bronx, Staten Island as the slippery gums. Queens? Fuck Queens. That cocksucker Jimmy Breslin lived in Forest Hills. Eldrick had no tolerance for newspapers. For him, Son of Sam was the last straw. It made him break out into a cold sweat every night that there was some dumpy killer who could look like you and me sticking lead in people's skulls. It made him break out in a rage to think about this *News* columnist Breslin being some kinda chum to the Son of Sam, getting that letter. And the papers that ran Son of Sam stories all the time, never stopping, pimping themselves out on the blood and gore for a quarter, Jesus Christ. Fuck them.

He was cleaning a mug, just swabbing away, when Lolita walked in with a freakshow. She was dressed hot to trot, the little goddamn mamacita. Hell he'd come in his chinos if it were allowed. She had on these jean cut offs, what the kids wear, and this tight top so her perky Spanish Harlem breasts could get through. Shit. He blamed her for everything, always had, and couldn't get over her.

He'd give anything for one go around. That'd show his asshole of an ex-wife. He was much better than she said.

"Welcome aboard," he said just to her, doing his best to emphasize the guy she was toting around didn't matter.

"Rum and Coke, Eldrick," she told him. He grimaced. He hated when she didn't say hello.

"Eh and what does this bozo want? Welcome to the Sly."

"Hmm," Archie said.

"You speak-ey the English?"

Archie didn't feel good without his mask and fedora. He felt nauseous, naked, and even Lolita's presence couldn't counteract that. She interrupted him. He was *close.* One, two more, he would've been in the dungeon of the Candies, and then he would've blown them right open, and then…he had an answer, he didn't have an answer. He was closing in. He wasn't. This time spent in the streets, it would all be…his thoughts always seemed to run out of breath. On the Force, it was more he never had time for breath, between clamping down on the street scum and scum in blue. He admitted he was glad to see Lolita. She was a taste you couldn't get out of your mouth. You rinse, you spit, it did no good. He was happy. He was pissed. He was working, he was close, he should've resisted. Any other broad and he would've. What woman had ever told Archie London what to do? Instead, he just went with her like a baby, riding in silence along the Sea Beach Express all the way to a shithole bar in Manhattan where some gray-haired fireplug was staring at him like he was wearing a fake penis on his forehead.

Once Lolita reminded him of the weather, he began to feel hot. On the job he always ignored it, letting events overtake elements. Mind over matter, et cetera. She appeared at Stillwell and he was aware of the sweat pouring sickly down his back, the way his undershirt clung to his skin, a geological stain taking shape. He felt the dampness of the pistol grip. Boarding the train, he touched it under his coat and he couldn't be sure it wasn't an old stick of butter he had stolen from his senile mother. He coughed loudly enough for Lolita to turn her small dark head and place a hand on his. She never said anything.

"Watch yourself," Archie said.

"Who? Me? You're telling *me* to watch myself in my own bar?"

"Yeah."

"Last fella who said that…he ended up in the morgue," Eldrick said.

Archie knew he was lying. His lower lip shook, his eyes flitted too fast, and his right hand, balled into a fist on the old counter, was clearly shaking. Scared little man. Archie took pity. He was balding and desperately trying to save it all with a comb over, his greasy hair swept into a crooked sidepart, the strands triangulating at a peculiar point near the center of his skull. 20 years ago, he may have been handsome and tough. Could've been those blue eyes.

"The morgue. Hm. How many dead bodies you seen?"

Archie moved closer. He was two feet or so from being in biting range.

"Enough in this fucking city."

"I've seen, let's see, 28 bodies."

"You sleep with all of 'em?"

"Hey, hey," Lolita chirped, not quite getting in between them but position-ing herself well enough for an uneasy détente. "Let's just relax. Put on the TV, Eldrick. Archie and I like the TV."

"Oh, do ya?"

A jukebox was playing Buddy Holly, one of the songs he made right before he died. There were six other people in the Sly Foxx, two of them in the corner smoking, the four others, all trucker types, jammed into a narrow booth. They had three beer pitchers among them.

"And I want some of that popcorn, too," Lolita added. "Not the stale kind."

"Not the stale kind, she says. Okay, princess."

Archie turned to her. "I'm going to go home."

"Why? Why? C'mon."

"This ain't my bag.'

"Nothing's your bag. You hang out with that stupid writer too much."

"I need information."

"Relax."

"Easy to do when you're 20. Harder to do when you're 40."

"That's not even that old. My dad's 78."

"Hmm."

"You'll like the popcorn."

He hated the popcorn. It was dry, barely buttered. When he bit in, he got as much kernel as fluff, and this was no good. He considered how he ended up here, with Lolita. Why this was the person who could make him do things he did not intend to do. Why there were captains and sergeants and principals and professors and coaches who never, for a single moment, commanded a smidgen of respect from Archie London, and could not even get him to bring them a glass of water if they collectively held guns to his head.

Lolita Velez. 21 years of age next week.

He kept eating the popcorn. Lolita sipped her drink. Eldrick Foxx, slumped and owlish, went back to polishing a glass, or whatever it was a bartender was supposed to do. Poor fuck. He still thought Son of Sam was coming for him next. He still imagined that pudgy shmuck David Berkowitz under his bedsheets, polishing a gun, wanking off. He kept a .44 magnum in the bar, down with the spirits. A dog talked to Berkowitz! Eldrick didn't trust dogs, either. This friend of Lolita's, he mouths off, he's getting the .44—that was a promise his trembling trigger finger would keep.

"Not bad, huh?"

"What?"

"The popcorn."

"It's bad."

"Let's get you drunk."

"I don't do that."

"Hey, I'm all done. Another rum for me, and get a gin and tonic here for Archie."

Eldrick nodded.

"Everyone drank on the Force so I didn't."

"You know what my brother JoJo says about cops? He says they're an occupying army and we're the colonies. Anyone who isn't white."

"They fail white and nonwhite equally."

"No, they hate us Puerto Ricans more. They're terrified of it becoming *Nueva* York."

"Hmm."

"Tonight's the night you tell me what goes on in your head."

Archie's head jerked up at the TV. In stuttering Technicolor, the beginning of an evening newscast came on, a man in a dark blue suit and striped tie glancing down at his papers. To his right, on a wooden prop of a television screen—a TV within a TV—the words "Riot at Sox Park" appeared superimposed over the image of a baseball stadium. Archie kept watching.

"Thousands of young people worked up by a disc jockey, his anti-disco night got out of hand, the White Sox promotion obviously backfired when the fans, the young ones, took the demonstration much too seriously, spilled out of their seats mobbing the field as you can see, the game was delayed over two hours. Police actually set up barricades to keep people out of the stadium. It was truly, truly an unbelievable sight. Lisa Landers is there with a live report."

Archie waited. The scene on the screen was a field of dancing maggots that, when he squinted to make them out, were actually people. The shot held there for two monumental seconds.

"Lisa Landers is not there with a live report. As you can imagine, the scene is pandemonium and it's not our policy to, uh, add to the situation."

Four anchors, three men and a woman, turned to each other.

"Fucking fucks," Eldrick said, staring up at the TV.

"That looks fun," Lolita said.

Archie was quiet. He clenched his gin and tonic. One sip was enough. Something, he understood, was coming, or had come already. This anti-disco night brought it. He had no explanation, no way to rationalize it. Then again, he was sure the future would mean the death of reason. Ronald Truncheon believed in organized conspiracies, pocket illuminati guiding so-called current events behind a gauzy curtain, all coincidences leading back to a small man in a dark room fiddling with a switch and an intercom. *Go here, go there.* Paranoia, yes, but also a blind trust in rationality: there were actors and puppeteers with minds and hearts who decided what was what, who killed Kennedy, who killed King, who ensnared and destroyed the hero of Archie and Truncheon's parents, Richard Milhous Nixon.

Archie subscribed to another idea. He wouldn't even really call it an *idea*. It was more anti-faith. Nihilism with *some* belief. He sniffed, he hunted, he fought, he came close to killing but didn't. He believed in justice, fully. He believed himself to be of better stuff than any other human in his immediate or distant orbit. Closest was Truncheon. There was no second. Not Lolita. Not this strange child with a gangster brother, a diabetic mother and a father who fled her family for Big Sur, where he starved while writing home lovely letters about his alleged communes with nature and the "invisible eyeball."

Archie had no classification for Lolita.

"Drink up, c'mon," she said, taunting him with those eyes. He could tell Eldrick Foxx felt the same way and hated him for it. Her feline eyes were a dusky brown, too large for her miniature, rounded face with its ghostly dimples. They were forever challenging whatever walked in front of her, never shirking, never shying. She made religious eye contact. There were legendary lovers, Lord Byrons and such, with those same eyes, and monarchs and warlords who murdered because it was easy. A wizard like Truncheon—a horndog like Truncheon—could expend an entire chapter on Lolita Velez's eyeballs, 10,000 words on the typewriter without getting up to take a piss. Lolita wasn't one of those "hot" girls you remember from high school, a prom queen or a cheerleader sporting the cleavage of an 18-year-old at 14. She fit no stereotype. You could peg her as one of the enigmatic ones, slipping in and out of shadow, laughing wildly at a joke in the hallway before returning to a seemingly unshakeable silence, her thoughts utterly her own.

Archie met her doing PI work for a client in Spanish Harlem—one of the only really rich Puerto Ricans up there, a man named Alfredo Borrero. Borrero years ago had belonged to a right-wing party or cult that plotted, but never carried out, an assassination attempt on a socialist congressman named Vito Marcantonio. Borrero told Archie he still regretted that Marcantonio, who had the gall to vote against the Korean War, died of a heart attack walking out of the City Hall station on the Broadway side, and not by his own hand.

"That red communist killed America every year when he was in office, and I hope he's tasting the tip of Satan's penis every goddamn day for eternity," Borrero said at least several times, forgetting what it was he had summoned Archie London, Private Eye, for. Oh, right: he simply needed to know if his wife was cheating on him.

"Tail her and tell me. She's slippery. The third's always the worst."

"Third?"

"*Wife*. I'm told the fourth one usually ends up the best, statistically speaking. But I have no appetite for a fourth wedding right now. I want to cling onto number three and see if we can make it work."

"That's heart-warming."

"Yeah, and if she's screwing that JoJo Velez, the kid in the hardware store, she's a goner. I will end her."

"You shouldn't do that, Alfredo."

"I don't pay you to talk back. I pay you to tell me what cock other than *my own* my wife is putting inside of her."

It was an easy case. In two days, Archie had closed it. Gloria Borrero, 52, was *not* sleeping with JoJo Velez, then 22. She was sleeping with JoJo's friend, Diego Polanco, 23. This was disorienting for Alfredo because he had grown so used to envisioning his wife sleeping with JoJo, the suave part-time cashier at their local hardware store, Rivera's. (JoJo would unexpectedly quit soon after the case.) It was like Alfredo had watched a porno of JoJo and his wife and was now being told that it was simply an actor playing JoJo. He could not accept this at first. It was a tremendous letdown. Alfredo was a man used to sketching out reality beforehand and forcing images and events to conform to the rules he had invented for himself. Any failures to conform were simply ignored and disregarded. This was how he charged ahead to make himself a six-figure man, a landlord to a vast, disheveled swath of the neighborhood. He was a man of a profound, and powerful, ignorance.

"It's JoJo!" he boomed. "I know it."

"It's Diego, a high school friend. They were feeling each other up in a Lenox Avenue phone booth."

"That's not sex."

"They went back to Diego's mother's place on 116th and Park. Diego performed cunnilingus on your wife. She performed fellatio on him. Then they had standard coitus, missionary position, until your wife demanded he 'drill that stone cold rod into me.' He did so. This lasted, in total, for 46 minutes. He ejaculated and she came as well, during the initial cunnilingus. No contraceptives were used throughout. They kissed when it was over."

"You *sure* it wasn't JoJo?"

Looking back on it, Archie figured Borrero got a real kick out of JoJo Velez banging his wife. Archie didn't have an exact reason; these sorts of fetishes, like finding a foot erotic, defy explanation. He could see Borrero grabbing his erection and rubbing mightily to the thought of JoJo on top of his wife, pogoing up and down, shooting spooge in her eyes.

During the brief investigation, trailing Diego out of the aforementioned phone booth on Lenox, Archie heard someone cry, "Your shoes!"

Archie looked down, then up. Standing to his side, one foot off the curb, was Lolita.

"Hey hey, those shoes are untied."

It was true. The shoelaces on his left foot had defied his double knot. He stooped to redo them.

"Yeah, thanks."

"What're you up to, anyway?"

"I can't say."

"You following my brother?"

"I can't say."

"He's done bad stuff, but probably not what you're after."

"You know that?"

"I know, man. Aren't you hot in that coat?"

"No."

"It's summer, man."

"I'm aware. I need to get going."

"Keep your shoes tied."

"I will."

"I'm Lolita, by the way. I'm JoJo's sister."

"Good to meet you."

"No name? No handshake? Isn't that what you downtown gringos do? A firm shake, a martini at the oyster bar, and a stogie on the 7:46 to Armonk?"

"Good to meet you."

"I promise I don't have a *disease*."

She stepped forward, grabbing his right hand with both of her hands and clasping hard, like an oyster shell closing over a pearl. The power of her grip surprised him. So did the tickle of heat in his stomach and chest. He hoped she would keep her hands over his for a moment longer than she did, just one extra second.

"Now, if you wanna know who that rich bitch is actually—"

"You know about my case?"

"I don't know about any case. But if you wanna know who she's screwing, doing the dirty dance all the time, it's *not* JoJo. JoJo's tight with his girl."

"I'll take that under consideration."

"JoJo is tight, I'm telling you. His pal Diego, well, he gets around. He's got the longest anteater uptown, that's the word. Wouldn't surprise me if some horny housewife like Gloria Borrero wanted to ride that for a few hours."

"I'll take that under consideration."

Ever since then, whenever he ran into her, he would feel a fistful of heat around his heart. He would breathe shorter, fight for the exact words he wanted to use. This was not a fight he usually had. He chose to speak few words and knew exactly what would come out of his mouth, plotting out entire interactions like a conversational grandmaster. He would never claim to be witty or articulate. He was just not sloppy. Sloppy words in this city could get you killed.

"Drink *a bit*," she said to him again, miraculously finishing another rum and Coke. Next Eldrick brought her a beer, a Budweiser.

"I told you, it's not what I do."

"He's a pussy," Eldrick jumped. "That's all. Never trust a man who can't take a drink."

"Shut up, Elly."

"Don't call me that."

"Then *shut up*."

"Hey, whose bar is it, anyway?"

"Department of Buildings says it belong to an I. Niederman. I looked it up."

"That's my landlord. I'm the bar owner. He owns the building. Some Jew in Brooklyn."

"I. Niederman. I wouldn't tell him to shut up."

"I'm this close to throwing both of you out."

Lolita stuck her tongue out. "Didja even ever meet your dad?"

"Huh."

"Old Double X. The Beast."

"Look at this little tart, reading her *Sporting News* back issues."

"Didja? I saw he had a son, Jimmie Foxx Jr. I never saw anywhere that mentioned Eldrick Foxx."

Eldrick's features noticeably compressed, the right angles in his jawline tightening as a row of jagged upper teeth peered out from below the lip, like he was preparing to nibble his chin off. He stared straight at her.

"Watch. What you say."

"Tell me, Elly, how did your daddy die?"

Archie did not look at either of them. He was following the newscasters collectively decrying the anti-disco night in Chicago, their pastel neckties aglow with indignation. An anchor with a sandy blonde mustache reported there were fatalities. The female anchor gasped unprofessionally.

"Get the hell out of—"

"*How?*"

"Of old age, like anyone else on this fucking planet."

"No!" Lolita slapped Archie on the shoulder. "Let me see if I remember the story the right way, my little girl memory is a little fuzzy, too full of rainbows and daffodils. The story goes that on July 21st, 1967, Jimmie Foxx, one of the greatest hitters in baseball history, choked to death on a piece of meat. Chicken, I believe. He was 59."

"I will not have you desecrating the memory of my daddy in this bar."

"He wasn't your dad and you know it. Admit it! If you don't I'm not coming back here. Archie and I can get juiced somewhere else."

"You…" Eldrick was not shaking with rage, exactly. He was close to stillness, save for a tremor in his index finger and the bulge of three or four capillaries. He glanced toward the spirits.

"You aren't his son. I come here and you tell lies to everyone. I don't like lying. You aren't anybody's son. You're just a guy."

"One more word, just one."

"You should call it the Sly Fox, one 'x.' Just one. I bet I got more homerun hitting genes than you, and I'm pretty sure my papa is a queer."

"Get out. Get the hell out. Both of you."

Lolita didn't stand. Archie was watching the TV, like Truncheon watched his TV. Eldrick turned and headed for the spirits. If tonight had to be the night, so be it. He had been waiting for chaos to intrude all these years, expecting a mass murderer to saunter in and blow them all to smithereens. Someone like Son of Sam or even just a strung out Latin kid from Lolita's neighborhood willing to kill for a dime bag. Waiting, waiting. But why wait? Why not *be* the chaos? You can change the course of other people's lives, bring destiny to their doorsteps. You don't have to be a passive actor. You don't have to be JFK in Dealey Plaza. You can be Oswald, eyeing his prey in the scope, one shot to insert himself into recorded history for all time, or at least until the sun incinerates the Earth. You don't have to wait. You can bend down like a good boy and retrieve the hidden .44. You can write the screaming headlines for tomorrow's papers. Let's see what Breslin makes of this: one bar owner shoots dead a 20-year-old woman and her latest squeeze, an ugly lug with a comic book name. Shoots them at point blank range, two bullets, straight between their eyes. The cops will marvel. *Two perfect shots. They don't teach this at the academy.* Hot damn. They won't even have time to think. No time to beg. No time to apologize for hurting Old Eldrick's feelings, Old Eldrick who has no warm body to love at night, no child to cry for attention, no friends beyond the barflies and maybe Jacko, an old cop he knew from his days playing billiards in Bay Ridge. Old Eldrick so afraid of life he must kill life. He was so close. Keep bending. You know where the .44 waits. Behind the vodka and the fake eau de vie. These people shouldn't talk to *you* like this, the son of James Emory Foxx who retired the second best homerun hitter in baseball history. They're wondering right now where you're going. They don't believe Old Eldrick has it in him. They're like mother: they *doubt* you, they belittle you, they see you as a shit stain brought to life, an accident to be wiped away. They see you as irony incarnate, the son of a drunk who opened a bar. Ha. Ha. The 5 o'clock news will be so excited for this story. The tabloids will orgasm. Who needs the summer of 1977 when you have the summer of 1979?

"Hey, we were just kidding, right Archie…"

Archie blamed the TV for delaying him long enough to not glimpse Eldrick grabbing a hidden handgun. He was slow to the draw, and had to put his hands in the air when Eldrick, purpling in the jowls, demanded they go up. Lolita followed Archie.

"That's right, hands where I can see 'em."

The guys in the booth scrambled beneath the table, but there wasn't enough room for so much beef, so elbows and thighs were left exposed to stray bullets. One of the men was quietly pissing his pants.

"Take back what you said, Lolita. Take it back, you, you bitch!"

"This isn't what you want to do," Archie said.

Eldrick jerked the handgun over to Archie's face.

"Shut up! This isn't your bar. It's mine."

"Okay."

"C'mon Eldrick, let's stop playing," she said. "You know I like you."

"Whore. Bitch. Both of you, a bunch of motherfuh…I should blow both your brains out. I should, I should!"

"Don't do that," Archie said.

"Ehhh, *why?*"

This wasn't a man who had the fortitude to kill, Archie figured, but there could be accidental discharge. Proceed with caution.

"You'll ruin your life. You'll be in prison for life. They'll torture you up in Attica. It's a shithole. Just put the gun down. Lolita talks sometimes, you can't take it all to heart. Talk is meaningless."

"I'll do what I want!"

The tears. Jesus Christ. Archie was embarrassed for Eldrick. He could see glittering beads in the corners of each eye, the birth of a maudlin trickle downward cheek. People today. Jesus Christ.

"Let's just take it easy, Eldrick. Let's ease that gun down."

"I won't!"

Eldrick fired the gun. Instead of blasting open a vital organ, the bullet exploded against a lonely dartboard on the wall, shattering it like a dinner plate. Assuming Eldrick, unused to firing a weapon, would be too stunned to do anything else, Archie slapped the gun out of his hand. It ricocheted off the counter and landed near Archie's feet. He picked it up. Two guns tonight. How fortuitous.

"You're a real son of a bitch you know that."

Archie smiled. He picked up the gun and aimed it square at the bartender's throat.

"Archie, no, don't do that," Lolita said, looking more afraid now than when Eldrick was aiming a gun at her.

"I should and I shouldn't. So many decision points."

"C'mon fella, you know I wasn't going to shoot you guys. You know…"

"I knew you didn't have it in you to kill. I, on the other hand—"

"Archie, stop! This is pointless."

She had a point. Paralyzing or killing Eldrick Foxx would do nothing to further any of his ambitions or give him answers. It would not end his hunt in the newspapers, newscasts, and subway turnstiles, his sense of waiting for a reckoning. It would only be one more dead body for the morgue to file, extra night work for a patrolman in the 9th. It would be a conversation starter. Water-cooler talk, the additional anecdote for the cabbie, another fear to account for before bed. A way to fill an uncomfortable pause in a dialogue. Might as well save the bullet.

"Go back to serving drinks," Archie said, tucking the gun in his jacket. "I'm getting out of here."

"Good idea," Lolita said.

They entered the strangling night. Heat was the word, the only word, the lone source of language among the stumbling drunks, savvy pimps, shrunken punks, and homeless pirouetting around the East Village at 2 a.m. You could almost hear the Lovin' Spoonful. *Hot town, summer in the city, summer in the…* fuck it, too hot to sing. Archie was feeling it now, worse than ever, the broil in his chest and back. He was feeling like a steak left too long on a grill. The night fuzzed at its damp corners. You couldn't get a grip. Admitting something, not quite defeat, he untied his trench coat.

"Let's go uptown, Archie."

"Why?"

"We can go somewhere quiet for a while."

"I'm going downtown, to bed."

"Just come with me uptown. What you doing Sunday? Nothing I bet."

More time with Truncheon. Bay Ridge to the Upper West Side, an hour and a half one way if he's lucky. Truncheon said he'd order Chinese Sunday and Archie would like a rack of greasy spareribs smothered in duck sauce. That was enough of a reprieve before he started on a new case, something about a wife suspecting a husband was a homosexual, though the exact details were lost to him right now. He unbuttoned his collar, tugged at his belt, and rolled up the billowing sleeves of his coat, his pale wrists laid bare in the halogen glare of Second Avenue. They were walking toward Astor Place.

"I got some things."

"Ride the train with me for a bit."

"Why?"

"I'm scared. Must you question everything? A girl doesn't like early morning rides around Manhattan. I read rapes are up 28 percent this year."

"You read too much, Lolita."

"I see you reading enough. And it's all my papa's fault. You name your kid after a book you like, and you get problems. Trust me, Archie, I'd be happy knowing less."

"That bar owner of yours has real problems."

"Eldrick? He's a sweetie deep down. You just rattled his nerves tonight."

"He tried to kill us. I was ready to kill him."

"And I'm glad you didn't."

"You were the one pushing his buttons you know, with that Jimmie Foxx stuff. You rile people, Lo."

Lo. He had never called her that before.

"I need to have my fun. We all die one day, so why not have fun?"

They hopped down the station at Astor Place. A shirtless man in smeared corduroys begged for nickels. Lolita tossed him one. Archie ignored him. He didn't believe in free money for the bums. It was a way for high-minded liberals to ease their guilt—not that Lolita was this way—and make them feel they were doing something good in the world when they were making no greater difference than tossing toenail clippings in the trash. The bums would stay bums. The liberals, those left in this hollow city, would keep their real riches. Archie could have a little more respect if one of these Columbus Avenue college professors offered to co-sign on a mortgage for one of these Boxcar Willies. That was a *difference* being made. Otherwise, it was all a waste, and too many seconds and words were wasted already.

"Hey so why aren't you a cop anymore?"

They were craning their necks on the platform to stare into an empty tunnel.

"Disagreements."

"What did you—"

"If you want me to ride with you, ask less questions. I need time to think."

"Okay, okay. Think away, Robert Oppenheimer."

So he did. It was a half-lie. It was more he had entered a period in which he didn't want to talk out loud. Too much language gets caught in your teeth. He could tolerate silence. He had spent whole days and weeks not speaking to anyone in the years since he left the NYPD. You let your thoughts devour you, swim in the past, garbage and all. You see your father, a Democratic Oyster Bay town supervisor after his stint in Albany, gripping at his cheeks like he was trying to tear them off, confessing everything to his wife in bed. Archie, 15, leaned against the closed door. *I'm sorry, I'm sorry, it's just, it's just.* He wouldn't understand for many years. His father and the other woman, the green-eyed one from the pool club. The ultimate triviality. The next three years were spent, for Archie, in a state of constant repression. He did not jerk off. He was proud of that! Leave that to the dregs with no self-control, no self-respect. Think of the time *wasted*: he did sit-ups and push-ups instead, graduating to clapping and one-handed by freshman year of college. He wouldn't be anything like his father crying at the foot of his mother's bed, his cheeks run raw. All that noise he made.

The train car was empty, except for a bum sleeping at the end in a bed of newspaper. He was old, 60 at least, and snored louder as they crawled uptown. He had no shoes and blackened feet. Lolita hummed to herself. It was a song, probably from a television show he or Truncheon had never watched. Certainly not *Welcome Back Kotter*. He should get off and go back home. Lolita could make it home on her own, she knew the streets well enough. She wasn't dumb or weak. She was…she was…he didn't really know. She could be playing him. It was possible there was even a Candies tie. Think about it: she fortuitously showed up on the night he planned to smoke out their nest, a night when he was clearly *flowing*. His reactions were perfect. If there were a night to inflict a mortal wound, it was tonight. Instead, he went downtown and played Cowboys and Indians with some maniac who pretended he grew out of a splash of Jimmie Foxx's semen. Truncheon must be rubbing off on him. He was seeing patterns everywhere tonight. Lolita Velez was an undercover Candy trying to throw him off the trail. Her pal Eldrick staged the whole scene. They each told the Chicago White Sox, via telegram, to torch disco records. The fatalities were all distant cousins.

Archie was the only untethered person left. Everyone else was hooked to something, compromised.

"Let's keep going up," Lolita said.

"What?"

"It's nice and quiet. Just ride to the end of the line with me. Van Cortland Park."

"I need to sleep."

"C'mon."

"I don't see the point."

"The point is the time before dawn is the best time to be awake."

"It's dark and then it isn't."

"No, it's like there's only stillness. You are alone, but on the cusp of a great thing. A new day."

"Okay."

"JoJo and I spent a whole year just staying up until the sunrise. We didn't miss a sunrise in 1977. Did you know that? Not one. All seasons. We spent the summer on the rooftop. You doze off to the sound of gunshots. I'm not too afraid of guns because of that summer. I'm only afraid of what guns can do to other people, not me."

"You should have some fear."

"You don't."

"I do. Things you can't shoot and punch."

"Look, you're talking, see? I knew I'd get you going eventually."

"I never liked parks. I like real nature or nothing. Parks cheat you. A deception for idiots."

"JoJo's been to the country, but I never have. I was in Westchester once. My papa never had enough money for vacations. And my mama ran away. He was a welfare queen, my papa. In all senses of the word."

"So he really was like that?"

"He had a boyfriend and everything. Rafael. It was secret but everyone knew. JoJo said he saw them putting their mouths on each other. How you have two kids, have sex with a woman, and then go do that?"

"I don't know."

"I know I'm not like that. One of my friends, Carmen, likes getting drunk and kissing girls. She's tried to kiss me four times. I'm not against it, you know, I mean, kiss what you gotta kiss. But I don't like the woman body. I think it's ugly."

"I don't know."

"You *do* know, Archibald. Stop saying that. You have an opinion. How about this? When we get to Van Cortland Park, last stop, you tell me that opinion."

"We'll see."

"You're the only cop, past and present, I like to talk to. And look at. You know that, right?"

"I guess I do. Here we are."

"I hate them all. JoJo hates them more. JoJo says the post-police state is possible and that by like 1990, the gangs are gonna take over and reform themselves and become the new government and then the cops will be outlawed and all the blacks and Puerto Ricans will be safe. The NYPD will be disbanded. JoJo says it's inevitable. Anyone collecting a cop pension is going to be executed, like the Holocaust but for police. He believes all of it. He walks around with the future on the tip of his tongue, the future frozen in his head, behind his eyes. He sees it so clearly he misses sometimes what's in front of him. I dunno if we're gonna get what JoJo wants. I think a lot more has to happen first. Besides, people like you wouldn't let it happen."

"I'm not a cop anymore."

"No, but you don't want the police going away either."

"I want justice. However it's gotten, so be it. I don't sweat it, the future of police."

"I think you do care."

"Well, you sure *think* a lot. But I'm the only one inside my own head. Sorry."

Archie couldn't make eye contact. If he did, he didn't know what would happen. He was bathing in his own sweat. There were canals wending around his groin, ponds in the concavities of his torso. He needed to stop glancing at Lolita's thighs, the hook of her knee, her calf glistening below the edge of the mustard-colored seat, one foot swinging lightly off the ground. A sock, off-white, sagged from her right ankle, bony enough to pinch between his slippery thumb and index finger. She recently chewed two wads of Wrigley's Spearmint and he could smell them on her breath.

"That's what you think, Archie."

The train was underground and then it was above ground, grumbling through upper Manhattan or the beginning of the Bronx, Archie couldn't tell. He never went up here. There could be opportunity in the future. Undoubtedly, turnstile jumpers were common, and criminals needed someone who was not a bumbling, overfed cop to push them on the righteous path. They needed him. He could start in the South Bronx, Morrisania, Melrose, trawl the streets for a few days to get a feel. It could be more productive than Stillwell. He'd do that after he took out Ras and the Candies. The Candies came first.

Beyond the windows, the night was aquatic, protean and entirely unreliable. He was glad for his two guns. He was glad—though he wouldn't admit it to her—that he was going to take her home.

"You think that guy's asleep or dead?"

"Asleep."

"What you think he takes? You think he's got drugs in his system?"

"I don't know."

"We should get him shoes."

"Yeah, okay."

"We *should*."

"Plenty of shoe stores open at 3:30 in the morning."

"We can just take someone's shoes."

"Who?"

"Someone's. I bet someone would trade."

"Trade what?"

She only smiled. Behind those lips was a font of staggering knowledge—or nothing. This girl, this woman—what was she? He tried to understand. People, in his experience, fit into one of a few archetypes and you just squiggled in the details from there. We aren't unique snowflakes. We're decent or assholes or venal or lazy or some unoriginal mixture. We come from the same cosmic lab.

Lolita had no lab, no precedents. He struggled to breathe fluidly in the heat. What, he expected it to let up? Van Cortland Park was near. Another stop. He played baseball there as a kid, just once. He went 0-3. Line out, strike out, pop out. An umpire chastised him for accidentally throwing his bat on the follow through. He apologized. *You do that again, kid, I'm throwing you out.* It was the summer of Mantle, Triple Crown, and Archie was wondering whether switch-hitting would improve his big league chances. Where were the scouts for him? He still believed Yankee Stadium, Ebbets Field or the Polo Grounds were around the corner. One big game, just one, if he just put all his weight into an inside pitch and crushed a monumental homerun. The one homerun he always wanted to hit, and never did.

"I bet you always have something to trade," she said. Her tone mixed the coquettish and the foreboding. Before he could unravel it, determine where in the past or future her intentions lay, they were entangled. The bum snored. Archie already couldn't remember who moved first and it didn't matter. With the fierce urgency of *now*—apologies to Dr. King—they were pawing each other apart, desperate for the first hint of nakedness. It quickly became a mindless fuck, in the most wonderful way that phrase could be used. Their minds and designs were elsewhere, their theories and pageantries of logic. Who was Truncheon, who was JoJo, who was Jimmie Foxx? They entered into a void of their own delicious making, the train car trembling to Van Cortland Park, his cock rambling against and then finding where it needed to be. Lolita knew what to do. She had him on top, like he was the pro, the man with a plan. *Bullshit*, the dying superego croaked. *Bullshit*. Her underpants were white and frilly, not what he expected. His boxers were gray. The pile of stray clothing—trousers, belt, jeans, boxers, panties, trench coat, fedora, loose quarters—grew at a proper pace beneath the row of seats. He had forgotten how to kiss and did it anyway, hard, all tongue with lips dragassing along, trying to play the part of older sophisticate. She was the kisser. His white ass flared like a distress signal in the air. The fucking was quiet, not furtive but hushed enough, as if there were some allowance made for the sleeping shoeless bum. They fucked like two kids reunited after a continent-shattering war, the kind that ruined too much to make the subsequent novels and poetry worthwhile. The train was slowing. Lolita bit at his ear too hard but he loved it. Keep it there. Once upon a time, they were stuck in a bar on the Lower East Side. Once upon a time, she surprised him at Stillwell Avenue. His knees ached on the seats and he told them to shut up.

This was the trick, because she was bigger than him. Bigger in every way but flesh and bone. She could swallow him. He could backslide down her esophagus and into an acidic oblivion. She could do anything.

"Our stop," she said. "Keep going, though."

They fucked as the train doors slid open. The bum did not stir. Soon, the MTA workers would be stumbling through in a feeble attempt to clean the car.

He had not done anything like this in a very long time. He had not abandoned himself. Archie London was discarded for someone else and he would be back in a jiffy, just after ejaculating into a woman two decades younger than him. When he did, the bum rose up, all of it just terrible clockwork.

"Ey whaaa," the bum growled through his beard. His glassy eyes met the couple in the act. His brain swam through the endless labyrinthine yesterdays defined by vacant train cars and hunger, joining the pieces as best it could. He was asleep for a long time. Days possibly. He scratched his nose, picked for crusty boogers in the hidden ridges. Hmm. His body had an idea.

"Eyy whaaa…" The bum was bum rushing them, toddling angrily from his corner seat to their own. Lolita was the first to scramble, throwing one hand overboard for her bra. Archie jumped up, his soaked dick displayed like a swollen lance. He grabbed his coat before his pants, buttoning up just as the bum arrived, his hands outstretched. "Lemme into some action," the bum said. "I wanna stick it too. Lemme in."

Archie didn't have time for his underwear because the bum was closing in on a three quarters naked Lolita. Here we go, *another* fight. He did feel relief from the heat with his haunches and crotch exposed in this way. He also was jittery about getting knocked around in the balls. The bum, thankfully, lunged for him and not Lolita, and he applied an elbow to the bum's solar plexus that put him on the ground.

Archie had gone flaccid; what would it mean, after all, if he hadn't? Lolita was almost dressed. There was the matter of hooking a bra and buttoning jeans, routine stuff even when you're under duress. They glanced up at each other, checked the bum one more time, and fled into the night.

They were on an elevated platform so they ran downstairs, Archie coming up the rear, Lolita scampering in front. They met the Bronx, sibilating now, the tongue of summer back in their nostrils and pits and shoulders, perky in the afterglow of sex. Archie could sprint the mile.

"You surprise me," she said. He noticed they were on another street called Broadway. He counted Broadways in at least three boroughs.

"How?"

"You're a lot more than you are. I think that's a good thing. I don't just read your moves."

"I can't read your moves."

"We're two books without any words. Just paper and imagination."

"I don't agree," he said. "I have a lot of words, somewhere."

He would learn to call this the night of Velez.

7

21st Century

Death, oh death. So much of it, and so soon. It's so easy to forget the only fundamental truth of life is death.

Sundra was alive with death.

First, Quentin Stellar. She did not stop thinking about him. Then, Chase Dimon. For different reasons, she also did not stop thinking about him.

She reviewed the events of yesterday.

They were all assembled in the auditorium to watch the time travel adventure. Sundra somehow knew they would not reach the Jurassic without a hitch. It would have been too easy. They were derailed somewhere else. From the numbers on the screen, it became clear they had arrived in 1979. Such a random year of no significance. Thanks to Chase's cameraeye—same tech Quentin died with—they could see the long lost world through his eyes. It was a mad jumble, flying discs and shirtless torsos and deranged chanting. This was why she avoided sports stadiums.

Then it all went blank. There were the initial stages of denial. A signal had been lost. 1979 was in a dubious position in the space-time continuum. Chase simply wanted some *private* time. It was conveniently ignored that the last images the party in the auditorium saw were of bright flame, the type that was not survivable. He and the boys had dumbly wandered into an inferno and died. She felt a tinge of regret for the scientist, Dr. Allen, who spent his last moments alive getting bullied. He went out on the opposite of his terms. Like Quentin Stellar. Who imagines getting shot out of the sky?

Being bossless, at least temporarily, in no way changed her position with Velocity Ventures or the nature of her contract. She belonged to them. In the vast premiumscape, conventional wisdom said she had nowhere to go but down. Conventional wisdom was not always wrong. This was the very best her life would be, benefits-wise. No other corporation offered so many choices for their employees.

She was due at work at 7 a.m., in six hours. She was awake. What was Rex doing? She checked her Gaggle but he wasn't there. She didn't sleep much anymore. Lately, she had been decoding the words Stellar left behind, parsing his digital lectures, bromides, jeremiads, and the like, feeling like the only real person on Earth. Stellar was going to do something very great before he died. He was really flying. The news feeds would not acknowledge he was flying above the city without the aid of tech. The feeds were unequivocal: Stellar *did not fly*. The police were taking proper precautions to shoot him down. You could never trust anyone today. What if he were a suicide bomber trying to fly himself into the Trojan Tower, a la 9/11? Well, far less damage would be done, for one. Hundreds dead versus thousands. Excellent security at airports made such a spectacular attack impossible. Terrorists preferred "soft" targets now. Trains, buses, unguarded public squares. You never know when death is near, when its fangs are so close to drooling all over your neck. Sundra would prefer not to die. In fact, if a djinn materialized right now in front of her—Gaggle-certified djinn?—she would wish for immortality. There would be little hand-wringing, fretting about all the friends she would outlive, the literally endless amount of time stretching in front of her. She would fly through the air and never die. She would find the means to transcend New York, the United States of America— she would live gleefully to watch the civilizations crumble, one after another, exposed for the farces that they are, this supreme waste of life. How many billions would trumpet their trivial accomplishments, their molehills on the Everests of time and space, while she stood back, immortal, and laughed? Her eyes closed. Immortality would not be wasted on her.

Morning light brought a new panic. She dreamed all of Stellar's streams, including the final video, had been wiped from Gaggle searches and WatchMe, the video-sharing website owned and operated by Gaggle. Her dream was made real when she began a search, her legs still beneath the covers. Her fingers danced unthinkingly above the screen, joined as much to the ether as her brain, performing tasks laid out for them at birth—tap, tap, search. Quentin Stellar was gone. Really gone. All the uploads, the copies of the uploads, even the threads—gone. She logged into her Bleater account, entering another realm under Gaggle's thumb, but found bleats, rebleats, and hashtags referencing Stellar had been purged. Ditto for WatchMe. For the hell of it, she slapped herself. No, this was not a dream. It was 5:02 a.m., she was very much awake, and the truth of Stellar had been scrubbed from the face of the internet. Harder said than done.

"Fuck fuck fuck fuck fuck," she said loudly, almost melodically. No one lived with her in this apartment, so she could curse as much as she pleased. "Fuck fuck fuck fuck fuck."

Even news reports, scrubbed. Where was the uproar about the First Amendment? She imagined a Velocity Ventures supervisor's retort: "Lol."

Here were the fruits of the ecstatic reports of yesteryear she read as a student, how journalism, that noble profession, would be saved. All those venerable institutions, like the *New York Times* and *Washington Post,* and the traffic-sexed start-ups like Pox and FluffFeed and the rest (well, to be fair, the venerable institutions behaved like traffic-sexed start-ups) had entered into paternalistic partnerships with Gaggle to boost their pageviews and make them profitable again, like in the old days of news on paper and advertising ignorance. Of course, allowing your news to stream directly on Gaggle to eliminate those pesky and precious seconds it took to download a story from another non-Gaggle site meant that Gaggle, suddenly, could play editor-in-chief for the limp-dicked news industry. Served them right. *Right?* You play ball with Gaggle, they'd eventually knock your teeth in, one way or another. They could get the ump and the fans to do it if they couldn't do it themselves.

So, exeunt Stellar. He never existed as far as the World Wide Web was concerned, so he never existed as far as reality was concerned. She was still impressed by the breadth of Gaggle's reach, its ability to continually erase the multifarious, convoluted blackboard of life and start anew, performing the equivalent of the ultimate control+alt+delete, shutting window after window until we arrive at zero. Task manager to the rescue. Gaggle Quentin Stellar—the input could be "Quentin Stellar" or just Quentin Stellar—and you would still find references to the man, the professor, the scion, but nothing to the last moments of his life or what was said. In this Gaggle universe, ironically, Dr. Quentin Stellar was very much alive. There was no evidence of his death anywhere. Were she so inclined, or just grief-stricken enough, she could easily fool herself into thinking she'd see him later today.

She would never be immortal, but Gaggle was plenty capable of pulling the trick for others. She looked down. A buzz, a text. She was needed. She was being summoned. Her supervisor, Mr. Chevy, needed a word. All lower case letters.

sundra need a word be in my home 740 thx

"Home" was code for office. A Velocity touch. Your desk, situated in a long row of desks in an open "collaborative" "bullpen" style, was also "home." Remember, you are a premium. You have work. So many don't. So many *zeros* out there, her father reminded her, and you can never join them.

"Once you're a zero," he had said, "you will never be anything else. Nobody's gonna contract with anybody who becomes a zero."

Indeed, it was gospel, and she would admit to being spooked by it. The Think Pieces, Gaggle-elevated, had made it plain as the bread in her cupboard: in this age of automation and globalization, having a job was a grand privilege, one that should never be taken for granted. One's ability to hold a job, to be contracted by a firm, was practically encoded in one's DNA. But unlike conventional DNA kept away from meddling scientists, this ability was plenty corruptible. Lose a contract, become a zero, and stay that way. *Don't you understand* that Velocity and McKing's and WatchMe and Gaggle and all their friends employ you to their detriment and out of the goodness of their collective hearts? Why, there are conveyor belts, apps, and androids that can do everything *you* do. Duh! So shut up and be thankful you've got a place to be, credits to earn, credits to buy shit with, an apartment that is not a hovel. You have so much. Don't whine. You're gonna burn your bra over surge-pricing at the subways? It's natural selection. And it could be way worse.

"You get what you get and you don't get upset." The immortal words of Gary Glassgarden. Also: "Suffer silently."

Time hopped forward, as it always did, and she was showered, dressed, and huffing to her subway stop, 12 blocks away. She followed the globs of premiums down the slanting steps, tasting and trying to spit out their warmth. She dug for her credit card to swipe at the turnstile. Let's see, it was before 8, rush hour, that meant she was right in the heart of surge pricing, especially since it was summer and school's out which meant school's *in* for the Metropolitan Transportation Company's coffers. Let's see, let's see, she stopped conjecturing and swiped. $21. So be it. Maybe it'll be $15 this afternoon. Hmm. Maybe not. She shoved into a crammed car, body bobbing and blocking with a pair of women that must have weighed 300 pounds each and looked young enough to have gained all the fat last week, and counted down the 16 stops until she was at work. She closed her eyes, opened them, closed them again, gave in and stared intently at her Gaggle, because why not? It was in front of her. It was so easy. An infinity, an eternity, just below her fingers, an extra dimension of reality—or is this life, this meatspace, the extradimensional slice? Gaggle could be Earth 1 and we were Earth 2. She considered this. Her digital self—Sundra on Bleater and Sundra on Sharespace and Sundra on WatchMe and Sundra in Gaggle results pages 1 through 26, the final 25 just other combinations of people and entities that mention Sundra or Glassgarden—was the ur-self, and all else was a lie. This was the reality the ghost of Quentin Stellar still decried.

The Queens to Manhattan jaunt along the KFC line was as long as expected. Delays were such a reality that they were built into her mental schedule. She was rarely disappointed. She liked it more when Honda had the naming rights to her train line, because she despised fast food and the constant holos of Colonel Sanders that assaulted her eyes in the train car, the ad streams that interrupted her Gaggle stream thanks to geomarketing tech. But that was life. If fried chicken was ever placed in front of her, she would vomit.

The underground wifi was spotty so she got her supervisor's angsty emails minutes after she was supposed to. They came in waves, twos and threes, and reminded her of a teenage Hitler, one who would never reach his full potential as Fuhrer.

Where are you??
Important, pls hurry.
On your way? text or call thx.
How far are you seriously
This is ridic pick up now
KFC Line wifi isn't that bad Sundra come on come on come on
Fucking really
This. Is. Important.
Sundra!!!!

For some reason, she had no fear of Sigmund Chevy. None. Mr. Chevy, an associate account supervisor at Velocity, the leader of a 15-person unit, shaved his head to pretend he had chosen baldness as his own destiny, rather than genetics telling him to sit on it and spin. Since the future had found no cure for diabetes, and the future was now, Mr. Chevy suffered from that as well, and medicated himself with Diet Coke. In another form, 30 or so pounds ago, Mr. Chevy could've been handsome; he had a southern Italian swarthiness, simple dimples carved into each cheek, and a general symmetry that, taken together, was above average. A good face (well, not the lack of hair) for a dating profile photo. Mr. Chevy had a wife, never named and never seen. It was not known what she thought of him. What was known instead was that his nipples were punished in the tightness of his dress shirt, as was the outer ring of his stomach.

The subway disgorged her in Midtown, hot and banal and crowded, and she hurried to where Velocity owned the top three stories of a 48-story building looming anonymously over Bryant Park. Her Gaggle was buzzing with Chevy missives. Like anyone else, she couldn't remember the last time she turned it off. It was becoming increasingly taboo to do so, especially when your employer would know the minute you'd decided to shut it down for the day or night. Turning off a Gaggle was a sign of laziness and disrespect for the hard work of your colleagues and employer, a sign of premature surrender. Who are *you* to say when work can't contact you? Who are *you* to determine the contours of your hours and days, the terms of a contract you've signed and which an employer will benevolently honor? Who are *you*, anyway?

The contradiction of America, she thought. The doublespeak. The twin engines of empowerment and degradation. Remember, you could do anything, but you were also ultimately worthless and thank people better than you for permitting your First World existence. The twin engines of the Age of Velez. What Quentin Stellar hoped to destroy and did not. Poor, forgotten Prof Stellar. What did he really hope would happen, had he not been shot down? That the masses leading their lives of quiet desperation would suddenly revolt after a flying man rudely interrupted their Gaggles and insisted on thoughtsyncing his spoken word manifesto? Was this the first of many flights? Was this simply the beginning of a greater and yet unimagined enterprise, one that would pull the curtain down on the Age of Velez? She could never know. She would also have nothing but memory, and the snippets she gamely recorded to her own device, to go on. She would have conjecture and her own will, her own hatred.

Because she was getting an idea, entering the soaring lobby of the 5th Avenue building, opening her eye wide for the retinal scan so she could be cleared and ride an elevator to witness Mr. Chevy's rage. Because the idea was *here*, in this city, a few miles south in the precipice of the Trojan Tower. Because the idea would be easy enough to execute, because the technology existed, because she was smart enough and no one would suspect Sundra Glassgarden, just another girl in the great big machine.

She thanked God she was not black or brown-skinned. As a white person, even a Jewish white person, she existed as the American default, the least suspect of the races, even as the majority minority future inched ever closer. No one would suspect her. A white person wanted to preserve, not destroy. She would exploit every stereotype baked into the American Pie.

"Good morning, Ms. Glassgarden," a disembodied voice told her when the retinal scan was complete. "Have a nice day."

Sigmund, Sigmund. Today wasn't a bad day to absorb some abuse. It may not even be a bad day to abuse right back. The elevator whisked her up to the 46th floor, she got out, thankfully saw no one she recognized, and opened wide for another retinal scan before entering the sprawling Velocity floor. Mr. Chevy was not high enough on the food chain for his own private office. Rather, he was in the open bullpen with everyone else, but he had slightly more space on the end for his desk. Velocity believed in transparency, so what he said to her would be heard by everyone else. This was regarded as a very fair system.

"Well, Sundra, how nice of you to arrive," Mr. Chevy said as soon as she stepped onto the floor, where most of her colleagues were situated, eyes trained dutifully on screens. "I never thought you'd make it."

"Hello, Mr. Chevy."

He rose like an aggrieved, but slightly doped up, ape. He did not look like he was ready to scream. This was better than expected.

"I want a word with you *in private.*"

Well, forget that. Privacy was bad. Perhaps she'd be getting terminated. Dad would cry, literally cry, sob on the floor of his Bay Ridge condo. *My daughter, now a zero, a zero!* She didn't want to be a zero but could enjoy the spectacle of dear dumb dad cutting loose. Let it fly, Gary, be *you.* A good cry could be healthy.

She'd prefer not to be terminated for obvious reasons. Also, she thought as she followed Sigmund Chevy to the "private space" on the other end of the floor, it could be a detriment to her nascent Plan. How to get clearance into the Trojan Tower as a zero? How to avenge Stellar? Basically impossible.

"I want to say this is going to be bad—you know me. But it's going to be something else."

He shut the door behind them in the "private space," predictably windowless and antiseptic white. There was a long graphite table, several chairs, and they each sat, Chevy landing hard. He snorted.

"Mr. Chevy," she said. His mouth opened to answer. She realized she hadn't planned on saying anything else. Just "Mr. Chevy." The syllables hung fat in the lifeless air. He cleared his throat. Cleared it twice. Despite the militant air-conditioning, he was sweating.

"So, Sundra. I called you in here because, well, you are getting contracted out."

"Okay."

"You can view this as a promotion or a lateral move. It's up to you. Your credits will be the same, regardless. You're being contracted to Devora."

"What am I doing for Mr. Dimon's wife?"

"She is needing more assistance at the Sea Gate estate. She is grieving with Mr. Dimon being gone, likely permanently."

"I thought he was being pulled out of the past, that it was all just a matter of lost reception, failure of the feed, missed signals…"

"No. Keep this between us for now, Sundra, but Mr. Dimon is likely gone, likely permanently."

"Yes, you said that."

"He, as hard as this is to say, died in the past, as did his son and the party he was with. A terrible mishap, a true tragedy. But Velocity needs to guard its time travel tech very closely, since as you know there are only a few companies who are dabbling in this field and we must retain our competitive edge, so the board thinks that for now, we must keep this as quiet as possible. Mr. Dimon made very few public appearances. His absence shouldn't arouse too much suspicion. If any of the news feeds want to know more, we'll put out a statement about an undisclosed illness, and kill him off quietly."

"So Devora is grieving."

"Yes, she knows the truth. The company is sending her extra staff. She hasn't left Sea Gate in several days."

"What does she need me for?"

"Anything. Everything. You're to report tomorrow."

"There's no subway over there, right?"

"Ride out to Stillwell, last stop, then take a bus. It's not that hard."

"Well, from Queens—"

"Are you complaining?"

"No, Mr. Chevy."

"That's good. I'll be honest. You're smart enough but I'll be glad to see you go. It's time."

"Thanks, Mr. Chevy."

"Watch that attitude with Devora."

"I shall."

"She is very *demanding*, I hear."

"I'm ready."

"Good. Good. Now, go out there and do your job. If anyone is suspicious, if anyone asks why you went into privacy, just say you're being transferred within the company. Nothing else. If anyone presses, say nothing. Got it? Otherwise, we can just terminate you. You wouldn't even be the first person we terminated today."

"I'll keep quiet, I promise, sir."

She kept her promise. Besides, she had few real friends at work other than Rex, so there'd be no reason to overshare. She weighed the pros and cons and decided this would be just fine for the plan.

Now she would call Rex. He better not be napping after work.

8

21st Century

Rex was on the KFC line, riding out to Sundra. She was lucky to be in a premium enclave with prime subway access. He had been wandering in deep Queens, train to bus territory, and tonight would be one of those nights, milling on an empty sidewalk until one of those MTC buses wheezed around the block to attempt to take you somewhere. It is what it is. Sundra seemed serious in her texts and he knew better than to disregard a serious Sundra.

He could use a nap. He would close his eyes one stop. One stop, that's all, he wouldn't really fall asl—

9

21st Century

Not too long ago, Chase and Devora Dimon's Sea Gate estate was not an estate at all. It was an exclusive gated community, far less exclusive than anything Chase would dare live in, but equipped with gates, a guard booth, and private beach. Whites afraid of the blacks in Coney Island public housing developments congregated there. There were more than 800 single-family homes built in the Queen Anne and Mediterranean style. By the time the public housing was razed for the Coney Island casinos, the Sea Gate residents had begun to move out, fearful of the wall-to-wall casinos set to rise on their little spit of land. So Chase bought out the last few hundred families and erected a beachfront estate for his wife, who hated the city. Chase lived mostly in a double-townhouse on the Upper East Side (in Russian oligarchic fashion, he had purchased two townhouses, knocked down the walls between them, and built a home to fit his ego, bowling alley included) and resented leaving Manhattan, even for summers in the Hamptons. Devora, the opposite, enjoyed the beach, the water, the quiet.

Chase also feared she was close to a "crack-up." The Sea Gate estate, nicknamed Castle Devora, came to be, replete with a mansion crafted in the Japanese feudal architecture Devora, an old Asia studies major, favored, and a great lawn for parties, polo, and whatever else people do on great lawns. A $7 million entertainment system was installed, which featured a rock concert-sized projector and the largest subwoofer in North America. It was never clear why Devora required this entertainment system, or the quarter mile-long swimming pool, when neither were actually put to use. Devora had the beach, after all. She rarely had parties. Perhaps that is just what people with money do; they have it, so they spend it. The first law of having money.

There was a three-story garage at the edge of the property—an architect managed the feat of making a garage look like a lovely, Meiji Era birdhouse—for a fleet of vintage automobiles Devora never paid any attention to. Collecting cars was not a hobby of Chase's or Devora's really, but somehow the Porsche Spyders and Boxsters and Rolls Royces and others accumulated like metallic, and highly expensive, mothballs in the Meiji garage. Chase rarely visited, so they said, and Devora, once ensconced in Sea Gate, rarely left. The casino boom never arrived as advertised. Neither did the mass of riffraff and derelicts that parasitically cling to any gaming facility. There was the Trump casino tower built over the old Coney Island Houses on Surf Avenue, and Zuckerberg, diversifying his investments after Gaggle acquired his proto-social media venture, tried his hand at an equally lavish casino and mechanized racetrack that roped in the old aquarium, tripling its size and adding, somehow, a blue whale exhibit (the whale, named Bubble, predictably died in captivity, ruining a handful of childhoods). Slot machines rose in the ashes of the Cyclone. A concert series was added, nostalgia dance-hop and rap acts frequenting a revamped stage in Asser Levy Park. All of it was a disappointment revenue-wise, though there was some respectable foot traffic during the summer months.

Looming fears of superstorms did not keep beachgoers from frolicking in the surf. It did not keep minor league baseball from thrilling the five thousand some odd people who enjoyed watching fresh high school and college graduates slap baseballs in the sun. The parachute jump was not demolished for a casino parking lot, though one magnate, Sammy Slamowitz of Sammy's World Amusements, proposed just that. Devora Dimon could live in peace, away from her husband and occasionally her child. The estate gates were built high enough to withstand all intrusions from the outside.

"Who is this?" a voice, just a voice, asked, bounding off the marble. Sundra turned. Another servant in a Nehru jacket glided into view, but she was not talking. A woman, black-haired but much older, emerged behind her, and she saw the three words had come from her mouth. The servant began to talk before she was interrupted.

"Who?"

"I was going to say—"

"*Who?* Speak faster, Ulivia."

"ThisisSundraGlassgar—"

"Okay, Ulivia. I appreciate the effort."

There was a song by Paul Simon called "You Can Call Me Al" and in it Simon sang about a "bat-faced little girl." That girl, Sundra decided, must have been the woman standing in front of her. Black-haired, wizened, pale, with gimlet eyes and gimlet lips and a hunch that hinted of whole weeks spent underground, the woman approached Sundra, who felt like a giantess in her wake. She blinked as if her face was flushed with light. It was not. The woman's hair was tangled in tresses that to Sundra recalled a medieval epoch never lived through, a time of wizardry and whimsy and readily available death. Her dress must have cost a lot; it shimmered aggressively. Sundra hunted for a few more adjectives but the woman was already speaking.

"So this is the one they sent me? This premie. A bit gawky for my tastes but if darling Velocity insists, who am I to argue with labor? Really, who am I?"

Sundra was silent.

"Do you talk? Say your name for me. Ulivia can't do the talking for you. Her IQ is not quite 100."

"My name is Sundra," Sundra lamely offered. She noticed the tapestry of weak blue veins in the woman's forearms. This woman who must be—

"Devora Dimon, but you knew that. Ulivia, can you make tea? I want tea. Sundra, what do you want?"

"I'm, I'm okay."

"Okay? Okay. I hope you prove more interesting than you are so far. Come out with me to the pool. Now."

So they went. Servants were silently and strategically placed in each room they passed through. The interior reminded Sundra of one very large wing of a museum simultaneously honoring our planet's rustic past and apocalyptic future. Flatscreens appeared to be everywhere, all turned off. Bonsai trees nodded. The inside lasted forever until they were outside, overlooking a pool that could be a stadium parking lot if filled with cement. Servants as ghosts patrolled the perimeters. White pool chairs and recliners waited for asses. Beyond distance fencing, and a phalanx of hedges, hissed the sea. All the servants looked like low-powered androids. Sundra suspected they were flesh and blood, but had no proof.

"Tell me, can you hold a conversation? I hope you can. I explicitly requested they not send me a dumb one."

Sundra stared at the pool, not making eye contact. "I converse fine enough."

"We are in the age of whims, Sandy. The final epoch."

"*Sundra.*"

"You're Sandy now. Sandy, what is it, your last name?"

"Glassgarden."

"Sandy Glass works for me."

"That's not my name."

Devora laughed like a matriarch curled over a Mahjong table, circa 100 years ago.

"No, no, but it is. Now it is. I say so. My whim, my rules."

"You can't change names."

"But I can. I will call up your supervisor now. Or, no, I will call up his CFO, because your boss is dead. My husband."

"I'm sorry for your loss."

"No you're not."

"I am. It's terrible. Chase Dimon cared so much, for the company, for his work—"

"Chase didn't give a shit about any of you."

"Okay."

"Let this be a lesson, Sandy. I am at an age when I want to instruct, to teach. I want to talk. I want to impart *wisdom* on my Sandy Glass. First lesson: I can do anything I want to you, and you can do nothing about it."

"What's the point of this?"

"There isn't any. I have time on my hands. Time that feels endless, but is actually fleeting. Sad but true. I want to teach you that, at least."

"I know enough for now, thanks."

"Do you?"

The bat-faced woman reared back and punched Sundra in the gut. Sundra staggered and dropped to a knee, where she was still three-quarters way to eye level with Devora Dimon. She was smiling. What a bitch.

"There. And what will you do about it?"

Classic schoolyard bully challenge. I hit you, you gonna hit back? You gonna cry? Sundra's been there, done that. She was surprised, but not rattled. She could do bullies. The psychology was easy to anticipate, deflect, and defuse.

"Nothing," Sundra said. She tried out hang dog.

"Hmm, well," and Devora drove a right heel into Sundra's forearm. This time, the hang dog look was real.

"Still nothing?"

Sundra tried not answering.

"You won't fight back? Maybe you get it then. See, this is the age of the whim, like I said. I have a whim. I get to act on it. My husband was like that. We made a nice team for a while. People like you, Sandy, you are subject to *my* whims. Modern civilization has evolved in such a way to put me up here and you down there, me in sharpened high heels, you in whatever discount dreadful flats you wear into *my* house. I am being simple enough for you. You get it?"

"You don't seem like you're grieving. They told me you'd need help with that."

"Who? That rooster Chevy? Your little supervisor?"

"Yes."

"I should have him killed. Maybe tomorrow. I can do that, you know."

"Murder is still illegal, I think."

"Murder is all relative in the court of law."

"True."

Sundra was standing now. She would be ready for the next strike. Hitting back would not be wise. She couldn't be wasting any time in jails or prisons. Rather, she'd absorb one more blow, writhe around, beg for mercy, and move on. It was a big estate. There must be ways to avoid Devora Dimon.

"My late husband—my dead, gone forever husband—would often argue. He was a mild believer in representative government, classical democracy. He believed there was something to be learned there. A value to be had. I laughed at him. He could never understand the future so he dabbled in the past, you see? His wealth was a glorious accident. He knew it too. He obsessed over what already happened, rewinding life, being able to experience the grand total of Earth history as one movie. Poor dumb Chase. He would tell me that American democracy has its place in the 'gorgeous mosaic of history.' Can you believe that term? The fool stole it from the History Channel probably. He thought you should keep up a democratic charade for the people and that occasionally it would prove itself useful. He believed in it morally. Why? I don't know. Do *you* know, Sandy? No, no, you only know what I tell you to know. And isn't that the point? That we've arrived at a moment in history where one human being can have such wonderful agency over another, where one's value can be so much greater than one's neighbor, like a man compared to a dog. I know, I know, I'm so blunt. Chase used to wonder why I couldn't lie more. Why couldn't I be nicer? You must wonder."

"No, not wondering at all. You seem nice enough."

"You won't save yourself that way. I can keep you here for the next 50 years if I want."

"My contract is—"

"I won't let you be a zero. I am extending it indefinitely. You are employed forever. Congratulations."

"Thanks."

"That tone in your voice. I don't like it."

"I'm sorry, that's what I sound like."

"What if I ordered you into surgery? We could reconstitute your vocal cords. We could make you sound how I'd like you to sound."

"I don't know, I suppose…"

"The age of whim coincides with the age of reinvention. No one likes who they are. They want to customize. They see the toys in the store, the apps, the dignified fun, and wonder why their dumb skin and bone can't be the same. Why can't we go in for an upgrade? Why can't we trade ourselves in? It's not fair. I told Chase he should do a wife trade-in every three years. He didn't quite agree."

"He loved you."

"I told him I'd do a husband trade-in every two years."

"I'm sure he loved you."

"You qualified your language. Am I doing that to you already? Making you doubt yourself? Self-esteem is reprehensible in the likes of you. It does nothing for the society as a whole. It holds us back. Imagine where we'd be without self-esteem. Imagine if the mass of boys and girls just sat down and shut up and did as they were told. We're maybe halfway there, but so much progress is left, so much unfulfilled. The smart people have their whims and the others must follow, no questions asked. Velez understood. I told Chase, this is a man who gets it. Right here. Never again will someone get it like this. He shrugged and kept trying to make stupid money. Stupid, useless money to pay for my subwoofer, my pool. Chase was a rich man who could do so little. A waste of net worth, a waste of life. He spoiled our son, the little brat. I miss him, I admit. I am not inhuman. I am not evil. I feel, too. Devlin didn't deserve to die with Chase. He could've been something."

"Been what?"

"Not his father. Not so stupid and useless. Money for money's sake, money for trinket's sake. Don't get me wrong. One, I am not evil. Two, I like things. Hence Sea Gate. I treasure it. But I also understand its stupidity."

"It's decadent?"

"No, stop with the morals. No moralizing here."

"Who did that painting out front? The man with the—"

"An Italian, a photorealist, Arlus something. I paid not enough for it. Beautiful work."

"Very detailed, very real-looking."

"Something so real yet so fake. All art judged by its approximation to reality. Chase liked art that he could understand, that his simple brain processed. He could deal with photorealism. I can deal with more."

Devora turned and shouted toward the sea. "Ulivia! Ulivia! I want my ArteMs., now! Now!"

Devora turned back and lowered her voice at Sundra. "I thought about installing little chips in their necks and tracking them around the house. I would have them as little blinking lights on my Gaggle and I'd press down and one would come to me, or suffer. Suffer an electromagnetic shock, internal, of some kind. I thought about this very hard. What stopped me? Inertia, I suppose. The effort. I enjoy flesh-to-flesh contact. It's easier for me to shout and kick them in person. I am stronger than I look, no? I can hurt you."

"You did hurt me."

"This is actually something only a few are privy to, but I used to beat the living shit out of Chase. Every few months. I would take my stiletto and pulverize him. Bite down so hard on his nipples during our rare moments of sex he sobbed. I once, before one of his stupid and useless meetings, broke his nose with the screen of my Gaggle. Just swung back and smashed him under the bridge. Oh, that felt good. It was so, so good."

"Did he fight back?"

"Once or twice. He was conditioned to be a good boy. His downfall, ultimately. I think my hitting him correlated with the increased amount of time and resources he devoted to this time travel scheme. He was convinced in 10 years or so it would be a lucrative arm of the tourism industry. Time tourism. Go visit the Revolutionary War. Go visit your grandpa's wedding. Try to rim job Marilyn Monroe."

"They did make it back in time. Something seemed to go wrong. The coordinates—"

"Yes, I was briefed. No need to *bore* me, Sandy. You bore me enough and you're dead. They wanted to go see the dinosaurs for Devlin and they ended up in what, 1979? A typical Chase mistake."

"1979."

"Now, Ulivia!"

A waifish woman in an olive Nehru jacket, Ulivia was holding a velour sack. She untied it and took out a white pill bottle. She pulled a small, palm-sized bottle of water from her pocket. Devora opened her mouth and Ulivia poured the water in. She opened the pill bottle quickly, dropped one pill in her palm, and then eased it, like a morsel of bread, into Devora's waiting mouth. She swallowed.

"Hmm, now now, who can I play with? Where's Friedrich? Or Randa-lander?"

Ulivia straightened her back. "I will summon either one, miss."

"Ping them and see who's closer."

Devora drew closer to Sundra. She smelled vaguely like lox.

"So, I said I wouldn't install little chips to track these premies, but that doesn't preclude Ulivia from doing the tracking. I find it's good for them to have hierarchies built in among their ranks. Ulivia is my chief, my little kapo. She tracks with her little Gaggle which in turn is synched to mine. She summons them when I tell her to. They learn to fear her approach and in turn know I am more powerful than her. You remove yourself from the lowest. In your absence, they make you into a god, a legend. This estate is big enough to miss people for weeks. I don't even know how many servants Chase has contracted to be here. I know the ones I like to romp and stomp. There's maybe 15, 20. The rest, I don't know. In the kitchen? Cleaning my pool? Dusting the garage? They don't care because we do free-range crediting around here. They're basically compensated in dollars. They can spend their earnings in whatever hovel they want and like it that way. You'll get that privilege soon, Sandy. Because you are lucky to be here, lucky to be serving me, lucky to be in service of my whim. Lucky to be here, in this age."

"I feel it."

"Do you? Let's see. Do you know what this pill that I swallowed is? You know, Ulivia. Do not tell Sandy here. Do not spoil the surprise."

"I won't, ma'am," Ulivia said.

"Get Hermes out for me."

Ulivia unzipped the cylindrical velour sack and pulled out what Sundra, from her relatively limited exposure to porn, believed to be an artificial penis and harness. What do they call it? A strap-around? A strap-on? The penis was white-pink, larger and thicker than the erections she'd tussled with, and flapped lightly from the black leather straps and o-ring. Ulivia gently handed it to Devora. Sundra tried not to change the expression of her face, straining heroically for neutrality in the wake of Devora stripping off skirt, stockings, and top, unhitching her necklace, barking to Ulivia to unhook this "damn fucking brassiere." Her light-starved skin was a checkerboard of wrinkles and moles pocked over visible bone. She did not look like a naked rich woman. Like neurons, little veins pulsed and fired on her arms and torso. A ribcage shoved against skin for freedom. Ulivia stooped obediently to remove Devora's underwear, pinching the elastic on each hip and pulling down. Nausea enveloped Sundra. She never could have foreseen this. Neutrality fled her. She was herself, dazed and unnerved, feeling her palms go wet. Devora was not wearing anything now. Her nakedness was elfin, otherworldly; she was a white flame on a floor of ice. No, *grass*, they were on grass outside, no ice, no flame. Metaphors were for the ill.

"Whooo am I getting, Ulivia? Tell me, tell me."

"It looks like Friedrich is in closest proximity. He is cleaning excess chairs in the pool house."

"Is he? Wonderful. I like his suppleness."

"Yes. I have pinged him. He knows what's coming."

"Good. Now Sandy, I want you to watch. I get a kick out of that. There's a one hour window to really feel the ArteMs. kick in. After that, the high is disappointing. Here, Sandy, I'll tell you. I'll ruin the surprise. First, I need my Hermes."

Ulivia slid the strap-on's harness on Devora. It wrapped her thin waist, dildo protruding from her crotch. The muscles in her calves and thighs flexed. Ulivia stepped backward, smiling just slightly, though not in the way that would indicate self-awareness. More pleasure in her boss's happiness. Devora was happy, happy to turn and run from them both, across the lawn, around the radius of the great pool and toward the cottage-like structure tucked into the corner, where waiting was her hunk of flesh. Oh, Devora could feel so young with ArteMs. thrumming through her. What Sundra did not see: Friedrich, buttery and blubbery, subdued in the pool house, Devora lodged in his back like the largest tick in America, yammering in his ear, biting his ear. Sundra walked closer because why not. She heard yowls, moans, grunts—the soup of sex talk. What Sundra did not see: the artificial penis, several inches longer and thicker than standard, penetrating Friedrich. She did not see the glacial sweat on them both. Friedrich had fallen to his knees, his fingers dug deep into the soil where Devora had forced him, the pool house's northwest corner. Sundra came close enough to hear it all and imagine the rest. If she had x-ray vision, the tableau would have been Devora pumping and pounding, her strap-on playing the role of woodpecker and Friedrich's butt the wood. There were other metaphors. Friedrich cried real tears. It was unclear if they were for joy, sorrow, or something in between, undefinable. His extra hundred pounds could not change the calculus. Through a gauzy flap in the pool house structure, Sundra saw their silhouettes thrashing.

She backed away. She had seen enough. How many more hours did she have here before she could ride the bus to the train and get away?

At some point in time later—someone could argue to her it was minutes or hours and she would've believed either—Devora came huffing out of the pool house, her scrawny face slathered in sweat. She did not look relieved. She looked fretful, angry, a bit ragged, like Friedrich had been the one with the strap-on doing the real fucking. Where was Friedrich? He never exited the pool house.

Well, Sundra thought, he may be passed out. Sleeping. Dead.

"Okay okay, that was something," Devora said as she approached. "ArteMs. always screws with my sinuses in the end. I forget that. I really do."

Ulivia, like a good phantom, was again at her side. Sundra never saw her walk up.

"Ulivia, get me my guns. I want to go hunting. My stress is not relieved."

"Yes ma'am."

"Tell Friedrich if he doesn't shape up I will be hunting him. Tell him the police department doesn't care if he dies. Tell him I'm not exaggerating. Tell him if he does not loosen up that asshole of his, he will be done away with. No, *no* euphemism. Killed. Say killed, Ulivia. Do this after you fetch my guns."

She turned to Sundra.

"Is there a gun you prefer? You ever hunt?"

"No," Sundra said.

"Well, you'll learn then. For now you'll cheer me on. I need to be positively reinforced."

"Okay."

"Let's get it on, then. I will go change. Ulivia will take you to the range."

Ulivia took her to the range. They traveled through a flying buttress of hedgerows, oversized koi ponds, gardens of unidentifiable flowers and fauna threatening at every turn in their maze-like path to devour them, turn them into fertilizer to further feed their growth. They walked for what must have been a half hour, right, left, right again, right further, left, left, around a round-about, toward what Sundra thought was the sea but in fact was another direction entirely, vaguely north or east. Several times she thought they had left the estate. She asked twice if they had. Ulivia succinctly replied in the negative.

"I do love to see the missus hunt," Ulivia said.

"What kind of, uh, game do you have here? Birds? Deer?"

"No, no, no. Missus Dimon would never hunt something so banal."

"Then…?"

"You will see."

"Of course. Of course."

They passed through a stone archway, the type seen in elite cemeteries, and entered a flat grassy stadium-sized field. She saw no game. At some point, she imagined, there would be genetically-spliced mythical creatures unleashed on the stage and Devora would chase them with an electrified crossbow. Fucked up griffins and sphinxes and chimeras and unicorns would romp around until they were promptly killed, only to be reborn in a lab days later. She had heard this was what the rich liked to do, murder the simulacra of fantastical animals, and Devora was certainly someone who fit this mold. A big, disgusting, magical animal to get a bullet in the brain. Ulivia stared blankly ahead.

"How long have you been with Devora?"

"Missus Dimon?"

"Uh, yes."

"11 years. Since my 17th birthday."

"Wow."

"It was such a wonderful opportunity for anyone, let alone any premium. The Dimons are so wonderful and important. They do so much for the city."

"So much."

"My goal has always been to gain Missus Dimon's full trust. I think I am almost there. She is so, so sweet and has so many friends, and I hope to be one of her very best, and if not that, someone to be of help."

"So sweet."

"How long have you had the pleasure of working for the Dimons?"

"At Velocity? Three years I guess. Three long years."

"How wonderful."

"Yup. Wonders every day."

"That was quite the romp Missus Dimon had today. One of her finer. She made very good time."

"Time?"

"Oh, she insists all her copulations be timed. I don't ask why. She says it's very important. But she made great time."

"Is great time fast or slow?"

"That's a good question. I would say it's in between. You want medium time. Especially with Friedrich. His endurance is exceptional."

"Wow, Friedrich. What a guy."

"He came at 17 also. He was here for three years when I arrived. We are both blessed to have known this as our adulthood."

"Blessed."

"Here comes Missus Dimon now!"

Here she came, riding in a capsule-shaped silver car. She sat in the front reading a traditional print book. No one else was in the car. Sundra was old enough to remember when people placed their hands on wheels, pressed pedals, and "drove" cars. How silly. The car stopped about 50 feet from them and Devora, closing her book, threw it out an open window. It landed, cover up, in the grass. Sundra couldn't make out the title.

"Ulivia, retrieve my shotgun from the trunk. Now."

"Yes ma'am."

Ulivia opened the trunk and took out a long black shotgun, a semi-automatic. Sundra knew nothing about guns, their brands or their capabilities. Its size dimly impressed her. She had heard laser guns were coming into fashion and wondered whether this would be like that, firing glowing red beams through the heart of a winged horse. Devora carried her gun past Sundra and Ulivia and entered the field, raising it as she began to tramp on grass.

"Summon them," she said, spitting after the second word. "I want them out here in 10 seconds."

"Yes ma'am."

Animals, real or fantastical, did not emerge. Ulivia produced a bright red whistle and blew into it. Sundra shuddered. One second, two seconds, three seconds hopped by, and she began to see the field was not empty. There were shadows struggling into people, then fully-formed humans, at least two, then four, then eight, a mix of men and women of indeterminate height and weight, most likely middling in all categories. They walked in their own directions as if they were trying to find separate bathrooms after long naps. None of them looked at Devora and her gun.

"Car!" Devora cried, and her silver capsule car roared to life, sliding in a path just to their right. Devora climbed in. "Sundra. Get the hell in. Now." When Sundra didn't move, Devora yowled "now!" and Sundra obeyed. Ulivia smiled placidly at the scene.

The windshield of the car slid down on Devora's side so she could point her shotgun straight ahead. It took Sundra longer than it typically would have to assess what exactly was transpiring in front of her: one of the wealthiest women in the world going out to hunt human beings with a shotgun. She fought and failed to find the correct words to fully describe the revulsion blooming inside her. It wouldn't matter anyway, because her words didn't matter here. All actions, all gestures, all feints toward actions would be performed in the context of Devora Dimon's wishes and desires. All of what made Sundra Glassgarden into Sundra Glassgarden meant as much, or less, than Friedrich's raw red asshole, because at least Devora could get a real fuck in with the guy. Sundra, well…her value was TBD, and it certainly wouldn't be augmented by her opinions or a display of morality.

In the Age of Velez, Quentin Stellar once taught, morality could not be quantified, and therefore was useless.

"You see that one there?" Devora asked, aiming her shotgun at a middle-aged man in a blue polo shirt. "That's Beame. He's first. He goes slow, so I like it. I like it easy. Struggles are a waste, and boring, believe it or not."

The shotgun fired, ringing madly in Sundra's ear. The bullet blew open the back of Beame's head. He fell forward, blood geysering left and right. He stopped moving.

"This is my favorite part."

The car accelerated toward Beame's corpse. The tires gobbled up the ankles, calves, legs, waist, back, and neck in one eye blink, and crushed the skull completely in the next. There was a minor thud underneath. Devora swung her shotgun to the side, a window sliding down to accommodate her soaring muzzle. Sundra felt vomit prancing in the back of her throat, waiting for the right signal. Devora cocked her gun.

"This one will be a little harder. Over there, that's Beame's friend, Wagner. Wagner is a type who likes to play games, run a zig-zag in the hopes of evasion, you know? Like an ant without a head. So stupid. More stupid than usual. The smarter ones die fast, believe it or not."

The car swerved left and chased after a second man, also middle-aged and whiter than Beame. He appeared to have more fat gathered around the midsection. Devora aimed, fired, and missed. The bullet exploded somewhere in the grass and Wagner, not exactly zig-zagging, began to run faster. "Shit." She fired again. "Shit." A third time. "Oh shit." The car sped up. They were side by side with Wagner, who was red-faced with close-cropped silver hair and the determined stare of a preacher. Devora aimed across the car so the muzzle would've smashed Sundra in the face had she not anticipated the shot and leaned back into her plush seat. "Oh baby, you fucking..." The bullet blew open Wagner's cheek and that was all. Confetti of flesh, font of blood. Sundra had never seen someone die in person, let alone two. The body rolled and bounced away from them as the car's momentum took them out towards the center of the field. The vomit was close now.

One more kill should do it.

"He was such a brute. How could he make me miss so many times? Ammunition is *not* as cheap as it looks. Especially with those unreasonable demands the Chinese and Koreans put on everything."

She turned to Sundra as if she would have an opinion on the import of arms from East Asia.

"Don't look so glum, Pris Stratton. They're *only androids*."

"What?"

They took after the third man, named Koch. Koch was shorter than the first two and globular, like a ball of snot brought to life. Still, he lived and breathed and presumably talked, and Devora was about to murder him. What should Sundra do? Cry out? Try to seize the gun? Kill Devora? She thought about what Rex would do in a situation like this one and she decided Rex would do exactly what she did: nothing. She regarded Rex as an equally moral being, only quieter, pegging herself as someone who, Stellar-like, would find injustice in the world and call it out for that. Someone had to. She watched old videos of "protest marches" and "civil disobedience" and marveled at the thousands of people who could be compelled to take time out of their work lives—or rare time out from their down time—to commit to acting for a cause that would provide them no immediate remuneration, no immediate change. There was a time when a mass of people, many unwashed, "occupied" a park not far from SoFi-DieBeca for a whole month. It was a general protest against inequity and while the goals, she admitted, were incredibly highfalutin and unachievable, it was still remarkable that people once were motivated in such a way. She had never seen a "protest." She wasn't even sure if she had ever spoken the word out loud. What Stellar had done was a protest, she decided. He had the same aim of any protest of old, no matter how ineffectual and outmoded they seemed: to raise awareness. Her stomach churned. What had these many protests amounted to? The long marches, the streets blocked, the occupations? *This*. All of it had led to Devora Dimon spending her family's billions to murder humans (or artificial humans?) on a hunting range on her estate. All of it had led to Devora Dimon taking some type of drug to get her in the mood for a raping. All of it had led to Devora's husband dying in the distant past. All of it had led to Sundra's life signed away to Velocity Ventures.

Don't forget the Plan.

"Now I want to go for the twin-killing. Dinkins and Giuliani. Two wily cats. I always get them, though."

The car accelerated once again, faster than before. Devora aimed at two figures in the rapidly approaching distance. Once was a man, one was a woman. The car drove first toward the woman, a thin brunette in tennis sneakers and short green skirt. She was jogging at an easy pace.

"Oh ho ho, jogging all easy, are you? Death is easy, life is hard. You will learn."

The woman didn't react. She was jogging, staring straight ahead. Sundra told her body to intervene. Throw itself at Devora, knock the gun away, change the outcome somehow. It was strange that one should even being telling one's own body to do anything. Shouldn't it just *do*? Shouldn't the invisible moral currents of the universe carry it forward? The jogging woman was at most 25, a young 25, clear complexion, the color of brown sugar. She did not expect anything, or look like she expected anything, despite jogging on a terrain of death. Didn't she see the corpses? Hear the gunshots? Devora cocked, aimed, fired. The sound was felt in Sundra's core, even in her vagina. She shook. The bullet struck in the thick of a bicep, knocking the woman sideways to the grass. She rolled soundlessly, the blood trailing along.

"What is wrong with you?" Sundra finally asked.

"What is wrong *with you*?"

"I'm not the one killing people."

"Oh, you really are so dense. I said it already. They're goddamn androids. Built for sport."

"Well, why don't you get them built to look like animals?"

"Because that's not as fun."

"This is sadistic."

"Would you rather me cull from my premium collection? Would you rather have it be you?"

"Well, no."

"Then shut up. You don't know anything. You are here until I don't want you to be here, and then I can go and hunt and fuck or kill you like all the rest. So count yourself lucky."

"Okay, I do."

"Sandy Glass, let me tell you something: you are going to live a very long time or a very short time. You are going to die in this world or a different one, like my husband. Who knows what the future holds? For reasons I don't understand, traveling into the future is much more logistically difficult than going to the past. Maybe simply because the future hasn't happened yet. I will tell you what I think, though. I am the most honest person you will ever meet. I am not like my husband, a hemmer and hawer, a sugar coater. I coat nothing. I promise you that."

"I appreciate that."

"If you continue to question me, I will throw you off this vehicle. I promise."

"I'll be quiet then."

"I need to focus now."

The car drove to the man, the first victim to look genuinely frightened. He was bald, trim, and dashed at a speed that seemed preternatural. Devora lined up her shot when the car had pulled beside the man, who was drenched in sweat and wailing. She could see the terror in his gleaming eyes and drool-slathered chin. He knew what was coming. He knew and he didn't want it. Anything but that. He'd beg if he weren't running. Keep me alive. The ebullient afternoon sun winked off his scalp, lending him a dash of whimsy unwarranted for the situation. Devora aimed. She shot left-handed, Sundra noticed. Did she always shoot left-handed? Did it matter? The man somehow ducked and the bullet missed. "Shit," Devora muttered. She reloaded. The man gained speed. He was running slightly ahead of the car, beyond the hood on a diagonal path. The car swerved in an attempt to run him over but he hopped away, wailing without taking breaths. Devora aimed again. The man did not duck but the bullet missed. "Shit." She wouldn't miss a third time. They both knew. Devora wasn't smiling at all. Her face made this seem like grim and vital work. Aimed, fired. He was struck in the back of the right leg, a non-fatal blow. He fell forward, face first. The wailing. Sundra feared she would never forget this freakish sound. She did not know yet what she would never forget. The car slowed, stopped. Devora, in her imp way, hopped out of the vehicle. She skipped across the field to where the man lay dying. Blood leaked passively from his torn thigh. There were ponds and canals of it near his feet, on his pants leg. His wailing was lower, more a growl, and he did not look at her. She drew the shotgun so the muzzle was within inches of his temple.

"You didn't get away," she said. "You had your chance and you failed."

More growling.

"I never liked your type."

The man opened his mouth and croaked out English in an unclassifiable accent. "You will be sorry. There are more like me."

"Correct, I ordered a large shipment of your prototype last week. They should be arriving tomorrow."

From close range, Devora was able to completely destroy the man's head. Sundra, leaning against the door of the car, slipped and fell, from the noise or the scene of bloody combustion, she could not be sure. Actual smoke trailed from the husk of neck that held a head that spoke to Devora. From her position on the ground, ass to grass, Sundra saw Devora as a little giant in her pumps and black stockings, her back elongated in the dusk. She did not want to get up. She really did not want Devora to turn around.

Sundra could no longer detach herself from this life, as she had been doing for most of it, dismissing her father and Velocity and even, to some extent, Rex. Ironic detachment, steely aloofness, the illusion of looking down on other people: all of it meant nothing here. Quentin Stellar understood. At least, he partially understood.

Sundra's Plan came back into focus, shedding its daydream gauze, its lack of immediacy. This was one mistake. Always relegating it to a safe future time when there was no safe future time. Death could kiss her on the lips in the next second. From now, until there was the freedom Quentin Stellar hoped for, she would work on the Plan and do nothing else. No one could know except Rex. She would trust Rex like she would a loyal dog. Dogs don't betray. Otherwise, if Devora even got the hint, she was finished. The present was finished. The future Stellar dreamed of would be finished, and the Age of Velez would be permanent, absolute, infinite. She was sure, ass on the grass, she had this sort of power to participate in stakes so high, galactic and intertemporal.

She was sure because she was Sundra Glassgarden, and that was enough.

"Oh, what are you sulking about? You keep that up and you're gone."

"I'm not doing anything. Just resting."

"Resting? We've hardly done anything."

"I'll get up."

"Do you want to kill one? Is that it? You feel you're missing something?"

"Why did you take me along anyway?"

"Because I said so. That's enough of a reason."

"Okay."

"You shouldn't be so dramatic about death. Do you know how many people die in this city every day?"

"No."

"I have a little counter in my room. It goes off every time a report comes in of someone dead. This is all deaths: murders, car accidents, sickness, old age. It tabulates mortality for me. Very handy."

"I've never heard of someone doing that."

"Chase never liked it. He found it morbid. He whined. Do you know there was a time when Chase expected me to do everything for him? He made the money, I was supposed to fill all other roles. I wasn't just a mother to Devlin. I was a mother to him. I would cut his meat for him, feed it to him. At restaurants, he would insist I order for him. I fed him, in a non-sexual way. Just cut his steak and fed him. This was early in our marriage, when I was less myself. The truth be told, I didn't become myself until a few years ago. I expect you, Sandy, had the advantage of becoming yourself at an early age."

"I don't know."

"I took time. I played Chase's dutiful wife for close to a decade. He needed so much reinforcement. He needed worship because of his sensitivities, his fears of falling behind and dying. I would wipe his ass in his early years. He would take his poos and then call for me like a little boy. 'I'm done, I'm done.' And he would get down on his knees, put his tushie up, and display it for me like one of those open-faced sandwiches. 'Wipe, wipe,' he would murmur, ashamed but proud. He loved the feeling of being taken care of, coddled, having someone scoop shit out of him with toilet paper. Rich little Chase. He grew up that way. His mother wiped his tushie. So I did it too. For a while at least. I wasn't yet myself. Eventually, I hit a breaking point, and I started to see who I was. I took the shit in the toilet paper and smacked him in the face with it. He couldn't even speak. He was so shocked. You may wonder why he didn't divorce me, throw me out on the street. There's an old-fashioned explanation, Sandy. I knew where the bodies were buried. That simple. I could go to any corporation in America and leak them prototypes of Velocity's time travel tech. I could tell them how they chose to short certain stocks. I could give them secrets about Chase himself, make his weaknesses public. I had pictures of his micropenis. Now that he's dead, I don't mind saying openly a man with a micropenis gave me a child. It's possible. He *tried*, Chase, in his own way. His little prick could get as big and hard as my thumb and he'd plow away, the semen going drippity-drip. What a grand, sad life he had. So rich and so stupid."

The car had driven off the field and through backroads of tall grass, the ocean water lapping behind.

"Chase made the mistake of forgetting about the ephemerality of life. He made the mistake of forgetting entropy. He truly believed he would find a way, soon enough, to be immortal. Imagine, that micropenis immortal. It's disgusting, really. He hired a few smart and lucky scientists to figure out the basics of time travel and then he mused it was only a matter of time until you could stall aging completely. He had an interest in cryogenics, though that won't matter now, with his remains incinerated in the 20th century. I thought that was funny, that his body will never be preserved, that any hope of immortality has been denied to him. I mean, I could order an android in his likeness. That could be of some consolation to him, no?"

"It could be."

"Don't be a fool. It's not consolation. He is dead. The dead don't get to be consoled."

"They don't."

"There was something endearing, I do have to admit all this later, about the time I spent wiping him. He had a little ass, hardly any fat, very flat, like smushed dough. Pimpled, a little purply even. Why? I don't know. There was a mole on the right buttocks cheek I got to know very well. The mole was dark red, like a dying star. I swear it glowed in the bathroom lights. I could just get lost in that dreadful mole. Chase became that mole. All his billions, his successes, his wonder, in that little mole glowing off his cheek. There may have been a microscopic hair or two reaching out. Who can truly remember? I wasn't yet myself, and the memories are a bit less crystalline from that period of time. I was a half-formed sort of thing, groveling my way toward enlightenment. Do you ever look back on what you were, and lament it all?"

"I don't know."

"Don't you damn premiums know anything?"

"Um, well—"

"I'll tell you something, if I don't get better conversation out of you, you'll be on all fours with Friedrich. He was frightfully dull once. I fixed him."

The car parked itself in a small lot and they got out. The sky was bruised with nighttime cloud cover. Sundra felt very weak. Even if they were android deaths, they seemed real enough, and she already foresaw the PTSD, nights interrupted by the images of exploding scalps. What was the point?

She might as well ask.

"Why do you like to hunt them? Why do you buy robots that look like people, that seem like people, and kill them?"

"Because I can afford to. Because I can. There is no other reason."

"It must be fun for you."

"I feel it is something I would do. It is me. You always end up becoming yourself."

"I've heard that somewhere before."

"I don't know what sewer culture you premies are exposed to, so I suppose anything is possible. You could be pretending to agree with me, to have heard something, to save yourself as a conversationalist. To save yourself from Friedrich's fate. But that doesn't work here. I don't like simple agreements, affirmations. Sometimes I do. Sometimes it's all I want. But if I don't want it, and you give it to me, you are very screwed. Literally. I will pop a pill and screw you."

"When you married Chase, did he know you'd be this way?"

"He had a certain conception of a wife of a multibillionaire hedgetechfund titan, and I agreed to this conception, before I became myself. I was someone else. Wife of Chase. Not Devora. It was a ruse I knew would have its end, and it did. I've been very happy since."

"So you're glad he died?"

"No. It's like being glad that there's a sunrise and sunset. They're bound to happen. He was going to die, one way or another. I suppose I'm pleased to have outlived him. His will was stupidly generous, and he lacked viable relatives. I have the vast majority of his assets."

A retinue of servants materialized as they walked close to a wing of the estate, west wing or east wing, she couldn't quite say. Her senses of direction and proportion were shredded. Devora was herself, but Sundra could not find herself. She retched, or imagined retching, watching a future clip of her body vomiting the entrails of her body. The clip sputtered in a loop behind her eyeballs. She needed time alone. A minute. An hour. A year. Time to regroup, to focus on this plan. Time for Sundra as Sundra knew Sundra. Time for before Sea Gate.

Turn back time. Go back. Time before Stellar, before Velez. Go back. Her pulse was atomic. Go back. Her eyelids drooped, stones weighted to the lashes. Go back. Her knee was touching the grass without permission. Time before, time after. Go. The plan. Koch, Beame, Giuliani. Don't forget your plan.

A cartoon of Japanese origin played in the distant past, a clip watched once and logged for never again, except right now, protruding from her memory.

When did she watch it?

Leading anti-hero to minor villain: "So I guess it's true after all. Androids do experience fear."

10

Lolita

I didn't have Santa Claus growing up. I had Marc.

To Bartolo Velez, better known to me as Papa, there was never a question of heroes and villains, sinners and saints, godsends and gofuckyourselves. Binaries ruled. Everything else drooled. He could be a man of books, faggot ambiguities, but he ultimately divided life into light and dark. He saw JoJo as dark. So they fought, not until the death, but until JoJo walked out.

Where should I begin this? Not from that night on the train. That's too easy. We'll start with how I started off the bat—Marc.

Marc didn't have a full name in our household because he didn't need one. I learned it later on, around the time I kissed my first boy: Vito Marcantonio.

Papa worked on his first campaign for the Congress in 1934. I was not yet born, nor would be for many years. The joy of JoJo and myself coming into this world, albeit accidentally, could not match the joy of Marc's rise, and Papa's belief that he was playing his part in the workingman's history, which he saw like a great ocean with waves that must be ridden to the shore. Papa was in love with the ocean, even if we lived nowhere near there and rarely went. He saw it in his sleep.

It didn't quite make sense. Not much did with Papa.

Marc came to our apartment once. I was not yet alive, but JoJo was, and Papa talked about this often, telling me how remarkable it was that this man could come here. This, beyond his failed stabs at poetry, was what lit him up most. Marc. A man of the people. Papa had a way of describing him, and I'll try to remember him here as Papa would, as if I were there. I have no obligations to him—it's not like he'll ever come see my baby—and it may seem strange that the daughter of such a person, who fled to the other side of the country to be alone with himself, his feelings, and his men, would feel this need to remember his old idol. I will state for the record, my own, that I don't think Papa was gay for Marc. Marc was not his type, ultimately.

Marc built a bridge in El Barrio between the Italians, the Blacks, and the Puerto Ricans, because he spoke their languages. He was Italian, a gringo, but his spirit was with El Barrio. This mattered because no one else was with us, certainly not the cops. All the cops were white and Irish except for one, Rincon, a traitor to his people who JoJo rightfully beat up as part of his initiation. Rincon had to go. He once made JoJo lick a turnstile after he caught him jumping. He knocked him over the head with his night stick afterwards. JoJo was dizzy for a week.

But I don't wanna talk about Rincon. What's the point? Word in El Barrio is he died last year of a heart attack. No one's seen him around. Everyone's grateful.

Here's how Papa described Marc, or might have done it when I was a kid and had the adult powers of perception and memory. I'm an adult now, barely to some people, but I've felt like an adult since I was five, to be honest. Childhood was never interesting. What was the point?

Marc treated his words like bullets, blast blast blast. He was small and dark, a dark white man, his hair so slick and black it glowed off his white skin like magic. He was for the workingman. No one is for the workingman, everyone is too afraid, too afraid of the bankers and money launderers but Marc, who they said carried a crucifix in his pocket everywhere he went, had the real Jesus on his side. Jesus of the poor, the down and out, Jesus on a cold and windy day on 125th when you're too hungry to wait on a bread line. Jesus on a day with snot making a music note on your lip. Marc was for the Communists sure, but the Communists were for you, the party of a square meal and a fair shake. Marc was against the bankers' war. When he came into this apartment, I had your mother make a steak, all the fixings, not any stuff from the Island, because I kept reminding her we were from America now and Marc didn't want no arroz con gandules. Marc ate fast. He ate like his teeth were bullets too. He had on a three-piece suit which he said he got discount because his cousin worked in a department store, and anytime I needed a suit, call him, go down to his office and he'd take care of me. I said thank you, gracias, thank you again. Marc spoke Spanish but I didn't want to give him that. We were Americans now. He was about to run for mayor so we talked about that. He had the look of a movie star, believe it or not. He was like one of those guys with a gal around his shoulder in the moonlight, driving a Chevrolet. He could drink his liquor straight. But he just had a beer when he came over. Your mother, thank God, cleaned out our best glass, usually saved for one of her damn brothers. Marc—he was a small man, physically, wiry and snappy in the limbs, and he moved like he was at the dance hall, even when he was talking of the most serious matters, like the capitalists killing the working man for profit or even how we needed to go back to the five cent fare. Fair was his fare—

You get the idea. I arrived a few years after Marc departed. It was a trade—my life, his death—Papa probably wouldn't have made. Certainly wouldn't have made it for JoJo.

I should be in some kind of school or work, but again what's the point? JoJo did a semester at City College. He said it was for losers going nowhere. It definitely didn't make sense for him, especially when he got in good with the Candies. Harder than getting into Harvard. It takes a while to really get in good with them. They don't fuck around. I told Archie this, that he's really gonna die one day if he keeps at it going down into their heartland. Look, uptown, Candies can't get you too bad. You got other gangs, other territories, they don't have as many pigs on the take. Once you hit Brooklyn though, hit south Brooklyn, it's like the Candies confederacy. They're about ready to make JoJo a general.

I hope he doesn't die.

So, like I said, I should be in some work or school, but who's gonna make me? Papa is gone. Mami left him, us, and went back to Puerto Rico with her brothers on a vacation that never ended. She says she's coming back but don't believe it. She wires up money occasionally so I guess that's nice. JoJo, like I said, is all set, so we're left with me. What do I do? I walk around a lot. I don't have any real friends my age because most chicks are basically kids, even when they're adults, and I can't deal with that.

JoJo had a lot of jobs but I've really only done waitressing in slimeball joints. I wouldn't mind one day working a few shifts in some Wall Street diner, serving scrambled eggs and French toast to the capitalist bankers Papa hated so much, even if it never was really clear what JP Morgan did to him. I wouldn't mind sucking up that clean air, no shit. Rich people are different. You learn that quickly. It's not the clothes, the hair, the make-up. It's the *knowing.* They aren't afraid of dying. They think money will keep the stink of death away. Death is everywhere if you're not rich. You wake up, crawl out of bed, you run smack into death. I get out of the subway at 125th and I'm jumping over winos and junkies and angry old folks. I'm getting ready to duck. JoJo taught me to walk with my head a bit low, down to the ground. *Don't make em suspect nothin.* Papa thought men like Marc were beyond death, or barriers to dying, somehow. Papa didn't know shit, in that regard. It was good he was out of the city by the time the blackout hit. He would've peed all over himself. He would've gotten killed accidentally, I bet. Papa wasn't important enough for anyone to try to kill him. You would've seen some guy ripping a TV from a shattered window and by accident choke out Papa with the cord. I spent most of the blackout smoking reefer with JoJo and some of his friends. I haven't really done reefer since. JoJo doesn't approve. He says it dulls you, makes you weak, easy to hit. All the Candies keep clean, he says. They deal plenty but don't take. Every week JoJo comes back up to El Barrio with a pocket of cash and hands out some to me. Between that, waitressing, and Mami's hiccup of bucks, I do okay.

What do I do these days? I walk the city, looking for him.

Not Papa. Not JoJo. Him. He's gone underground, the bastard. But I know the underground.

You know, I'm just getting to think about having a real kid come out of me. I knew plenty of girls in the neighborhood who got knocked up. One girl I went to school with, Nina Hidalgo, had a kid at 14. She was knocked up by this huge cocksucker Ruben Carrión, big fat 19-year-old sicko with a furry mustache and everything. I actually tried to kill him. JoJo talked me out of it, said it wasn't worth it. *Don't waste your first kill on Rubencito, chica.* I had a plan for Rubencito. I knew where he lived, a tenement on Park with his mom and three sisters. I had a plan to lure him, take him on a date and cut his throat in a movie house. I liked thinking about the plan a lot, thinking about watching him bleed out as the film flickered overhead. This, of course, was before I was having a baby.

I don't really think this way anymore.

It sounds dumb, like I'm some white social studies teacher, but you carry a baby, you carry the future. I've been thinking about that a lot. I knew a girl, Carla Reyes, who had an abortion when she was 15 from some Jew doctor on the Upper West Side. The Reyes family was one of the few in the neighborhood with money so her dad, who worked construction I think, pretty sure he was up on the Twin Towers at one point, paid to have the baby go away. Why did they live here if they had money? If I had money, I'd be with the abortion doc on the Upper West Side, enjoying the fresh salamis and pastramis in the delis over there. Anyway, the abortion fucked her up big time. She was real glum after that. I'd say her eyes always seemed like they were fogging over, like maybe she had been crying yesterday but was done now and was thinking about crying again. She ate less. We talked only a little bit afterwards. She never came out. I asked her if she was going to see *Star Wars*. I thought the guy who played Solo or whatever he was called wasn't bad looking, for an old white guy at least. She didn't say anything. Or she said she wasn't gonna do it, shrugged, walked away. Nothing interested her. I think if she had to do it over, she'd keep a baby, because it's better to have the life and put up with the shit than to have no life at all. If you have an abortion, you start out with a loss right away, you gotta carry around this phantom with you, and there's no way you won't find yourself years from now, maybe waiting for a train downtown, thinking what could've been, could my baby have grown up to be an astronaut or Reggie Jackson or a junkie, because it's all possible, and possible beats nothing, an un-person? I don't know. Something to think about.

But I don't like the Church telling me what to do with my body either. Priests don't know anything. God's not gonna tell me what I can do with my womb. It's complicated.

JoJo wants me to check in with a doctor. I don't wanna. I took a test. I know what I am. What's a doctor gonna say? I only want to check in with one person.

It's a bit shitty but I spend my days looking for him. It's not always like I'm *looking* looking, leading a search party or yelling his name from a street corner. I'm just looking out. Always. Any man's voice could be his voice. Any snort, any growl. Any jacket and tie. Any trench coat. Any five o'clock shadow. Any sounds of heavy footsteps. Any tap on my shoulder. Any shadow, to be honest.

They could all be him.

JoJo calls it yo-yoing. You get on a train line and go back and forth, end to end. A true yo-yo is where you end up where you started. So I yo-yo on the Lexington Avenue line, all the way into Brooklyn and back up here. This was yesterday. You figure of the thousands of people pushing in and out of the train cars one has to be him. That's just odds. That's just math. I always had a decent head for math. In the 7th grade, I had a teacher, Mr. Franks, who said math wasn't for girls. I didn't know what to say. He was old, balding, white, so he had to know more than me, a Puerto Rican girl with a lot of hair. It seems to me that the paler your skin and the less hair you have, the more authority you get. The master race is white as the surface of the moon and hairless. Alien. Races are funny. I know JoJo thinks the race revolution is coming, and soon all the whites will be thrown into the street and killed for their crimes, slavery and everything. Their *systematic dehumanizing oppression*, he says.

I don't hate white people. I thought about this yesterday, as I yo-yoed. White people are just okay. I almost feel bad for them, especially if the revolution is coming, as JoJo predicts (I am doubtful). White people always seem the most disconnected from the world. The most ghostly, in a way (not because of their skin color). They're so of the world, such a default, you don't even notice them—they fade away, like clouds passing in the sky. They don't notice themselves. They don't know struggle, life lived in the negative, so they don't know anything. I think of super-powered babies. They don't even know what to do. Ever see a white person walk north of 96th Street? Ever see how big their eyes get, how tight their jaws get, how they have the *ho shit I'm in the jungle* look glued on their faces? See, they'll always be afraid of us brown people churning at the depths, waiting to rise up, but I ain't got nobody to fear rising up *on me*. I'd rather punch up then have to look down. That's just me.

I already thought of a name. I don't care what he thinks, what he tries to do if he shows his grubby face again. It's *my* baby, I'm carrying it—him or her. If it's a girl, I will name it after me. Why do men only get that privilege? What kind of bullshit is that? I will name her Lolita Joaquin Velez, after me and JoJo. If it's a boy, I have two ideas. One was to name him Archibald for obvious reasons. That idea is getting thrown out. The second idea, believe it or not, comes from Papa, at least indirectly. We never had bookshelves because Papa didn't want to pay for them or build them (he couldn't build a damn thing) so books, stuff Papa swiped from the library or maybe got on discount down in the Village, would be lying around everywhere, the floor, the beds, the bathroom, you name it. One of the books he always had was a book of poems by someone named Octavio Paz. I didn't know much about him and I didn't learn how to read in Spanish too good. So I can't tell you whether the poems were worthwhile, not that I'd have anything to say about poetry. It was just always around, so I have a warm feeling whenever I hear the name. It's familiarity. It represents a time when Papa really was a Papa, when he wasn't running out late nights, crying in his room, vowing to leave for California, then finally leaving. *Octavio*. It's not a bad name. If the baby is a boy, I can live with it. It will be my say. Not his. Until he shows his face. Then maybe he gets a say.

I don't want to admit I'm looking for him. I'm not one of these white girls from the movies. I'm not pining for *my man*, my hunk in white shining armor. At the end of the day, who gives a shit? I look in my own way. It is what it is. JoJo will be back soon and we'll go out and get dinner, maybe the Mexican place all the way by the East River. I'm getting hungry.

That does remind me—last week something very weird happened.

Yeah, I can't believe I forgot. How could I? It happens. Life moves so fast you forget life. It's a dream, really. The samurais said death was an awakening from life. I sometimes believe that. Especially, given what happened last week.

So I'm walking down Lexington. I think I was going to meet Leddy, a girl in the neighborhood. Someone on the outside would call her a "friend" but to me she was another body, another shadow, but let me get on with it. I'm walking down Lexington and what do I see but a little white boy. I mean, little isn't the right word. He was stuffed, all rolls and two chins with a rich boy's glow, his stare wide and blank and lost. He was wearing nothing like I'd seen before around here or anywhere. A shirt with a lot of weird colors and logos, a real fucking space cadet. He looked very tired. Beaten. Shuffling as much as walking, a bit of drool in the left corner of his mouth. His teeth were whiter than his skin. He was short and had some flat silver and black thing on his wrist, almost like a watch but definitely not a watch.

He was walking without watching where he was going and bumped into me, like that. Out of a script.

"Hey," I said. "Watch your step."

I tried not to be too mean. Clearly the kid was lost from the Upper East Side. Went north of 96th Street like he wasn't supposed to, didn't listen to his gringo parents. Oh well. I had sympathy.

"Uh, sorry."

He had a bit of a sooty face, like he'd been playing in a dust field. And there were weird tears on his clothes. I thought I saw dried blood. Who knew a kid like him could get rough. Maybe he got his ass kicked on the other end of the neighborhood, his daddy was lecturing at Columbia and he made the mistake of staying outside the gates too long. He really looked lost.

"Where you trying to get to?"

"I don't know. Just looking for food. No one takes cards or chips or scans around here."

"You trying to pay a bodega with poker chips? *Hokay.*"

"I figured at least you could take credit cards. I got one for my birthday last year. No one's got any machines for that. I was hoping maybe the supermarket would have one. I also hoped there'd be something to detect net worth. You figure at least there's a fallback? Retinal or finger scan? Nothing. There's nothing. This is a nothing world."

"What the hell are you talking about? You look real out of it, kid."

"I'm gonna sit down."

He sat. Slid right down against the brick side of a building and sat on the sidewalk. There was probably dog shit 10 feet away.

"If you pay me back, I'll go get you a soda."

"You can detect my net worth? You can do a scan?"

"I don't know what you're talking about. You don't got 50 cents?"

"No. Where I'm from, we don't do cash."

"Then how the hell do you buy anything?"

"I told you. Cards. Scans. If you have good net worth like me or my parents they scan you and you get what you need."

"Uhuh. Lemme guess. This is some new social experiment on 72nd Street?"

"No."

"You know what, you're in such bad shape…I feel bad enough to just spot you a soda. But no other gifts."

"I'm really hungry. Any snack would be good. I don't need Coke."

"I'll get you chips."

I went and got him a bag of chips. When I came back, he was still sitting there, staring straight ahead into the street. A bum walked by and stared straight back. He lost the fight and walked on.

"What's your name, anyway?"

"I'm Devlin."

"Hmm. What kind of name is that? I guess I can't talk. I'm Lolita."

"That's a nice name, sure."

"I got named after a stupid movie. Or book. Or both."

"A movie. That's cool."

He was eating the chips like it was the first time he'd ever seen food. He practically swallowed the bag in two bites. If he whipped out his dick and started fucking the chips, it wouldn't have even surprised me. Crumbs were splattered like little salty stars all over his face but he didn't care.

"So let me guess now, you got no tokens for the subway? You need that too? Too tired to walk downtown?"

"I don't have any tokens. I haven't been on the subway here."

"I've heard that you rich kids just get driven around in black cars everywhere. Subway's too dangerous for you."

"That's not it. I'm just really tired. I'm gonna go sleep somewhere."

"Well, I got no place for you. I mean, I don't wanna just say you would never have a place, it's just there's barely enough room for me in JoJo's pad. One more body—nuhuh. He wouldn't have it. JoJo wouldn't like you anyway, sorry."

"I saw a park not too far from here. I'm gonna go lie down."

"You talking about Garvey?"

"I don't know. Yes. Maybe."

"You sleep there for five minutes you'll be robbed blind, deaf and dumb."

"I'll figure it out. I've figured it out so far."

"So what's that on your wrist anyway? It doesn't look like any watch you get at Macy's."

"It's my Gaggle. It's no use here. I get no reception. Not enough satellites in the sky. It still can run on some functions on solar but I need a charger to get enough juice for any of the good apps, and I left my charger at home. My dad said next year I could get it grafted to my skin to charge from my bioelectricity, which is best. You're not supposed to do that until you're 18. Dad said it was okay though."

"You must watch a lot of TV."

"No, only really old people watch TV."

"Um, okay. You be safe out here and get home okay. If you're in trouble, well, I'll give you my brother's house number. I don't usually do that. I don't like to do that. JoJo won't like it. But I'll do it. You don't got a pen or pencil, right? Paper?"

"No, I'm not an old man."

"What the fuck does being old have to do with a pencil? Anyway, can you remember a number?"

"My Gaggle can record."

"Okay. Tell your giggle."

"*Gaggle.*"

"Okay. Sure."

It went like that. I wondered if the kid was on drugs. You don't see fat little white boys on drugs, but we live in strange times, right? I figure I'll keep an eye on him while I'm keeping an eye out for *him*, the other him.

I figure a lot of things. I figure I'll be okay tomorrow. I figure my baby will be okay.

I figure I'll see Archie again.

11

21st Century

"Memoirs are a strange thing. How to make your life into words? How to rearrange these events into a false narrative? How to remember? How to pretend to remember? How to even do this when I have so much more living to do?"

Ulivia, at that moment, whispered to Broxton, the dining servant working under her, to bring out the brisket to Missus Devora and her guest. Broxton nodded and tried to as silently as possible deposit the main course on the two plates. Ulivia clicked her tongue. His form was off, elbows out, too much clatter when the plate made contact on the table. Broxton would be punished later. That was clear. Now that Missus Devora had tired of Friedrich, and his sexual recalcitrance, Broxton would be next. She almost felt bad for Broxton.

"Oh, you worry so much. It's silly, really. I never understood how you could fret. I never worry. What is there to worry about?"

"Death. A bad book."

"Bad? Good? Who cares? It'll sell. Everyone will want to stream it."

"Who pays for things anyway? All these words, words, and more words, all of it empty symbols of the past life."

"Are you worried about sales? You need the money that badly? Do you need little old me to take care of you like the old days?"

"For my next campaign. Can you be president of the world?"

"Octavio," she said, clearing her throat, "you'd find a way."

The secret service were told to wait downstairs. The ocean view dining room's ambience would have been sullied by the presence of men in dark suits and ear pieces. Were they more of a target now, sitting by a window, guards waiting downstairs? Perhaps, but for aesthetics, Devora Dimon would take that risk. She figured she had lived long enough anyway, or by a simple law of nature she could survive an attack. She certainly knew she carried out her life in a way warranting the occasional attack. She accepted this. Long ago, she had decided compromise was silly, perhaps the silliest notions of all to permeate Western liberal thought. If we are all fated to die, why not live your life as brilliantly as possible? Why settle for less? For most, these were clichés, trite utterances floating like driftwood through their waking hours, either to be acknowledged or ignored. If she wanted to enjoy a meal with the former president of the United States in full view of whatever drone or copter that wanted to take her out, so be it.

"A way, a way," Octavio sang. "Yes, there is always a way. I learned that in eight years."

"Eight of the best."

"Yes, a fundamental revision of the compacts of capitalism and democracy. A rewrite of the American Dream. Oh, and the Indians finally won the World Series."

"Take credit for all of it, darling."

"It's so nice, sometimes, to not have to decide anything. I ask my wife to pick my meals for me. She combs my hair. I'm tired of the decisions."

"So you come here."

"I'll never forget generosity. When I was flailing in New Hampshire, Chase's super PAC kept me going. His money. Your money. I was a nobody. A slick, boyish Latino by way of Harlem and SoCal. A little baby. I learned, really learned then, how precious a dollar is."

"You're past that now. You've got your story to write."

"My story. I only have lies on my tongue. I'd like to tell a few truths."

"Dirty secrets will get you hype. Tell them how you averted war with Russia by sleeping with the prime minister, Marina whatever."

"You know, that one is almost true. Almost."

"Poor Nivea, married to a philandering president. Is there such a thing as a non-philandering president?"

"No. I don't think so. They said Obama didn't mess around much."

"That was so moving, your eulogy. The Hispanic president, with such soaring rhetoric, as the *Times* might say, paying tribute to the original trailblazer. I almost had tears."

"I guess that's the point of a memoir. I'm supposed to remember. Sit here and live in the past. I flew here from California to live in the past for an hour.

"I'm sorry about Chase, by the way. I should've said this before. I am very sorry," he added.

"He only has his stupidity to blame."

"Well, it's tragic, anyway. And your son."

"I miss him. I hope he can be retrieved."

"Is it possible?"

"I have some smart people trying to figure that out."

"This brisket is excellent, by the way."

"Don't lie. I hate it."

"Devora, it's good. Don't kill a cook over it."

"You've gone soft in old age."

"I've gone something in old age. Ruminative. Misty-eyed. Something…I need some hot tea."

"Ulivia!"

Ulivia, and not Broxton, filled former President Velez's cup. What a handsome man. Her knees shook. Broxton couldn't have handled the task. He was doomed. He could not rise to challenges like Ulivia could. Sometime later tonight, he would find his nipples in clamps and testicles slit and wonder, *why oh why was I so incompetent?*

"Very good," he said after sipping. "I think I regret a lot. That's the problem. A memoir of regrets. People will probably like it. I won't want to read it."

"Don't be a baby, Octavio. I don't like it. You know what will help you forget a regret? Blowing the brain out of an android. It's like sex."

"It was never a sport I could embrace."

"Hmm, well. Your loss. What are you calling the book anyway?"

"It's looking like *The Age of Velez*. I'm not a huge fan but the publishers like that."

"So sweeping. So despotic. So you."

"I think if we lived honestly, 'we' as in not 'you' but 'we' as a society, we would apply labels very different. This was a lesson I had hoped to teach."

Ulivia gestured furiously to Broxton to bring out the white truffle platters. Missus likes her desert early, as she's finishing her meal. She told that oaf Broxton. Why can't he listen?

"The professorial Velez. A great speaker, with such a fine touch for people. Preach, Octavio. I have my truffles. I have time. You gave us all, finally, *time*. The great Velez gift. Premiums gifting Ents white truffles. A lovely life."

"This is what I'm supposed to write about."

"Don't sound so guilty, so whiny. What is it, what are you so—"

"I didn't go far enough, Devora. That's what I want to write. That's what I can't."

"You can write whatever you want. You more than anyone."

"No, I can't. I didn't make the world ready. For starters, eight years, two terms—that is not enough. I sit here or on my ranch or in downtown LA and think that, every day. There just *wasn't enough time*. I got halfway there, maybe. There were too many obstacles. A Congress that didn't understand *enough*. A cabinet that was too ahistorical. I should have fired them all the second I realized it. I should have been unafraid to kill my own. I would put that in the book."

"So far, so good. And what else?"

12

21st Century

Sundra was on the Bleater line down south, to Brooklyn. It ran above ground most of the way so she got to press her nose to the glass and gaze out on the rooftops, the single-family shantytowns and apartment blocks that made up the old neighborhoods. She saw decommissioned antennae, crumbling chimneys, blacktops and church steeples, a tableau of asphalt and half-raised middle fingers. All premium territory. Cheap to live, but not cheap enough. The afternoon sky was late gray going on black, the sun ducking away, autumn lurking. She saw dead leaves, a smattering of orange and gray at the bottom of a retaining wall. The train lurched, sputtered, waiting just outside Newkirk Plaza for reasons clear to no one. A voice gargled over a loudspeaker. She did not know what it said. The few people slouched in their seats stared into their Gaggles, the sound and light pleasant on their soft cheeks. Her Gaggle was blank, conspicuously so, and soon she would get a few dirty looks if she didn't start absorbing herself in all it had to offer. What kind of deviant would just want to stare into space or be alone with her thoughts?

This was actually Bleater line C. Bleater bought the naming rights to three train lines, all of which had marquee routes straight through Manhattan and Ent territory. C began in Brighton Beach, traditionally a Russian enclave and now a hodgepodge of Latinos and Hasidic Jews, and ended in the northern Bronx, a hinterland Sundra knew little of. In between, there was plenty of Manhattan and the northern end of Brooklyn, where Ents congregated and spent their credits. On the southern end, where she was headed, lived premiums and zeros, side by side in what could charitably be called harmony. You had a lot of ex-cons down there too, people who racked up enough unpaid traffic tickets to lose their voting rights. She remembered again what Stellar had said: the Ent's right to vote was *irrevocable*. Of course, he also labeled American democracy a sham, so who really wanted it? She didn't know any premiums who had lost their right to vote to be particularly upset. The government, the media, constitutional rights—these were all abstractions to most people pulling triple shifts at the Kings Highway Olive Garden or desperately applying an extra layer of reinforcement to a seawall following the mutating aggression of hurricane season. The rights meant little. She wasn't sure, truth be told, how much they meant to her.

She was sure that she needed a way out from this place and that Stellar, in his short life, had pointed a way. Beautiful Quentin Stellar. She loved his ideas, and even his body. She didn't believe that Christ died for our sins, but she could be convinced that Stellar did.

Baby steps, Sundra. She turned on her Gaggle to watch a news feed. One at a time, and you'll get there. When should she share the full extent of the Plan with Rex? She could envision his reactions: intrigue, shock, horror, fear, and then acceptance. You could easily take his temperature. She watched the train pass Avenue M and she turned back into her Gaggle to be like everyone else. The success of this plan depended on her seeming like any other American. A hint of sedition or sabotage and Velocity, along with the full force of the police, would be on to her. She would be tortured. Even death wasn't out of the question, given how ready juries were to hand down the death penalty for premiums who committed crimes against Ents or their entities, their property.

Her father once mocked her for mispronouncing Ent.

"Ahnt," Gary Glassgarden croaked, "*not* ehnt. Ahn. Ahn."

"Okay dad."

"Don't roll your eyes, Sundra. This is important. You keep saying words wrong and you'll end up a zero. On the scrap heap of life. No one wants to be there."

"We should get to say words how we want."

"I don't know about that. Imagine the anarchy if we all did what we wanted. Imagine the chaos. How nutty."

Nutty, indeed. She had experience in that. Traveling down to the ass end of Brooklyn to meet under the cover of night—or late twilight, at least—with a Hasidic warlord would certainly make Gary Glassgarden uneasy. A mass of Glassgardenian men allow the order to be the order. They are manna for the Age of Velez: pliant and afraid, all too happy to take it on the chin, again and again, until bedtime.

The world needs Garys. An army of Garys slinking into the future, an arm raised limply above the eyes, squinting, whining, *don't hit me, please and thank you.*

Sundra was sure she wouldn't end up like that. Not if she were riding a train to Yaacov Yankowitz's domain, where the Velez system meant precious little in the heat of eternal Hashem.

Devora Dimon would not be able to get her soon. This was almost as important as freeing herself from Velocity itself. After today, Devora wouldn't be able to track her. Yankowitz would take care of that. The more Sundra contemplated her week with Devora, the more she was sure the human race itself was imperiled if she didn't act soon, if the Plan wasn't fulfilled. Devora was the Age of Velez's greatest product, its prime export, and therefore what would first disappear if all went according to the Plan. The Plan, the Plan! So real yet so mythical, she couldn't even articulate it to herself anymore. It existed as an allusion, a flicker of light in the sky, the remnant of a dream in the moment when you're finally awake, tasting the bitter ash of morning. All of that shit. Sundra, one stop away from Sheepshead Bay, thought about the androids.

Did they feel pain? Did it matter? The delight in Devora's face. The thrill she felt in eliminating an imitation of human life. The fake blood and fake brain matter looked real enough. After that first run on the range, Devora took Sundra a second time, and it was very much the same. Devora murdered, Sundra watched. What was the point? Sundra had been dispatched, in theory, to soothe a grieving and very important widow. Instead she had found a megalomaniacal despot so in love with life she could kill pretend people all day and night—not to mention that she raped her premium servants nonstop, also day and night. It was that drug, ArteMs. Sundra had never heard of it. But she was terrified that Devora, who did not discriminate between male and female anus, would turn toward her relatively blemish-free, nubile(ish) body. Sundra had never thought of herself as pretty, assuming only someone like Rex, a bit slow and forever slavish, would want a go around. She considered it a few times, though her brain always passed. Rex wouldn't be for that.

Just like she hoped she wouldn't be for Devora. She'd rather get a bullet to the abdomen and take her chances then face a hopped up Devora and her V-2 dildo.

Thinking of this, she got off at Sheepshead Bay, an above ground station sunk in sooty darkness. All the lights were out, or they were never installed. Gaggles glowed off wrists and palms like Japanese lanterns and Sundra found herself following the procession, walking down the hard steps to the street below. Empty soda cans, candy wrappers, sludge, and used condoms greeted her, along with a row of men slumped off the curb, smelling like shit. In the

Ent and more upscale premium precincts, homeless and zeros (well, was there really a difference?) were effectively cleared from the streets, locked up, and occasionally euthanized. Crime had gone down, so it was tolerated, even by liberals. Sundra liked the idea more than she could admit to herself. It was so easy. Who wanted to have all these unpleasant-looking people clouding your vision, living so unpleasantly on the streets you tried to walk and conduct your worry-free life? The police contractors who handled homeless professed their humanity, said the indigent were caged with the utmost care and respect and whisked in comfort to the nearest euthanasia shelter.

Out here the cops didn't seem to care. A man in a black hood and shredded jeans was pissing against the metal gate of a shuttered shop. Sundra could see the glimmer of a penis and she gagged. She looked down in her Gaggle for the address: 2207 Avenue Y. It was almost a mile away. Whatever. The sun was down, the air was warm, and the homeless hovered like the undead. She set off down the road forking up ahead. Her Gaggle commanded her to take the left fork. A few shabby Russian bakeries and tea rooms were crammed into the flat, two and three-story buildings on her right. She saw a bank, a former condo tower, and a church that she doubted, given the unruly shrubbery and battered brickwork, was in use. The streetlights were off, maybe permanently. She wished she had a firearm. This may be the outskirts of Hasidic territory, she thought, but it's gang territory and the Hasids pull their strings. They supply the money, the arms. They even join in, from time to time, beards blazing.

The dark in this city shouldn't *be like this.* She was used to Manhattan's lunar glow, the rhapsody of LED and halogen and even flame itself, her skittering footsteps timed to the metronome of a city that could never let you go, for better and worse. New York, in the gyre, could never be fed enough to go quiet, to crawl backwards, ass-first, into the nothingness of original life. The countryside where she had never been. This was like that. No homeless, no zeros, no Ents. Nobody. The opposite of hierarchy is anarchy, but this was not that. There were laws undergirding this navel of Brooklyn. She just did not know any of them.

Maybe she should have come with Rex. He could've lent some flabby muscle to the operation. He was a loud mouth, a klutz, too much of a liability ultimately to take down here, where the crackle of a twig could be heard for a mile. She saw a large drone purr overhead, taking photographs of her or the night sky. She saw one car on a wide, two-way avenue called Ocean. A flatbed truck followed. To the right, her Gaggle said, was water, the so-called Sheepshead Bay.

Her Gaggle, responding to a news pulse, began warning her about reports of Russia Alliance drones in American airspace, a fleet spotted northwest of Massachusetts Bay. Nothing ever seemed to come of the reports, but they unnerved her in their own way, despite her reflexive disbelief in the feeds. The American government fed data directly to the feeds and an editing algorithm made them consumable for Gaggles. From what she understood, the algorithm accounted for the probability of false or mistaken data. Algorithms could lie too. For as long as she could recall, either Islamists or Russia Alliance drones were threatening the destruction of America, land of liberty and freedom.

On her Gaggle's drone map the drones were like snowflakes, alone and beautiful in the dark. America sent drones to the Russians too. Even she didn't really know what the war was all about, the scuffles over foreign territory, sovereignty, digital fingers pointed in wholly digital directions that could never mean anything to her. She walked onward, across the street, around an abandoned CVS pharmacy. The windows were cracked and oddly fogged, teal and green graffiti slathered over a long side wall. She could not read the symbols. In a chained off parking lot up ahead, a man was swimming in a dumpster, growling to himself. He must have hopped the fence. She saw his yellowed teeth and ruddy eyeballs, his whole face like an eraser's smudge, the features blurred in the whirl of trash. He turned to her. She locked her gaze on her Gaggle. He had no Gaggle to stare into. Poor man. He flitted back to his dumpster, plunging two hands into the black. She hated the Gaggle, its hold on her, and even how it made her hate those who lived a Gaggle-less existence. The device was her unwanted lodestar, the third arm she was born with and could not amputate, no matter how much she willed it.

Now that weeks had passed and all references to his death had been effectively scrubbed from all digital space, she could see how crucial the Plan really was, given that Stellar had failed. There had been no revolution of consciousness. No uprising, no protest, no debate. What else could have happened? Nothing, of course. Hence her certainty in this being the single course of action. It was comforting, in a way, because she never had to make a decision. She never had to stare deeply into herself and ponder whether breaking the law was necessary when other resorts remained, penultimate plans that did not depend on bloodshed. She never had to choose. Stellar died, the world chose.

What would really happen when she was successful? Would men be hunting for garbage outside abandoned pharmacies? Would someone like her be traveling to the world of a warlord—a resourceful warlord, granted—to have a microchip illegally removed from a right index finger? No, no, no. It would be another world, and therefore better. By default. This she had to believe in, even irrationally, like the first martyrs who through their deaths would imagine an eternity with big brother Christ. She had no regard for religion and was quietly amazed God's hold on humanity had persisted so long, given the catastrophes that forever visited man. Following the Plan amounted to a form of religion, she had to admit, setting aside some rationality for *belief*—an emotion grounded in nothing but the emotion itself.

She saw she was on Z, checked her Gaggle, and began walking north toward Y. The block was tree-lined, with flat multi-family homes colored a dull shade of red, curtains drawn, squat stoops jagged and empty. A lifeless place. In the city, there was screaming glass and searing light and the feeling that, even with death imminent, millions could die together in a perverse kind of harmony. Here, on the icy outer rim, death would be solitary—as it should be. Here was where the grandmas and grandpas, no longer of use to anyone, felt their brain or eye or bladder transplants give, life seeping out and eternity barreling in, pleas for help dissolving on leaf-strewn windowsills. In trousers or sweaters or floral-printed skirts, their once fashionable tattoos faded to a pond scum gray, they would fall, cracking their heads against cold floors. She watched this play out in her head, a loop of anonymous deaths. She saw the drool, the drying of drool, the beginning of decomposition, bone to dirt. No matter the money we make, the companies we found, human bodies will turn into crap and go back to the planet. She turned back into her Gaggle. It told her about her heartrate, cholesterol, white blood cell count. It told her everything about her she ever needed to know. The AllRecord feature kept running recordings of every spoken word in a 100 foot vicinity and stored it in a cloud, automatically filed by date and time, to be pulled out at her own convenience. Memory and Gaggle had become synonyms and these dying, alone people—in her imagination, at least—were without tech, denied the ability to accurately account for their lives. So sad. So freeing. Her mind said to admire their detachment and commitment to a solitary life, imposed or not, and her heart said to fear it, *flee and get the fuck out of here already*. The Plan was not worth a solitary death. Her Gaggle gave thermal readings and could tell her that the houses she was passing were unoccupied, though two at the end of the block had three and two residents apiece. If a rogue gangster, a hungry zero, sprung up on her and tried to kill her, she'd at least know.

Stupidly, she had come here without a weapon.

She was three blocks from Yankowitz's dwelling. Thermal readings showed more residents on Avenue Y, almost enough to give her the feel of being in a real populated neighborhood. A dog, unseen, barked. Sparrows and pigeons landed in the gutter, pecked at nothing, flew away. She tried to just look at the world for the world, Gaggle-free. Shed the digital lens. Watch light with a naked eye. The junkie in Queens—a trusted junkie, granted—with the Yankowitz connection told her that she needed to turn her Gaggle off once she was within a block of the house. It was all for security reasons. If police drones did a fly by, they could pinpoint her Gaggle signal and trace it to Yankowitz's layer. The jig, whatever it was, would be up.

He said to knock on the door five times. It was a primitive system, counter-intuitive. That was the point.

She thought about her friends beyond Rex. This was a game she sometimes played: count the number of "real" friends, those she could trust with more than occasional company at the bar. She counted none. All failed her in some way. All were not Rex. They lacked the loyalty for a mission like this one. If pressed, they would turn on her, rat her out, flee to the warm embrace of law and order. They were all children of the Age of Velez. That was the difference. Rex hadn't made a decision; Rex was Rex. In any epoch, he would be Rex. This was unique. So many people were simply of their time and nothing else. Good when goodness was in vogue, murderous when it was convenient.

Would Yaacov Yankowitz live in the new world? She had no answer.

If this were 10 or 20 years ago, she knew she would be paying Yankow-itz's crew in untraceable cash. Given tree shortages and general distaste for the tactile, Sundra hadn't handled cash since childhood and knew of no business that still took anything other than credits. She couldn't just do a simple credit transfer to the account of Yankowitz or a subordinate, given how easily the police could deduce that she was paying for a highly illegal service. The reliable junkie had told her, she was going to purchase a substantial amount of grocer-ies from a certain supermarket in Queens for the next month, a supermarket that also happened to be a front for one of Yankowitz's cousins. She would pay slightly more for the goods to make up the difference (a percentage calculated at Yankowitz's discretion) for the expense in labor and whatever other miscel-laneous odds and ends required to run a supermarket that was a front for the Hasidic mafia. This apparently had been Yankowitz's payment system for years and no one had figured out the truth. Sundra felt relieved about that.

She was not interested in prison time or martyrdom. She could tell the ghost of Stellar about that: you died for a cause, but I choose to *live* for one.

Despite the arrival of night, several streetlights refused to turn on. She had heard about budget cuts threatening city services, so it made sense that the shortfalls would be felt here, where people who did not matter congregated. She hopped between light and dark, one corner washed in a blaze of blue-white, the other all black. A cat skittered around her feet and disappeared under a fence. She could hear her own footsteps. Thermal readings were low. No people, no life. Now she needed to shut it off because the blinking dot on her Gaggle told her the house was near. Leaves on the ground, not even fall. Leaves everywhere. Brittle tree branches, gaunt tree trunks. She hunted for a moon in the clouds, found nothing.

The house was two stories, squat and brick, with two doorways. It looked like a very small apartment complex. She went for the red door with the numbering that the junkie said would be his. Five knocks. On the fifth, her knuckles slapped the wood (was it wood or hard plastic painted like wood?) loud enough to create an echo, and she instinctively turned around to see if anyone was watching her. No one was. An empty car cruised by (lovers fucking in the backseat, unseen?) and headed for an intersection her Gaggle could not identify because she had shut it off.

She heard a rustle behind the door, a shaking, and it was open. A man in a dark coat and a sable hat peered out from a musty vestibule, a gray beard mushrooming off his jaw. He was short, thin, and looked as if he held too much despairing knowledge for a single lifetime. When his lips moved and his mouth opened, she could see how derelict his teeth were, like shards of glass improbably and painfully jammed into his dull gums.

"Yeaas?" he said, not looking up at her.

"I'm here for, uh, I'm Sundra. I was told they were expecting me. For a *procedure.*"

"A procedure. Good. We are always happy for the company."

"Always glad to provide it."

"Right this way."

She followed him down an unlit hallway. His jacket appeared to be silken, with a subtle pattern of flower pedals. She again wished for a weapon. A darkened hallway was a recipe for an ambush. Other than her Gaggle, she had no valuables on her, and the Gaggle was not an upgraded version that the market craved. They would be ambushing her simply to take a life.

She tightened her fists. Why not? She had no martial arts experience, no punching flesh experience. Time to learn on the job. The old Hasidic man didn't look too tough. If he came with a knife, she would parry as best she could. Kick him in the shins, the nuts. Inflict lasting damage. Her heart beat faster, her breaths grew shorter. Her pulse was making an attempt to escape her body. With a little more effort, it could burst free.

"You are Sundra Glassgarden, yes?"

"Yes."

"Only the smart fools come down here. I am glad. The world needs more smart fools."

"What do you mean?"

"You are living by faith. Not faith in our God, Hashem, but faith that this procedure will work and you will never be caught. That with this procedure, you will be able to proceed anonymously to accomplish whatever unsanctioned task you must complete. There is much faith in this, without all of the required logic. It is logical to come here to pay for smart people to do the procedure. After that, well…that's faith."

"I never really had a religion."

"We withdraw further from God every day. God draws away from us in turn. We are in the most Godless time yet, with more yet to come. Our God, easily enough, is this technology. But we falsely believe it is eternal. I am a man of science too. I know this planet only has so many years. We play the game of the temporal, when eternity is the only smart man's gamble. If the planet will be ruined one way or another—the climate ravages us, the wars get us, the sun swells and consumes us in its death throes—what does any of it matter, except God? There's a logic to that, you see?"

"I see."

They stood outside a doorway. The man barked something that sounded like Hebrew.

"Hebrew, right?" she asked. Why she felt the need to clarify, she didn't know

"Yiddish. The tongue we have fun with."

"Okay."

The door creaked open, showing another hallway. A solitary lightbulb dangled overhead. She could taste the dust, the mold and rot. There was a faint smell of wood shavings. Their feet were loud on the floor. No one was in front of them, even though someone had to have opened the door. Her eyes searched independent of her body, hungry for light and familiar form, another old man in a jacket to tell her everything was okay, this was not her death. Life comes tomorrow. The next day. You will succeed, Sundra. You are a woman of destiny, *we promise, we promise.*

"Excuse these appearances. We move frequently. This never gives us any time to decorate, to show our taste."

"That's okay."

"You are in luck. I hear Rebbe Yankowitz is near. You may just meet him. Very lucky."

"That is."

"Now, just sit here."

A lamp turned on. She was in the equivalent of a kitchen area, with cupboards and a sink and a little black table for dining. Three empty chairs waited for her. She picked one at random, sitting hard on the wood. A film of dust covered the tabletop. It was hot in here, she realized, a heat to close your throat and drown you. She couldn't see any windows. Just blank plaster walls. The man who led her here vanished into another room around the bend, where a bedroom might be in this miniature apartment. She missed her home. She missed the comfort of knowing where every chair and cockroach waited. She missed assuming she hadn't miscalculated somehow, overrated her gumption or other people's trustworthiness or just the general idea that she would turn out okay. She sat and counted in her head. If she made it to 10 and wasn't dead, she had done something right. The light overhead flickered. She could hear conversation in that knotty Yiddish language. For reasons unclear, she imagined she would never hear anything other than English. She knew some Spanish and that was it.

The man who led her in returned with another man, this one also bearded and hatted. He was taller, fuller, the muscle in an otherwise trim operation.

"You understand the terms of agreement?" the bigger one asked. "Where you must shop?"

"Yes."

"Good. Because if we see you are not following through after the procedure, there will be problems. I am just trying to be honest. Not trying to be threatening. We do not want you to be uncomfortable."

"I understand."

"Good!" he smiled. "We have that out of the way. I will be performing the procedure. I am Moishe and this is Dov. Dov is my helper. Dov told you an accuracy. There is a chance Rebbe Yankowitz will come here."

"I know, very exciting."

"Yes! We live in very expectant times. I feel there is a shift underway, a great change coming across all people."

"Oh no, not this," Dov said.

"Yes *this*. I can talk to our guest, can't I?"

"You can do whatever it is that contents you."

"*Good*. All I am saying is, we are in momentous times. I think, in the next few years, we are going to see the world behaving very differently. People are going to see that God is closer than they think."

"Hah this is bullshit. Who is coming, Jesus?"

"No Jesus. Jesus came. He came and died."

"Just do the fine lady's finger and let us be done. I am hungry. Nothing is open late down here. I would complain, but for those censors. I tell the Rebbe, let us stick to operating in free speech zones but no, of course, for safety we come down here, to *Shithead* Bay. Fooey."

"Stop your complaining, already. Why can't I talk to the lady here? We get so few female visitors. My wife, she never wants to see me. Ha. Ha. It is a punishment for her."

Sundra laughed nervously.

"You are wasting time, that is why. Simple, simple. Go on and do it."

"Here, let me prick you first to dull the pain," Dov said. "Then Moishe will go right ahead."

Sundra saw there was now a black satchel of medical equipment on the table and unrecognizable electronics. It occurred to her, as she was about to have her employment microchip removed and therefore commit a felony, that she did not foresee the physical pain. She had been living in such a subjunctive state of late—wishing and wanting and imagining what was to come while icily disregarding the absurdity of her present—that she ignored the reality of a blade, a needle, or any medical appendage sanding away at her skin, even if these characters said they could dull the pain. Because how could she really trust them? Trust anyone? This was a central operating tenet of the Age of Velez: if people could fuck you, they would. We are evolving toward ever more rapid and efficient ways of fucking others and getting fucked. You can be Devora and do all the fucking, figuratively and literally, or you can be someone else, getting fucked. She chose to see herself as neither, but that was not accurate or objective. She was not in a position to fuck anyone.

She closed her eyes. Men, they close their eyes too. They do it tightly, more reluctantly. Their fear of death and pain is more ultimate, more lasting, because their gender lies to them. They believe their cocks make them greater than they are. They buy that trick. You see a man close his eyes and he is a baby again, begging for his mother. What is it about men and their mothers? The same as women and fathers, she supposed, except Gary never held any great allure for her beyond what he was: a good enough dad who thought a lot of wrong things. She shut her eyes and embraced the inchoate electric shapes behind her eyelids. She decided she would be more afraid if she were a male. This gave her some comfort. Were the eyes of these two men closed, they would cower and shake.

Women, then, are comfortable being victims.

No, no. That can't be right.

She felt a burning in her fingertip, a surge of pain that almost made her scream, except it went away by the time the scream was ready. It was forgotten. Unlike most people, the idea of a microchip embedded in her finger disgusted her. Yes, it unburdened you from flashing your work ID at the sleepy-eyed security guard. Yes, there were the discounts to be had at businesses which partnered with Velocity. Yes, turning on and off lights with the wave of an authorized finger was nice.

She just had no interest in being anyone's property.

And now she wouldn't. Yankowitz's men would illegally extract her employment chip and she would no longer be trackable. On her own, and with what she knew Stellar had left behind, she had enough tech to make the Plan at least marginally possible. Rex would be needed for one last trip up the Magnum Tower—after that, all would be set to go.

Thank God getting a gun in this city was now as easy as getting a cheeseburger.

"Almost done, almost done," the Hasid, she forgot his name, muttered. His breath was like a tobacco-stained finger up her nose. She sniffled.

"Okay."

"Very good," the other one said. Her eyes were still closed.

She knew there would be a scar. That could be one giveaway if any authorities ever caught on. A legal microchip removal came with a quick skin graft repair. Unlikely that with an operation like this she would have such a luxury. She'd have be careful, keep the right index finger as out of view as possible for a vital finger on her dominant hand. This wouldn't be easy. Maybe she should say something.

"You are doing very good."

"How else would I do?"

"Erm, just good."

"Well."

"Just hold still. You do not have to keep your eyes so tight."

She opened them. The light was blotchy and bright, her vision temporarily blurred. She preferred the darkness of her own design. Her finger burned in a distant way, like it was a planet skimming the edge of her personal solar system, there but not there. They had numbed it. She did not even know if she had a finger anymore. She was afraid to look. It was easier to keep her eyes closed and ponder the nature of gender, the readily transmogrified human form. Now she couldn't feel her hand. What the fuck. Her whole hand. She stared at it, confirmed its flesh, fought the illusion. She had a hand and she must remember.

"Now, we put in the dummy," he said.

Right. Shit. How could she forget? You can't just take out a microchip from your employer and turn yourself into a zero. Your access to credits, transportation, housing—all of it goes up in smoke. The Plan would be to have a dummy chip replicating the functions of her Velocity chip that could be shut off so cops couldn't track her. Hashem bless this Hasidic mafia and their ingenuity. It would cost her months of shopping for marked up goods in a sham supermarket, but it would be worth it. She felt another needle and dared not look. She found a spot on the blank wall, a discolored patch in the shape of a square. She left her gaze there. She decided it was easier to shut her eyes again. Welcome dark. Enter dark. She tried to burrow inside a memory. A Stellar lecture. Strapping, butt-chinned Stellar, a scrumptious martyr if there ever was one. What would she do to him? Was it wrong to have a sex fantasy about a dead person? Either way, it was here, presenting itself: his shirt unbuttoned to show pecs as smooth as fiberglass, gleaming in the sun. He smiled and took her by the arms. His forearms, tanned and taut, asserted themselves, and she forced them to embrace her, hug her tight so the bulge of his penis could be felt against her inner thigh. His sweat smelled like maple. When he spoke, it was nothing, the afterimage of actual language, irrelevant in the wake of his bright teeth.

"Almost done there, girl. We are almost…"

"It's okay."

"Very good."

She felt them letting go and opened her eyes. The room was unchanged. Why should it have changed? She looked into the soft eyes of the two Hasids, their innocent criminal work done. Her mouth felt dry.

"Where is Yankowitz?" she asked.

"Ah yes. If he is not here now, he is not coming."

"I see."

"Do not despair. It is not personal. He is just busy."

"I know. I wasn't really expecting him."

"Now give me your Gaggle. We are going to program an app to shut down your microchip when you choose. We are disguising it as a weather app. My advice: do not let any friends use your device. Keep it to yourself. Someone tells someone, someone tells the police, and you are on death row. That simple."

"Yes."

"You are brave for coming here. A young woman, alone."

"What, a woman can't travel by herself?"

"No need for an attitude. I am just making an observation. My wife Libby would never come to a place like this."

"Yet here you are."

"Here we all are. How marvelous. Almost done!"

She emerged from her own mind to see that, indeed, a minute or so after the declaration, they were done. The tools were put away. Her finger was scarred and felt fine. There was no Yankowitz to be found. No guns in her face either. She stood up, and the two Hasids looked kindly and very old.

"Well, thank you."

"Let me have your Gaggle. We will add the app."

She handed it over. Others she knew would be more reluctant to part with a Gaggle. That was another irony. Despite the destruction of privacy as a concept, people were still protective of their property, particularly Gaggles. There was a whole class of grand larceny designations for Gaggle theft. She watched the Hasid—she had already forgotten his name—glide his long, bony fingers over the screen. More and more people weren't even touching their Gaggles anymore. Touch was becoming passé. You go full 4-D immersion, live within the device, argue and date and debate with the digital ghosts flying through your face, because there is no such thing as a face as we know it in meatspace. He tapped and swiped with a smile, like an old-world craftsman stooped over his tinker toy. Now, with his work done, her work could begin.

"You are making yourself into quite the threat," he said. "You know how this country handles its threats."

"I know."

"If you need help...well, I would say come to us, but you may end up incurring a debt you cannot pay."

"I'll stay away then."

"Yes. That is one lesson I've learned since boyhood. When in doubt, just stay away."

She left him, glad and afraid.

13

21st Century

"I truly detested the American Dream," Octavio said. "You could blame my communist grandfather maybe, who I never really knew until he was about to die. My mother, as you know, had me young and I lived in a shithole in Manhattan for a few years. East Harlem. El Barrio. We had no money, nothing. I never met my father. My mother didn't want to talk about it. She'd clam up. *You have no father.* So I was the kid with his mom's last name. She was a Velez, I was a Velez. My uncle was in prison. He killed a cop and wasn't sorry."

"I think I learned about all of this in one of the stupid *New Yorker* profiles."

"Yes, many stupid profiles. Deep dives into my life. Journalists in hunt of *telling* anecdotes that would demonstrate who I was, violate the law of small sample size and use some scene out of my life half-remembered by a nitwit I barely knew a half century ago to illuminate some basic element of my character. I dealt with many of those. Especially after my first Senate race. That's the nice thing about a memoir, I suppose. A story being told on my terms."

"Chase loved the American Dream, you know. That's why he supported you. He told me, *this boy believes.* He was truly an idiot."

"I gave off that appearance, to be fair. I was very good at it."

"Maybe the best."

"I hated anything that smelled of communism, socialism, or collectivism because of my grandfather, who from what I could tell was an abysmal failure as a poet and a person. He was a pathetic man. He thought in soundbites alone, no nuance, just canned 30's-era retrograde nonsense. My mother didn't seem to care for him too much. We didn't have much and I was left to my own devices. I realized at a pretty young age the American Dream was an effective lie, one of the best told in history. I knew the truth, the implicit truth: we are a nation built on the backs of slave labor and genocide. A slave nation. Our heritage is bondage. Everything else, our ethos and values and ideals, flows from this single truth or trickles in its shadows. Enslaved the blacks, killed the

Indians. All else is tangential at best. So I promised myself, in whatever I did, I would eventually be honest."

"*Eventually.* That's endearing. If you told Chase that, you never would have gotten his money. He believed in the country that was so good to him."

"If I ever was in a position of power, I told myself, I would try to be honest to the vision of the United States that transcended the lie of the dream, that got closer to the truth. We have prospered because of slavery, both literal and de facto slavery. Obviously, I could never say this when I was president. I could never win saying this. I could never say that the constricting of the futures of so many was the only way a few of us, the very best, could have a future. My great lament, Devora, is that I never went nearly far enough. I could have remained for a third term. I had a loyal military. I could have raised their pay, promised them perks unimaginable to them, the chance to come as close to godhood as they ever wanted. They'd call it a dictatorship, sure, and maybe that's what it would have been. Octavio Velez and the Army refusing to leave, invalidating the election, declaring himself president for life. Did I love the job that much? No. I'm happy enough. I have everything I could have ever needed. I left office with a 64 percent approval rating. No one really understood what I did, what I wanted to do. You did. Chase might have—"

"Don't be generous. Chase certainly did not."

"My dream, to put it bluntly enough, was to end democracy. Not for me—I wanted the legitimacy it conferred upon me for eight years—but for my successor. It's such a dishonest system. It's a trap, really. The people are the rats, democracy is the cheese and the trap, wrapped into one. You think it's good for you. The trap comes down and kills you, but you don't blame democracy. We're not a strong country anymore. The economy grew in the last six years I was president but the numbers were hollow, and they only took on real strength when we saw the beginnings of the premium system, honest enough excepting the name, which my advisers insisted was necessary to sell to the public. They weren't wrong. But why should I have to sell it to the public? I will write *that* in my memoir. I, a smart person, understood it was best, and so did a cadre of very smart people who had studied the issue for years, men and women with doctorates, law degrees, medical degrees, you name it. Why should the mob know more than them? It's illogical, really…"

"Oh, don't get so worked up."

"But I am, damn it. I want to," he was sweating, his face taking on the color of a pale eggplant. "I'm here and I will."

"You certainly will."

"Why go through the kabuki theater of it all? We're getting closer, at least. I'm happy to see you give your premiums no illusions."

"None at all."

"That's how it should be. They're entitled to know exactly what they are and how they should be treated. I just think about all the progress this country could have made if we had cast aside the dreams and lies, put our feet on the soil and said *this is what this is, and nothing else.* Imagine."

"I'm imagining." Devora yawned.

"This is serious."

"Autocracy, democracy, Devoracracy. What difference does it make?"

"It makes all the difference, Devora."

"Ulivia," Devora waved her hand. "More truffles."

"That's all you people think about, truffles."

"What people? Rich people? What would you rather me consider? Alternative modes of being? I love you, Octavio, I really do. You're a national treasure. But this erection you have for the platonic ideal of government needs to go away. Either you will it away or you need to fuck something. Let it out. Lead a military coup. Stop lamenting."

"I just could've done so much more, if I had stopped playing but their rules, if I had drawn up my own…the great change that—"

"Jesus Christ. The truffles, Ulivia! Please, now."

14

1979

Naked, naked, naked.

What was it with this century? He was often hungry and often angry and often afraid. Angry at the situation, of course. Hungry because all he had been taught about monetary transactions was useless here. Afraid for reasons pertaining to the aforementioned unresolvable issues.

Naked was how he thought of himself and everyone else. They had nothing. No tech in their hands, on their wrists, in their flesh. There was no digital space. No internet. No virtual reality. No way to actually communicate with people. He looked at his arms, pale and exposed in the summer heat. He had nothing. The reality of the world was just this filthy block he was wandering down, and not all he could access if he could just get the fucking Gaggle going. What he'd do for one hour on Bleater.

Never had he been alone with his thoughts like this. There was that time dad made the ill-fated decision to take the family camping and they went wireless for two volatile days. The whole family was ravenous when they got back home to Manhattan. Mom, who he was becoming legitimately afraid of, was giggling to herself while dad tried to stay deep in streams with clients from work. This was ultimately home at its best. No one talking, everyone gaggling, the combatants withdrawn and therefore at peace. It wasn't until the accident, and the apparent end of everything that he knew, that he began to think about how inadequate he was now, and always had been. He suddenly had endless hours to contemplate what he didn't like about himself, as opposed to his old life, when the time simply didn't exist. He shook repeatedly—this was new, the discovery of regret, catching his puffer fish reflection in window after window. He never, in the old life, gazed in a window. Why? The Gaggle was for gazing. Anytime spent outside its boundaries was wasted, inefficient, and stupid.

Now, all time was stupid. He felt naked on 125th Street. He had to look at the wild, retrograde city, inhale the foul smells, feel the non-air-conditioned breeze. How many times since he first landed in Chicago and watched every-thing go to shit did he instinctively glance down at his hand, expecting the shimmer of his screen? How many times had he expected the ping of a message sent directly to his brain via a telepath app? Already he knew in this new old world, what was practically medieval, that he was a "fatso," a "gringo," and "Pillsbury doughboy." Only fatso resonated with him at all, and this wounded. He could've gaggled the other terms but of course he couldn't.

Every thought seemed to begin and end that way. I'll just gag—oh, wait.

And then, like the closing of one window and the opening of another, there was Lolita.

It was night three staying with her, after she had run into him shuffling in a daze. She was the first person, other than a mentally deficient, govern-ment-funded policeman, to spend more than 10 minutes talking to him. He answered the questions and the police didn't believe his answers. They asked for a birthdate (they thought his answer was a joke), a social security number (he'd forgotten), and where his parents were (dad was dead, maybe, mom was at her place near Coney Island, maybe), and even fed him. When he said New York, the mentally deficient Chicago policeman tried and failed (not surpris-ing, obviously) to get in contact with anyone who knew a Devlin Dimon. They said they had no choice but to put him in "foster care" in Chicago. He didn't know what this meant, but it sounded foreboding enough, so he did what he knew worked with mom at least: sobbed. "Take me to New York, take me to New York." The mentally deficient police said if they did not find a relative in New York, he would go to foster care in New York, and that was the law, he had to follow it. Devlin knew of his father often bragging of how he could write whatever law he wanted. He wished for that power. He wished for it almost as much as he wished, every few minutes or so, for the blank screen of his Gaggle to show life.

What to make of this world. The food was woefully underlabeled. He never really paid attention to nutrition or calorie counts, but the information on the bars and bags of chips that Lolita supplied was lacking. There were pens and pencils, which he had never used, only heard of. The tendons in his right hand burned after single usage. The only screens were on televisions. These televi-sions were not internet-capable. They simply showed "channels" or streams which you passively watched until you rose up from your seat to press a button or knob to go on elsewhere. He had cried so much from Chicago on the way to New York that he was beyond crying now, even though these limitations on how he could enjoy himself made him want to shake and sob. He had to get back. Had to. Losing access to your Gaggle was like being told you could never go to the bathroom again.

"What are you doing?" Lolita asked, after she had walked in to find him with his face pressed into a couch cushion. "You fucking spaz."

He didn't answer. He couldn't say what he was up to—he was hoping time taken away from looking at his blank Gaggle screen, coupled with a garbled prayer he had just invented, could bring it back to life. He had done this with failed electronics before. Prayer. He was a man by Jewish law so he was man enough to ask God for what he wanted.

"Get your face out of the couch already."

He said no, but she didn't hear it.

"I'm counting to five."

He wrenched himself from the couch. "You aren't my mom."

"Nope I'm not, space boy. But you ain't paying rent, so tough shit."

Space boy. She liked that one. He might as well be an extraterrestrial. He had as much in common with this world as a Martian would. The rituals, the slang, the low-tech…it's funny, you know, how in the time travel movies the guy going back to the past gets to amaze the past people with the tech from his present and even throw in a few predictions that seem bizarre, but are true. How fun it all looked. He should be telling them about September 11th and thoughtsyncs, and here he was on a couch that smelled like old cat. Old fleshy cat, not synthetics. He would curse more, but he felt tired and hungry again. Always hungry. This world never had enough food.

Invading aliens were supposed to be conquerors, feared for their knowledge and command of unimaginable gadgetry. He was the opposite. He sighed loud enough for her to hear. It was not that he missed his mommy or daddy—it was more that he missed being *somebody*. There are only so many days you can be the stranger, the boy out of place, the weird-looking kid at school. In his school, Holly Prep, he was more than somebody: the son of the man who paid for a new fitness center, a bio lab, and an android operational enough to teach introduction to Spanish. Respect was paid to him, to the Dimon brand. He couldn't even do a search on other relatives here because there weren't even basic, operational computers! Nothing. He had asked Lolita several times, nicely at first, about whether she had a tablet, a smartphone, or even an old desktop he could use. She just laughed at him. No one had anything. "Look kid, if you want to search, you gotta keep walking the streets or I can tell the police."

"No more police," he said. "Not that."

She had never heard of the internet. No one had. He struggled to understand how anyone could meaningfully connect with anyone in this place. You talked on a telephone. That was technology. Disgusting. He stood up and sat down. He felt like erasing himself. Not dying, just leaving his body and becoming a ghost for a few days. He could glide unseen around the place, slip between walls, enjoy the breeze, and figure out what the fuck this place was all about.

Lolita looked very sad to him. It wasn't something he was used to seeing. His mom, the sad one, was often more bored than sad. His dad was never sad.

Lolita was pretty, though. Her belly, protruding out from her sky blue t-shirt, didn't change that. Sad but pretty.

"My brother JoJo is coming later. I'll have to explain to him how I let a space boy stay for free, when I barely have enough to feed me."

"I'm gonna go."

"No you're gonna stay until we can figure this out. A white boy like you keeps walking around here like you were, you're gonna end up in the East River."

"Does it flood a lot?" he found himself asking. He remembered the huge downtown flood last year. It overran the barriers. He cried all night.

"Uh, no?"

"That's good. A good thing. Good news."

She turned and walked over to a small table near the front door crowded with strange papers with words. He had felt them before and they left a funny inky residue on his fingers. It looked like someone had taken a news feed and, for some reason, put it onto paper. He mused about what a waste of time that was and considered it was something he might have done in second grade, a misguided art project that taught no one anything. He would get a gold star.

"So tell me, in the future, how many Mars colonies do we got? Are we fucking Martians? Are there projects on Mars? Do they let Latins on Mars?"

"Probes landed and took pictures but no one has ever been there."

"Huh? I don't believe it, space boy. You never went there?"

"My dad did orbits of Earth with the tourist shuttle and I think we had an investment in the first moon colony, he said, but no one went to Mars. Not me. No one."

"What a sad future."

"Not really."

"If we ain't getting to Mars in the 21st century, then what's the point, space boy? What's the point of any of this?"

"I dunno."

"Tell me who's gonna win the World Series this year."

"I dunno. I can't look it up. My Gaggle's dead."

"Super Bowl."

"My Gaggle's dead."

"Stanley Cup."

"My Gaggle's dead."

"NBA. Knicks?"

"My Gaggle's dead!"

The shout took them both by surprise. He hadn't raised his voice beyond what could be described as a furious whisper since he accidentally ended up in Chicago, on the exploding baseball field. He hadn't really allowed his body to admit what his Gaggle-deprived brain slowly understood. He wasn't going home. He was here, and would always be. The tears reluctantly crept out, one and two and three, smearing his vision of her and then the floorboards as he mashed his hands into his cheeks, trying to hide it all. The tears poured out. He was shaking, wailing, grinding his hands so hard against his skull he believed he could destroy it and take himself away from here. Become the ghost. Fly away. He felt her arm around him and the tears fell harder. If he could not crush himself, he would pour it all out until he was a sack of dead skin on the couch cushion, a pool around his empty sneakers. He moaned. The tears wouldn't stop. He didn't like to cry. His mom said he wasn't crier, never cried as a baby. He never cried in school. He would never cry in front of his dad. Why cry? For a flood, for a terrorist attack, but not for life, not for a sunny day in July when he should be at home, gaming with friends.

He had never spent this much time in the presence of premiums before. Never ever.

"It's okay, kid. It's okay. I won't ask you anymore. It's okay..."

Her arm wrapped around him completely.

"I wish it worked," he managed to say.

"What worked?"

"The Gaggle!"

"We'll get it to the hardware store, I'm sure—"

"They'll have a charger?"

"Yeah, I bet they will. I know a guy, he can do it."

"He has a charger?"

"He's handy. He could make one."

"It won't work."

"It could."

"No," he wiped his eyes. "Forget it. Forget it..."

Several minutes, or even an hour, dripped by. He wasn't sure. She had brought him paper towels and he blew his nose raw. Afternoon had bled into twilight, and he stood up to walk to her bathroom, which was smaller than the closet in his bedroom. He wobbled in the dark, failing to find the light switch buried in the scuffed yellow tiles. The pee rushed out. It smelled, which meant he needed to drink more water, which reminded him that he in fact was quite thirsty. In the darkness, he tried to make out his reflection in the foggy mirror over the sink. He could see dried mucus under his nostrils, just above his lips, and a red terror in his eyes. He gripped the sides of the sink.

Time skipped, then dilated, in his tears. In one moment, he was bent over, trying to hide his crying, and in the next he was back on the couch, a wad of paper towels in hand. The front door of the two-room apartment was rattling and in stepped a man. Lolita, reading a glossy paper publication, stood up and walked over to the door.

The man looked to Devlin like he had stepped out of an anime. Black hair cascaded past his shoulders and a beard, with a no-nonsense thickness, swallowed his face. He was tall, looming over them both, and his brown arms were carved with muscle, hairs sprouting from his wrists to the crooks of his elbows. He was smiling in a way Devlin could not recognize. His teeth didn't look like they were brushed. When he stepped forward, the sounds of his calf-length boots hitting the hardwood floor were like muffled gunshots. A black bulge at his hip showed he knew the sound well.

"There you are. A rare night in for Lolita Velez. I never thought I'd see the day."

"I'm turning over new leaves every time you go outside. I've lost count of my leaves."

His loping strides terrified Devlin. "Let's meet the new member of the family. Temporary member or permanent? Let's find out."

He extended a large hand. It hovered like a hostile satellite over Devlin's forehead and fell, landing where his pudgy, damp hand could grip it. The handshake was not tight.

"He was crying," the man said to Lolita.

"Yeah. He's homesick."

"And where's home?"

"Manhattan," Devlin coughed out.

"Well, lucky for you, though it might not look that way, El Barrio is as much Manhattan as the Upper East Side so we can get you home before the ten o'clock news comes on and bores us."

"I told you JoJo, he says he's not from here. He's the space boy. The future boy."

"Future, huh?" The man, apparently named JoJo, turned his gaze back to Devlin. "Where from?"

"I'm, uh, from 20—"

"I gotcha, 21st century. That's enough for me."

Lolita was rummaging in the cupboard. She pulled out a silver can of tuna fish and used a hand device—a non-electric opener, apparently—to take the lid off.

"How's the land, Jo?"

"Well, it was an easy day. I met with a boss down south. The Candies say they're having trouble with an ex-cop in Coney Island. *Your* ex-cop."

"He's not my anything. I don't see him."

"Then get rid of that baby."

"I don't want to talk about this right now. Especially in front of the kid."

"But I do. I busted my ass all day, yo-yoing to the end of Brooklyn, and I want to talk. Express myself. All I ask is an audience. Willing or not."

"Not willing, Jo."

"Okay, *Lo*. But I want to say something and I'll say it. You keep making a tuna sandwich."

"No bread anyway."

"Man oh man, they talk about the Depression being so bad, you know, but at least there were bread lines. Imagine that in El fucking Barrio. Free bread! Put a sign for free bread in the Lincoln Houses and watch what would happen. Bring back those days with Uncle Sam's free bread. Then your sandwich would be taken care of."

"What, you back to getting high?"

"No. I get a high just being here."

"Telling people what to do. You used to be better about that."

"It's a dangerous planet out there, *hermana*. I just need to start looking out more, as do you. You need to stop trying to track down a Candies target. You gotta stop looking now."

"I'll do what I want."

"You go out every day, yo-yoing up and down the city looking for your lost love—"

"Shut the fuck up. You don't know anything."

"You go out, tracking this thug, who's got the stench of white imperialist cocksucker all over him. You think Mister White Bread, with his old NYPD badge, is gonna take you out of here to a white picket fence in Levittown or some shit? Is that what this is? He's gonna be a good papi?"

"Really JoJo. Shut the fuck up."

"No cause this needs to be said. In front of the space boy or not. He's old enough to know reality. You gotta cut this shit out, Lolita. Right now. I can't have you out there looking for him. I'm getting a lot of shit about my little sister, who let this gringo thug Archie—"

Lolita, the can opener in hand and trembling, stepped toward her brother.

"I swear to God, to Christ, you keeping talking like this and it's gonna end badly."

"This is shit I'm talking about. We need cooler heads. The revolution, when it's all said and done, is gonna need logic after rage and passion. Do you get it?"

"You're delusional, JoJo."

"No, *you* are. You're gonna get killed. You and your baby. Archie London is skulking around in the Candies' nest, hoping, like a true dirty cracker, to single-handedly stop them. He has no plan. He's like a roach. I keep this shit quiet, you know—if they knew my sister was involved with—if *they* knew..."

"Chez Velez would be ruined, I know."

"Lo, you're not seeing—

"I see plenty. I see you don't want a white baby popping out of me. You want me to go end it still?"

"There was time. You may as well have it now and give it up."

"What I do with my child is my business."

"If the baby's here, it becomes my business. Don't you see this is all for your own good? You can't be going Archie London-hunting. That ship's sailed. You'll be killed."

"Let me worry about me for once. You always need to play daddy. You're not my dad. We don't have one anymore. You don't get to take his place. It doesn't work that way."

"I'm looking out for you."

"You're looking out for *you*. JoJo Velez wasn't always that way."

"Let me try again. It's been a wacko kind of day. There were a lot of moving parts. Here's the deal: it's very clear Archie is the Candies' public enemy number one. He has an obsession with them, and now they do him in. They want him dead. That's it. I dunno why he's messing with them—they're a powerful gang, but there's others, and I don't know what they did to him. Sooner or later, he'll be dead. That's how it works. You can survive for a while on their hit list. Maybe they let him dangle. But the more you go out there, looking or not looking for him, pretending to not look but looking anyway, the more likely you're gonna be dead too. That's all there is to it. And if you're dead, your baby is dead. I'm not gonna lie. I hate the idea of him being inside of you, him doing this. I know you said you wanted it—"

"Yes, I did."

"Well people mindfuck people. That's how white power works. The white establishment's a mindfuck and we're in a war against that. We're winning the war. The Candies are helping on that front, so that's why I go with them, but you know I'm not one of them at heart. I'm *me*. I fight for the future, not shitty turf on Mermaid Avenue."

"Fight for the future, spit on the present."

"It's not like that."

"If you love the future so much, talk to space boy. I'm going out."

"You stay in and eat dinner. I'm cooking."

"I am going outside. If you try to stop me—"

"What? Tell me."

Lolita, who was a foot shorter than her brother, stalked forward, coming within inches of his chest. She looked straight up at him.

"I'll get you out of my way." She said this barely above a whisper.

JoJo, his smile long washed away, did something which amazed Devlin: he moved. A man so much bigger and tougher-looking gave way for this small woman. His back, so straight, seemed to slump, and his eyes fell toward his boots. She walked past him and shut the door.

"She'll be alright," he said to Devlin. "She'll come to her senses."

Devlin sat back down on the couch. He didn't know what else to do. He was very hungry.

"You must be lonely, huh? I know what it's like when you're a kid and you can't find your parents. It's real rough."

Devlin mumbled "Yeah."

"I almost believe you, you know? Actually, fuck it—I do believe you. You don't look like you're from around here at all. At the minimum, you gotta be European."

"I'm from here. Manhattan. Just not during this time. I came here by accident."

"So tell me about that."

"Lolita just makes fun of my story so you will too. Forget it."

"No no no," he took his giant strides over to him and plopped down on the couch, shaking it. "I'm all ears. Go ahead. I need a good story. Today was garbage. Real garbage. Lo's gotta get that better. Garbage days mean garbage nights."

"So you're Lolita's brother."

"That's right."

"She's...she's tough, but I think nice. I like her more than all the other premiums around here."

"That's a nice compliment."

"What do you mean?"

"I mean, calling the Puerto Ricans premiums. It's back-handed, coming from a little white boy, and I could punch you in the face, but I'll let it slide. I'm no longer in a fighting mood. In a fucking or sleeping mood."

"How is it back-handed? I mean, that's what you are, right? This is definitely not an Ent neighborhood. That's a fact."

"Do you drop acid? That could be what it is."

"I don't know what that is."

"El. Ess. Dee."

"I don't know."

"Okay, well, anyway. Ents and premiums. Nice slang. I can't keep up with all the racist prep school lingo."

"It's not...it is what it is, I mean, it's like calling the sky blue."

"Uhuh. Like honkey is just another word for white."

"I don't know that word."

"Boy, they really shelter you on Park Avenue, huh?"

"I don't live there. My dad's building is in SoFiDieBeca."

"What is that, an art installation?"

"A neighborhood. It's my home."

"What is this, a tree house on Park Avenue?"

"It's downtown near Tribeca."

"You're full of surprises, aren't you? Lolita found a winner."

Devlin sunk deeper into the couch.

"Look, I'm not trying to be mean. You're just an odd duck. Nothing wrong with odd ducks. You hungry? I'm gonna make chicken and rice. Lolita likes that."

"Sterilized?" he asked, echoing his mom's warnings post-chicken flu out-break.

"No, what—wait, yeah. Totally. I sterilized Mr. Chicken myself."

"Okay."

JoJo turned around to cook. Devlin rarely watched anyone cook because the servants prepared food in a back room, nowhere near his room or even the kitchen. He imagined cooking as an intricate, unknowable process, fit for only the best premiums in the city, like JoJo. JoJo almost carried himself like an Ent. That was interesting, considering the squalor in which he, Lolita, and everyone in this place, a part of Harlem, lived. He seemed powerful and confident that his power could not go away. Devlin tried to focus on JoJo and not his silent Gaggle, the lack of neuro-notifications from his social networks making him feel so naked and alone. Only one person at a time spoke to him. What a multitude of voices there once were. How wanted he felt. His brain was so lit up, so alive. Now he was a darkened Christmas tree. That's the image that worked. All the lights still hanging, waiting, but the power cut.

All he could do was stare. His eyes ached.

"You like lemon on your chicken?"

"I guess. Okay."

Then JoJo did something that made Devlin gasp. He produced a cigarette, non-electric, and began to smoke indoors. This was flat out illegal. Any basic smoke detector would alert the police and he'd get put in jail for the night or worse. JoJo inhaled deeply and blew out a thick cloud of law-breaking smoke.

"What are you doing?"

"What?"

"You're smoking. How could you?"

"What're you, one of these health nuts? You sure don't look it, with all your jelly rolls."

"You're gonna get arrested!"

"It's not a joint. Relax. Just a cigarette."

"It's illegal."

"Not in this country."

JoJo puffed on it again. He was giggling.

"Lolita does always pick winners. She has the knack."

JoJo was smoking the cigarette within cancerous range of Devlin now. Devlin was sweating madly, his heart jackhammering in his chest. At least the fear overtook the loss he felt for his non-functioning Gaggle. There was nothing like impending death to sharpen someone's focus. Where were the police in this crap world? Were they invented in the 21st century? Smoking was such an obvious, detectable crime. He shuddered to think of what other crimes were committed here, crimes going unpunished. He imagined each sin as a rat scuttling below the floorboards, threatening to burst into the light and gnaw at his toes. If there were not Gaggles, this meant police couldn't track criminals, which meant terrorists could be doing whatever they wanted. This whole city could be rife with terrorists. How could JoJo be so relaxed? Just smoke? He might as well chug lighter fluid. Killing himself on the inside as terrorists kill from the outside. JoJo was in Devlin's face, with the cigarette, and he wanted to scream.

"You know, when I was about your age, I learned how to smoke."

Devlin was holding his breath. If he breathed in even a whiff, he'd be a goner. He could only imagine what his respiratory reader on his Gaggle would say, if his Gaggle worked, if he had a charger, if he was back home, with mom and dad and his apps.

"All you gotta do is put it between your lips and breathe in. It's easy and you look cool doing it."

"No..."

Oh no, he spoke next to the cloud, which meant he breathed in, which meant the cancer. Oh no oh no. Where were the police?

"It feels so good. There's nothing like a nice cigarette on a cold day. Just lighting up at the crack of dawn, feeling that rush. The column of smoke."

"No..."

"I tell people, it beats coke. A real good expensive cigarette is better than coke. It's personal. Coke's impersonal. The best stuff doesn't get you high because you're high already."

The cloud was all around him. He was surrounded. He would die here too, by cancer or untraceable terrorists. It was only a matter of time.

"You need to smile more, kid," he finally said, walking away.

15

21st Century

"Finally, the damn whites. I love a white truffle. They're the best things the Italians have given us," Devora said.

"I—"

"Don't say fascism, Octavio. That's too easy."

"I'm not a fascist. You misunderstand me. I just want honesty in government. I want this democracy business to better reflect reality. I'm tired of playacting. 30 years of playacting—that's what my political career amounts to. I could've done it. If I had been stronger, more decisive…truly unafraid. I dropped the gun. That's what mattered. I held it, and when I held it, I had history and the future twinned in my palm. Fused together where they needed to be. And I dropped it. Do you think I *care* that I happened to be a Hispanic president? Do you think I go to bed at night celebrating being a silly token for yet another race, even an ascendant one?"

"I never thought you cared."

"You know what democracy is? Marketing, PR. It's the ghost of something that never existed."

"Brilliant."

"A ghost who never had a body. A ghost born a ghost."

"Such a metaphor."

"You're starting to grate on me, Devora."

"I keep few friends for a reason. The more you have, the sicker you are."

"Friends are useful. But I'm not here to talk about that."

"You're here because you need me to help you lie about what to put in your book. Unspool another thread of reality, dear Octavio."

"Tell me about this time travel tech Chase was mixed up in."

"Now you want to know."

"Tell me that, at least."

"Tell you what? Are you pretending your government R & D wasn't involved in their own experiments years before my dear darling Chase killed himself trying to give our son a bar mitzvah present to never forget?"

"I just wanted to compare notes."

"Put it in the memoir, *The Age of Velez.* 'Time travel fails, every time.'"

"We know it's possible."

"Did you go back in time? Did you have sex with any of Thomas Jefferson's slaves?"

"Your language never ceases to amuse me."

"I want to know how far the American government got. My Chase died in 1979, you know."

"1979, impressive. That is far back."

"You've gone further."

"There was an internal rule about not tampering with anything pre-Revolution."

"If there's been tampering, that means the present has changed."

"Imperceptibly, maybe. I'm told this is an inexact science. Do you think the coming age of time travel will ruin us or free us? I should posit that in my memoir. Blow the lid off *that* secret. Maybe we could reverse climate change."

"I doubt that. Besides, we're adapting. The seawall around SoFiDieBeca is holding. Real estate prices are good. My investments are good. Chase's disappearance has not impacted Velocity's valuation, believe it or not. The markets didn't view him as essential."

"I do fear that one day someone is going to do something bad with this technology. Very bad. You've taken the proper precautions, Devora? The idea of featuring this at a children's party was very reckless."

"My obligation as a mother is to entertain my child. Not worry about your country or you."

"That's a bit selfish. We're all Americans."

"I'm proudly singing a song of myself. I'm not a neurotic. I'm not you. I understand Ents have their own country, that America is papier-mâché, a front for the right people to live out their destiny and proceed through their mortal years unimpeded by the nonsense of a force-fed, illogical cult of equality. I'm the honesty you wish you had. If I were you, Octavio, I would find my 10 strongest men with the 10 biggest guns and get to work. I wouldn't sulk in the mansion of one of my old donors. Figure out what you want, already. History will laugh at you otherwise."

Octavio was suddenly silent. He pursed his lips and rested his fist under his chin, like he was being interviewed on TV again.

"Do you think anyone wants to kill me?"

"You?" Devora smiled, brighter than she had all day. "*Of course.*"

16

1979

In 1963, the Dodgers came home. You could forgive a boy for buying a bleacher seat in Yankee Stadium to see them one more time in person, to rekindle the memories of all that was taken from you. Enough has been said and written about the Dodgers' bitter divorce from Brooklyn, their flight to Los Angeles, and what a harbinger this was for a city sniffing decline, and now careening into the gutter.

In 1963, the wound was fresh. Archie had only been on the Force two years and still hoped time could reverse itself to bring the Dodgers home. Charlie Ebbets' cigar box of a ballpark was a disgusting range of cheap housing now, but if you stood on the corner of Bedford and squeezed your eyes tight enough, you could still hear one of those lolling, half-empty games in the navel of the summer against someone like Phillies, nothing much to think about, just the boys in blue pushing toward another pennant. Archie was sure he'd be on the field soon enough. He was convinced, in the fall of 1955, he was the best hitter in Nassau County, even if he wasn't. No evidence pointed to this fact other than the evidence of hope, but this was often enough. He would grow, get better, get scouted, and be up in the bigs by 1961 or 1962, after a little seasoning in the minors. He wouldn't be a bonus baby. He wasn't *that* good, okay. He would put in his time, pay his dues, ride tin can buses in hard-to-pronounce townships and maybe get his cherry popped in one of those roadside motels, a pretty dark-haired baseball-mad dame to teach him how to be a man. The future was the easiest part of his life.

In 1963, he wanted the Dodgers to lose. He wasn't a baseball player. He was a New York City police officer, carrying a Smith & Wesson .38 special and earning $144 a week. He didn't feel any less betrayed than he did in 1957, the year he turned 18 and the Dodgers scurried west. He wasn't any less furious. That was step one to making his future less easy. That was also step one in a longer, unending lesson: your vision will not come to pass. How you perceive yourself in the future tense is inevitably a deception.

He was a Yankee fan that fall. He had grown up, like any Dodgers fan, reviling the Yankee teams that consistently crushed his Dodgers' hopes until 1955, Podres and his complete game shutout, party at the Hotel Bossert. But the betrayal had been too much. The O'Malley/Moses cabal which sent his team away meant he would never, in a thousand years, be a Los Angeles Dodgers fan. He still hated Los Angeles, California, a bleached expanse of filth and idiocy. New York was worth redemption. Were it up to him, were he the one holding the keys to the coming apocalypse, Los Angeles would be first to go. He could smile imagining Chavez Ravine in flames.

Yet there *he* was, a Jewish boy like himself, a Jewish boy made good. A bonus baby. A local hero. Prodigal son come home. He *believed* the Yankees were going to blow out Koufax in the first game. He made a 50 dollar bet with one of the dumbest lugs in the station house, Jimmy Leary, that the Yankees would not only win the Series but win game one. A two-part bet he couldn't lose. Another local boy who didn't pitch for a team that deserted New York was on the mound, Whitey Ford, and it was true that Slick was never one of his favorites, a little pretty boy blondie from Astoria who, he assumed, took it straight in the ass from Mantle and insisted he wasn't a homosexual, just a kid blowing off steam. Koufax threw a lot harder than Ford. He was simian, really, in his approach: fastball, curve, all raw strength, no deception. He didn't use his Jewish brain much. He didn't tell Woody Allen jokes. He just went in there, dark-haired and grave, and threw his two fucking pitches and no one could meet the challenge. Archie was sure Koufax, back in New York, would wilt under the pressure of pitching in Yankee Stadium. How many Dodgers teams of his youth had similarly dissolved in the heat of 67,000 hostile bodies? That was the Yankee secret sauce: in Ebbets, even as a visitor, you felt at home, because it was the rumpled uncle of ballparks compared to Yankee Stadium, a violent older brother who played college football and earned the unconditional love of your parents. It was Archie's shift that afternoon and they had him out on Pitkin Avenue stuck in a patrol car. He made the most of it, hiding a transistor radio and pulling it out in time for the first inning. His partner, a kid named Charlie Cicotte, didn't give a shit. Archie's heart fluttered. It was time, for once, to be on the right side of history, pulling for the Yankees at home against a franchise that deserved to rot in hell. What was West Coast transplant Sandy Koufax against these Yankees, each one mythological long before they had a chance to retire and end up on a plaque? He turned the volume up, Harwell and Garagiola crackling through, ready to sing to him in the eventuality of a Yankee first inning rally.

Archie slapped his knee. Told Cicotte, who usually spent his shifts at an OTB, to get the fuck out of the car. What do you mean, he asked. How could Archie explain? Koufax just struck out the side. Kubek, strikeout. Richardson, strikeout. Tresh, strikeout. A sickening omen made worse when the Dodgers got four in the second. Mantle, Maris, Howard, the real Yankee meat, came up in the bottom of the second. Archie felt the nightmare unspooling around him, the slow seep of blood. Cicotte wanted back in. Archie said stay the fuck out, Imma lockin the door. Mantle struck out. Harwell sounded elated. Maris, the second M of the M&M boys, struck out. All up to Howard, the Yankees' first black, who enraged Italian-Americans everywhere when he forced Berra to left field. Howard popped out and the inning was over. *He ties a World Series record, how about that. Five punchouts in a row for young Sandy Koufax...*and he let Cicotte back in, promising he'd beat his brains into the Brownsville gutter before the day was out. He knew then it was over. The Series. The Dodgers would have their victory *again* (don't forget the '59 thrashing of the White Sox) as a team representing a city that did not deserve a baseball team, or anything: did not deserve roadways, office buildings, schools, and peace. He shook the steering wheel. Cicotte said something about checking in at a storefront off Pitkin that wasn't Jewish anymore and Archie didn't react, just sat and seethed as Koufax went the distance. The whole series was like that. Drysdale beat Bouton 1-0 in game three. Peppy, flashy wop he was, almost tied it up with a homer, but didn't. Game four, the clincher, was appropriately in Los Angeles, and Archie had lost his 50 bucks and the feeling in his knuckles after pounding the steering wheel too many times. Koufax wrapped it up. Who else? Series MVP. Archie would never get his team back. He could see the alternate universe of Brooklyn World Series victories so clearly, almost touch the reality that never was, but then it would whiz past him like a high Koufax fastball. Looks like a strike, ends up a ball, you swing anyway.

He was walking the Coney Island boardwalk, thinking on this. It was going on nightfall and the beach was not as crowded as it once was, back when the regular guy and gal wasn't scared shitless to be walking in sandals to the train after dark. He smelled salt and wood and even, faintly, a burnt corn dog. In total night, he would be Vengeance again. Vengeance alone. Six weeks since he went to Truncheon's apartment. Seven since Lolita, seven since she delivered the news. He said he would be back and he didn't break promises. He just needed time.

The weather would not change. The weather was changing. Both made sense. He tugged at his coat, surveyed the wreckage of humanity. He was coming up on the Brighton Beach baths. Soon, they would approach. He could admit he was asking for death on the eve of his 40th birthday. They would come in numbers if he kept tempting them. It was important to know risk, and he was never naive enough to not believe that on one night, another moment in the flotsam, the Candies could hurt him. This was what a dying animal did: it bit, it lashed, it gnashed. It would devour its tongue if it didn't get him. The Candies' death could be his own.

Ras Locka. Come to me tonight. I am preparing. I am prepared. I have a gravesite for you.

"Do you really think an apocalypse is coming?" Truncheon, yawning, asked during their most recent conversation all those weeks ago.

Truncheon, defying the embargo, had procured Cuban cigars, and was smoking one in his living room.

"No."

"1980 will beget 1981 will beget 1982 and so on. In 2079 they will ask if the apocalypse is coming in 2080, and I, long dead, will have an answer."

"I said I don't think that."

"The arrogance," Truncheon puffed, and rummaged for crust within his thick right nostril, "of the living is assuming they are alive during a pivot point in history, a time of *great change*, a divergence, if you will. The weather is changing, they say. This cannot continue. *This.* They look at their palms and the sky and write odes to themselves."

"That is what you do."

"My books are the opposite of odes. They are markers of weakness. They are the excess thoughts, the rancid runoff, that I must purge myself of."

"To earn yourself money and awards. Critical appraisal."

"One day I do think mankind will be cured of this sickness, this compulsion, to *create*. To write. Violence, and then peace, will be the final language."

Archie thought about this. He did not offer an immediate reply. The gears of language, in fact, seemed to be stuck.

"These cigars are wonderful," Truncheon said. "Medium strength."

Walking now, he remembered that Truncheon's television was not working. His couldn't get reception for some reason. Hence the bout of loquaciousness that Gabe Kaplan and his sweathogs would eventually cure. He had heard

Soviet emigres were starting to come into Brighton, replacing the old-timers, people with his own lineage. He had no affection for the old-timers or the emigres. The further he withdrew, the more he found himself counting the ways he was like no one else. The longer he spent away from Lolita, from the domesticity or lack thereof he'd have to reckon with in the coming days and years, the more he was sure of his mission. No future was secure without the elimination of the Candies. The ineptness and immorality of his former employers, the New York Police Department, stunned him into a rage, a fugue that he chose not to break. He had lost track of the faces smashed, the kneecaps cracked, the pistols whipped. More were falling by his hand, but there would always be more.

How many *more* years could he do this before he was satisfied? This was the question Truncheon's face always asked without forming the needed words. He was neglecting the private investigating. A waste of time, work for imbeciles, work that nevertheless paid his rent, which he was purposefully three months behind on. The landlord, a Greek with a wart shaped like Crete, would knock once a week, breathing against the closed door. Archie never answered. He disconnected his phone when the Greek began to call. Let him rot. Let him live out his decline.

Vengeance left the boardwalk at Coney Island Avenue, stalking down a stretch of quiet, cream-faced co-ops. He fingered the heater under his jacket. He liked to check for it like he would for his own pulse. He was at his best, his sharpest, with a weapon near. He could feel his entire body constricting, coiling to a definitive point, the self needed for combat. Effective combat required an equal disregard for the past and future, a quick snapping of time's arrow. Combat required Lolita to be gone, and he had therefore been engaged in some form of combat for more than a month.

The child's name. What would it be?

Up ahead, he had his night. The machinery of luck—machinery he was sure he had built himself—brought him here, to Coney Island Avenue and Bright Beach Avenue, a shadow-swallowed rib of the city, the Brighton Beach Line's overhead throttle shattering dreams every ten minutes. He saw the men in black masks and arm bands, Candy-red. He saw the bulge, saw enough, calculated the exhausting seconds until they were inside the store, holding it up for cash. An initiation raid. Candies dealt in bigger stakes but the hold-up was the proving ground, the minor leagues. How do you know if a prospect is ready for the Show? Watch him perform.

So he ran as silently as he could, his coattails flaring like the baby wings of a pheasant. He was getting faster because he was lighter, because he was eating less. His bones were hollowing out. Stripped naked in front of a mirror, he was built like a refugee, every muscle twitch necessary for a life-saving action, to be determined. A six-day beard encroached on his jaw.

The bell of the jewelry store rang out as the two men entered, Vengeance their shadow. They were young, with high school builds and olive-to-copper skin, far-flung recruits, he figured. He did not give them time to draw their guns, to resist. He gave no time. He was beyond that. Justice, if done right, could not be delayed. This was the problem of the United States: the legal system knotted up with this mothball democracy—the thinning and infinite strands of twine that made up these geriatric penal codes—could not begin to adequately contain the filth. Truncheon may think him arrogant for presuming the tipping point was nigh, garbage spilling over the rim, and in a theoretical framework Truncheon could be right—the human race, whichever cohort tended to be alive at a given sliver of time, was presumptuous. But not Archie, not Vengeance. He knew. Every action he took brought the world closer to redemption, closer to the kind of place he would want to exist in, and maybe, one day, he could allow his own child to exist here too. History was littered with the corpses of those who sought to compromise justice. He would tell Lolita this someday. Law enforcement was flawed because the law was flawed and the enforcement was selective, predicated on skin color, class, disposition, and the state of the officer in question. Vengeance was beyond that.

How often had they laughed at him when he suggested the year-end goal for the department should be a crime rate of zero percent? That aspiring for anything else meant you were not supposed to be in the department? Archie was speaking in a foreign tongue, a future tongue, and he would have to force them to understand. They were seeing it already in the number of Candies he was returning to the earth. These were small-time thugs and gang leaders alike. He was closing in on Ras Locka. If he fell, criminal enterprise in New York City would be set back a half century. It would be like killing all the mafia families at once. Compared to Locka, the mob was tame, because there was a comforting fluidity to their enforcement, ways to strike from bureaucratic sidedoors and still mutilate them. Their inverted moral code was predictable. Locka, in many ways, was Vengeance's true counter-image, a fellow student of history, pure in his intentions to commit unvarnished evil.

A Manhattan-bound train galumphed overhead, screeching to a halt to gobble a handful of riders at Brighton. The train almost masked the chime of the jewelry store. Vengeance crept inside. The men were eyeing a sapphire display case in the box-shaped store. They did not keep their hands on their weapons, wherever they were concealed. This nonchalance was an invitation to strike. Vengeance didn't need more than one hit to have a permanent upper hand.

"What're you, what is this—" a rounded man behind the counter sputtered, his hands swimming in the air. He did not know who to trust. Vengeance should have been enough, but the man wanted more. His face was ruddy, old-world Irish, an invitation to die in the new order. A miscalculation: the new order did not come quickly enough. It never could. The thinning carapace of government would ensure that. The two Candies sidled closer to the man behind the counter and in another second they would have to be disabled. Vengeance was not stealth now. He followed them abruptly, each footstep blunt against the wine-colored carpeting. When one of the men attempted to reach into his back pocket, Vengeance's hand met him three-quarters way. They both turned.

"Tell Locka the jig is up."

"What?"

"I'm fucking coming, that's what," and he slugged him in the gut, sent him gagging backwards, equilibrium stolen. The second kid, younger-looking and frailer in a logger shirt and stained black jeans, spun and ran. He was caught in the threshold of the door and shoved outside, hard enough to stumble into a parking meter. Vengeance did not like his face. It shared too much in common with a field mouse. Hard black eyes, an overbite that could double as a snout. In an uncorrupted parallel universe, he could've let him go. The kid meant no harm. Look at this face.

"Okay, okay, I don't want no trouble."

"You are trouble itself. This means you do not want yourself. A quandary."

"The fuck man, I was just picking out a bracelet for my girl."

Vengeance swallowed the kid in a chokehold and brought him to the pavement. He laid a knee in the small of his back, digging deep. "Candy doesn't taste so sweet."

"I wasn't doing nothing," he moaned. "I was just going shopping."

"You were trying to stick up the jeweler."

"No I wasn't."

"You fucking liar."

The next minute was lost to him, which meant he was doing good work.

He had some rope saved from another job, enough to tie the kid's hands to a No Parking sign on a deserted side street and break the important bones in his face. He spat blood, cried blood, the corruption leaking out. When he was gone, Vengeance would be one step closer to the world that needed to be. He was doing the hard work for others. One day, they would canonize him.

"Tell me where Locka is."

"I dunno, I dunno what that is, Locka—"

"Wrong answer after wrong answer."

He left him tied there to track the first kid, who had gotten a head start but couldn't be far. Turned out he was sprinting down Brighton Beach Avenue, the broken shadows from the track dancing off his back. Vengeance was faster, always, and got a knife into the back of his arm just past a grocery on Brighton 2nd Street. He too was full of similar sounding words, though he gave a name. "I'm Sammy Kessler, I'm not in no gang, I swear man, we just do this colored armband thing it's a joke, an inside joke" but Vengeance wasn't going to be fooled. Withdrawing the knife, he used the last bit of rope to tie him to a drain pipe hanging off a shuttered storefront. The kid had a growth of stubble and no beard, his eyes wet and dark and pleading, like a diseased dog's. Vengeance had to decide. Would they be added to the kill count? Any of the Candies allowed to escape alive could regroup, would regroup. They would create a mythology of vengeance—they as the aggrieved party, as opposed to the foot soldiers of entropy—and come with reinforcements. The logic was clear here. Both kids needed to die. He put the knife down and worked him over for a bit, punches and kicks, the basic shit for a basic kid. He was begging for it to be done. *Stop, stop. I'm not who you think.* Vengeance knuckled the windpipe to keep him quiet. A dog barked, a babushka saw them, waddling in the opposite direction. If the Force interrupted, that would be a problem. Explaining justice to police was not possible. This kid wasn't giving him the information. Where Locka hid now. *Where, where, a street, a number, give me what I need.* Here was Vengeance, on the verge of begging. A tooth came loose, dangled, fell, rolled in dried gum. He would try the other one. Back to the No Parking. *You stay here.* He found a mess bloodier than he remembered, and the lies dribbling out. No amount of pain would get him to cough up the address, in the little he tried to speak. He said he did not know. I *dunno Locka, please mister...*he could hear Truncheon, owlish, telling him *enough, enough, back on the subway now, this isn't your day* and he would tell this voice to return to its body which, given the time and day, was welded to a sofa. Vengeance wavered. His fists only seemed to sink deeper into the fleshy loam without offering what should have been his. Without light—knowledge—beneath. Was he operating under the faulty assumption that, if dug in deep enough, he could find light on the other side? Was he simply spitting in the face of physics? He threw an upper cut and watched the kid's body sag, his knees beg for pavement as his wrists remained tied in place. He did not speak anymore. His eyes were shut. He bent forward, as if he was trying to pray. This wasn't how it was supposed to be. Where was the information? How could both keep lying to him? He clamped on his cheeks, thumb applying force from one side, forefinger from the other. If he kept pressing, he would get what he needed. He wouldn't leave empty handed.

"You son of a bitch."

"Please..."

"Tell me."

"Please..."

He mashed his cheeks so he had the face of a duck. He slapped him hard enough for a new spray of blood to dampen his glove. Now, he would have to make this worthwhile. Time was limited. He couldn't afford to waste it. Locka's cancer would spread for every burned away second. The fury built. Let the Force deal with the body and flail around for a perp. There were witnesses but he'd disappear. No one was better at that.

Ask Lolita.

"You have one more chance to tell me."

The kid's blood-streaked face was now limp. He did not stir.

"One last chance."

Vengeance fingered his knife. How to do it? In a world in which God died or never lived, justice was left for us, the living. Justice was left for those who could understand it, serve it, mete it. Without God, it was easily perverted, and this was the problem: between the Candies and the police, only he had this power to save justice from itself, and therefore save tomorrow. If he had Truncheon's words, he could have explained it already, jotted this into a few clean sentences and carried it around with him, under his coat. A writer was ultimately a translator, little else, and Truncheon was one of the very best. He could convert justice into language.

"You really got the wrong guy."

Vengeance craned his neck to see the man who owned the voice. The kid was barely breathing. By the time the man, bearded and long-haired like a lost hippie, stood within spitting distance, Vengeance had receded. Archie peaked out, surveyed his fists, the night, and the new arrival. He stood, poetically enough, in the halo of a streetlight.

"Poor sucker. He met the great Archie London. Always unfortunate," the man said.

Archie did not recognize the man, who looked closer to adolescence than manhood but floated over the sidewalk like he had lived far longer. Hearing his first and last name spoken out loud was more unnerving than he would admit. Only his eyes were visible, and the fedora was on, so this interloper had to have had some special association with Archie or know someone who did. Was there a mole from the Force tailing him? He would've known. No one would've sneaked up on him. Moles were easy kills.

"Who are you?"

"Me?" His smile was liquid, as if it could drip off at any moment. "Let me tell you something."

He moved closer, near enough to kiss.

"Tell me," Archie said.

"I know exactly who you are, and you better keep doing what you're doing."

"And that is?"

"Staying away from El Barrio. You stay away from her."

Archie felt a burning in his chest.

"You don't tell me what to do."

"I'm telling you, sucker. You try tying up *my* hands. Especially in that fucking clown get-up of yours."

Archie was used to swinging first. He missed the jawline and got the side of the skull, a glancing blow that probably hurt him as much as it hurt the other guy. He was tall, thick in the chest, and Archie could tell he knew how to box. It was in the footwork. He came back with two quick jabs and Archie was off balance, blocking rather than attacking. They grappled and Archie went ass first into a row of garbage cans, metal and refuse exploding all around them. He wasn't used to pain and disorientation. A steel-toed boot missed his teeth but mashed enough of his neck for him to feel the band of fire in his windpipe, and he was crouched, regaining strength for a charge that should have ended with the other guy's head smashed through the Ford's windshield parked in front of the pump. Instead, Archie threw his hands up and failed to understand what he was up against: someone with an equal belief in his indestructibility. A forehead came screaming into Archie's, a proud headbutt, and he felt the opening of a once unseen fissure in the world. Blood pooled, muddling the night sky he could still see. A train was grumbling, stopping, grumbling. The guy, the man-boy, stood above, imitating a titan.

"I'm JoJo, by the way. So you know the person who's gonna eventually send you to the grave."

"*Send*," Archie spat. "What, are you afraid to say kill?"

"Blame the comic books I read as a kid."

When JoJo turned around to walk away, Archie knew he had an opening. Even if JoJo was quicker, he would not have time to deflect a precise knife strike. Archie could get the spinal cord and it'd be done. Another night on the job. He didn't move. He spat again, tasting his salty blood, hating it. Human beings were animals. Always and forever. He was here to lift them up, help them, save them—but why? Why bother anymore? Let the Candies run New York. Let the rot set in. Let this place be JoJo's graveyard by the year 2000. He rubbed his jaw, his eye socket, fingered the swelling. This would take some real patching up. At least get up off your ass and return the favor to JoJo. There was time.

He could kill him.

One, two, three, four. Seconds slipped from him. The blood would not stop. He wasn't moving. JoJo vanished up the stairs, going to wait on the train platform. He could catch him if he moved. One, two, three, four. Catch him and what? Why was his body failing? He rubbed a finger beneath his raw nostrils and saw a bright new streak of blood shining in the overhead lights. He sighed.

That was Lolita's brother. Now he could go back uptown.

17

21st Century

Guns were easier to come by in the Age of Velez. After the terrorists showed they were keen on so-called "soft targets," the baseball stadiums and subway platforms and art museums, there was an emerging consensus that it couldn't hurt to carry a weapon. The local Democratic governments still resisted, at least rhetorically, but a popular, handsome executive who also happened to be a Democrat was saying something very different, so they paid heed to President Velez and loosened restrictions that Sundra understood to be gospel when she was a precocious child. The local Modell's, as well as smaller sporting goods chains, began to carry assault rifles along with footballs and tennis rackets years ago. Her contract with Velocity included shopping rights at Modell's. She made an old-fashioned trek to a brick-and-mortar store to make a purchase.

The charming thing about the old Modell's on Chambers Street was how they employed humans at the check-out counter. There was no need, with scanners and Gaggles, to do that, but the company had a homespun belief in putting some flesh and blood in their stores. Sundra didn't care either way. She burst in and went straight for the guns. She felt like she was channeling the spirit of Devora Dimon, chugging so madly towards weaponry and fantasizing about taking target practice at the Chelsea Piers shooting range. It was a good place to take kids.

She saw Rex was idle on Gaggle, an odd development because to go truly idle on Gaggle was a rarity. Not long ago, Gaggle introduced a feature that let you stream in sleep, running a thoughtsync through the REM stage and allowing friends to watch the approximations, in full dimensional color, of dreams. To go idle meant to disengage, a major social crime and almost a minor legal crime. She never worried too much about Rex, but she was curious as to what could be keeping him in the void. He wasn't the introspective type. He wasn't one to defy norms.

Over by the Mets and Yankees jerseys, in an elegant display just off the stairway leading to a basement filled with sneakers and hoverboards, were the guns. Modell's carried seven different brands of assault rifles, two dozen guns in all. Sundra voiced her intent to purchase the AR47-A and G2A-Heed and her Gaggle transferred the funds immediately. A pallid clerk, pinged on his own device, inched over to complete the purchase at check-out. He was tall and thin, more wisp than flesh, and his eyes were puffy from a process similar to crying, though he had not been crying. He was lucky to have this job, she thought. No, don't think that. That's a Gary Glassgarden thought you borrowed. He isn't lucky. *He isn't.*

But the Velezian logic was so easy here. Modell's didn't have to employ any humans at all. No one really did, come to think of it. Hence a system to protect the vulnerable, the mass of premiums. They were all lucky to be contracted, to even be property. In the old-old days, in the time of African-American slavery, there was the alternative of being a person whose skills could be in demand in a labor market. Today, there was the slave's life or the zero's life. The Ent life—to be a Devora Dimon, laughing god-like in the stratosphere—was fiction if you did not belong to them already. No amount of hard work would change that. No amount of laboring within the confines of law and order, of doing as you were told, would change that. She watched the clerk ring up her guns silently. How little he really knew. Freedom was there, in the barrels of those weapons. He just needed to train them elsewhere.

Lower Manhattan did not throb on a Sunday like it did during the week. She was grateful for that. She boarded the Cheetos Line at Chambers Street to head uptown and off to Queens, her firearms in black cases. She could be carrying a guitar. Strum strum. The station, after she scanned in, was fetid as always, and she at least forgave this because she wasn't being surge-priced on a Sunday.

Storms of black and gray rats swirled on the tracks. Two trashcans on the platform overflowed, soda bottles, sandwich wrappers, and a torn pair of jeans bursting over one rim. A pair of junkies filled a wooden bench, nodding off, nodding on. The wait began. Her Gaggle could tell her a train was 33 minutes away, but it was usually off. The MTC was still replacing a century-old signaling system, and with the cuts that came down from the state, it would be done sometime in the next millennium. Til then, she and the rest waited, playing the game of tiptoeing at the platform and squinting into an abyss. A man in a neon-colored coat sauntered near a No Exit sign, just off the end of the platform, and began to piss. He didn't look like a junkie and Sundra did look at the fleshy blur of his penis dangling out, soft but threatening. He wasn't taking much joy in it. It was just something to do. She thought, at some indeterminate point of time, she smelled burning meat. The scent mingled with the piss to create the smell of war, or what she thought it could be at its most banal and brutal. Her Gaggle beckoned, and she streamed basic porn—Eiffel Tower and ass to mouth—until the train, 43 minutes later, groaned into the station and absorbed them all, junkies and pissers included.

She was falling asleep when she heard the pounding of boots. They were stopped between Canal and Union Square. This was how it was done. At this point in her life, she could play guessing games to amuse herself: which police contractor was stomping through their lives now? The white V armbands told her it was Vektor, known for their exacting commitment to overreaction. Vektor routinely killed the most civilians, though precincts they patrolled would usually report reduced crime rates after a few months to a year, allowing all sins to be forgiven. There were seven Vektor men, and they all managed to stare straight ahead in the subway car, finding fascination in the backs of their bullet-proof vests. Their machine guns were pointed where they stared. To be afraid was beyond the point: there was so little you could control once police entered the scene, it was best to give way, imagine yourself soil being trampled on or sky waiting silently overhead. She knew to keep her breaths short, tight, movements as close to her body as possible. Noise was discouraged. For a premium employed by Vektor, there was much incentive to shoot, given the threat of termination that perpetually hovered over any patrolman who saw his crime numbers spike. If you were assigned to the 5th Precinct and grand larceny or murder ticked up enough, let's say 8 percent, you could be out of a job and homeless, given a police contractor's fear of losing a lucrative municipal contract.

The Vektor cops tramped to the end of the car and stopped. One checked his scanner. During sweeps for terrorists, it wasn't uncommon for a cop to take a body with him. It meant he could log activity and show to his bosses the sweeps were productive. An interrogation justified a salary. An arrest, even better. No one even watched. Their Gaggles were held up, and she could see the flickers of neighboring thoughtsyncs on her own screens, alerts about mental meet-ups she was not invited to. It was unlikely that any of them were chatting about the Vektors, though. One, it would seem suspicious. Two, who cares, when they're sweeping subways cars all the time? You never know where a terrorist threat is lurking. Might as well play it safe.

A teen with piercings in his lip, eyebrow, and ears was pulled to his feet by a Vektored glove and told to get against the wall. The car wasn't moving. Sundra decided to look up. The kid had the swarthy skin of someone who Vektors would profile, not quite an Islamist but close enough for a pat down or beat down. He was cuffed instead and the Vektors shoved him through the train door when they pulled into Union Square. Her Gaggle screen, like all the others in the car, blinked "If You See Something, Say Something." She decided to peel away and take a nap until her stop.

She saw herself, saw him. Saw them both. She was flying, gun in hand, straight for Octavio Velez, though she knew it wasn't possible that he could be fully-grown in 1979. No, he was born a year later. He could not be a man, smiling, his black hair slicked, his body electric in a trim blue suit the color of a moonless sky. She could not go faster. He was standing, waiting. His face begged for death. She saw Stellar above, floating into space, pleading with her. *Now, now.* All she had to do was fire. Velez was smiling, unmoving, ready. Deliver him death. She pulled on the trigger. Nothing came. There were bullets but they weren't firing, or she never loaded the gun in the first place, or they were simply apparitions, disappearing into nothing as soon as they left the barrel. Velez shook his head. She knew she'd missed it, he wouldn't stand still, he would go back and live his life knowing he had successfully shackled the future. Stellar called from the sky. *Sundra, Sundra. SundraSundraSundraSundra—*

"What?"

It was her Gaggle trying to wake her. It sensed she was sleeping for too long a period of time without interacting with it. "Sundra, dear. Where are you?" It pleaded from her wrist, an artificial child in need of love. She was four stops away. She said she was here, she was interacting, streaming, friending. Holos of women in ecstasy played overhead, eyes closed, mouths agape, their bare glistening bodies trembling in the grasps of monumental orgasms. "ArteMs.," a soft voice cooed, "will give you a real reason to scream."

She thought about this. At her stop, she had ArteMs., Devora's drug of choice, on her mind, and when she saw him there, alive, after he had disappeared from the Gaggle and therefore life itself, she felt it wasn't sufficient enough to simply say hello and embrace him, that the moment, now that she carried her firearms and they were so close to saving the world, demanded much more.

"Rex," she exhaled, her feet moving faster than she imagined they could. "Rex."

He was slumped-shouldered outside the doorway of her walk-up, sucking on a lollipop. Stepping out of a shadow and into the Swiss cheese glow of a nearby delicatessen, she saw why he was not smiling as widely as she was: the swelling in the lip, the black eye, both cheeks thick with bruising. She held her gasp. He waved, arm bent at a right angle, like he was late for the class he hated most. "Rex, my God..."

He didn't say anything.

"You were gone, I figured you were...well, I don't know. I could never concoct an explanation. You disappeared for a few days. What the hell happened?"

"I...I'm scared to say."

"Are they on to us?"

"Who?

"Anyone? Did they mention the Plan?"

She remembered, in fact, she had never even spelled out the Plan entirely to Rex. He knew fragments, hints, enough to hazard a guess but not enough to betray her to the authorities. She was safe in that way.

"No, which one, you mean—"

"I have the weapons. Step one and step two, complete. I told you about my adventure to Sheepshead Bay. They're expecting you, too, by the way."

"I don't wanna go."

"You don't *want*, what—" She stopped herself, remembering the beating evident on his face. "You have to go down there. You're expected."

"I'm not doing this, Sundra."

"What changed? What happened? Please tell me."

"I don't know," he turned away from her. "Someone may be on to us. Vektors were doing a raid and they picked me up. I was at Governors Island for two days. There was no light in the cell. They asked me my name and hit me. I said I wasn't a terrorist. It didn't matter. They kept hitting me. I was let go. That's it."

He didn't sound like her Rex. He was quiet, sullen, never making eye contact. Why was he just waiting outside her apartment like a lost puppy? She had an idea.

"Stay right here, Rex. I'll be right back. I've gotta get something at CVS."

"CVS? Okay."

Rex watched Sundra walk off to the CVS across the street. His ribs and cheekbones ached and the images in his mind would not congeal into the familiar, easy thoughts he once knew. It hurt badly to laugh. He knew he would be docked for the days he missed work and it was even possible they'd terminate his contract, since it was now on his record that he was processed at the Governors Island prison complex. He wished he understood why. Doughy and pale, he did not profile as a terrorist, and expected this privilege of his physique to keep him free from such hellholes. He expected a lot. What did life look like before Governors? He remembered ice cream, easy music, sleeping, jacking off. Now all of these things seemed unreal and impractical. It hurt to move his jaw, to chew. He leaned against the door, crossed his arms. If Sundra never came back, he could stay here, not move, and freeze himself. He would join himself to the architecture, become a wall, plaster, brick, maybe a doorknob. An easy way to live out your life. No one could suspect you of anything. You weren't prey.

It was funny. When they had beaten the shit out of him for centuries, but what was in fact two days, they were polite. They asked him how he was. If he was hungry. Where he lived. *We're done here. You did well, Mr. Umbra.* Asking where he lived was disingenuous because they knew. In the state he was in, knots of fire tying every exposed surface of his body, he was grateful for being asked. Courtesy went a long way in jail. He was led out of his lightless cell to a parking lot blessed by the sun. He was carefully belted into a black unmarked van with tinted windows. He gave them the address of Sundra's apartment without thinking about why he should go there. He saw he had been allowed to reintegrate his Gaggle and should have messaged Sundra immediately that he was alive and okay and coming to her home. But he didn't. He stared at the screen, now bright with life, and did nothing. He waited. The van drove slowly, kindly. Few bumps, as if the road knew what he had been through, the hands like steel clamps on his face, the feeling of cold cinderblock against his cheek. The driver, a bulky East Asian with a chin beard, waved him off and wished him a good evening. He seemed to mean it.

Rex wasn't hungry. He should have been. They hardly fed him between interrogations and beatings and he could remember, vaguely, being ravenous at the end of what was likely the first day. The hunger eventually left. Maybe it figured there were more important things to worry about. Sundra, the Plan, his job, his life. He knew how fortunate he was to be serving Velocity. His mother had warned him he was going to end up a zero if he didn't bust his butt. *You aren't as smart as the other boys.* It was true. He had no right to be let into Velocity's offices, not among men and women so smart they could all run the country if they had to. He would tell Sundra to forget the Plan. Be more grateful and forget it. What's the point, really? He didn't know what she was thinking and if he ever did, he figured it would end up amounting to little and making the wrong people mad. He did not want to make any more people mad at him. He was tightroping over the abyss and Governors Island always had room for one more body. *Let's stop making people mad, Sundra.* He would be a better person so Vektors or Dreisini or whomever would have no reason to take him away again. No way was he going to risk doing what she wanted, getting his Velocity chip extracted from his finger illegally. No, Rex Umbra followed the law. He was not a criminal, a terrorist. That's what he would tell Sundra when she got back from CVS. *I am not a terrorist.*

He was thinking this, over and over again, when she returned with a plastic bag. Unlike him, she was beaming. He even heard her humming. The bag swung at her side and Rex imagined an old-fashioned mace, spikes and all, and saw in the forward momentum of the bag how he could be bludgeoned to death.

Locked up in Governors, he began for the first time in his life to imagine eternity: the stretch of time that his death would be, centuries layered upon centuries, how the default would always be Rex Umbra, dead, not Rex Umbra, living human. This predictably terrified him. He wanted to cling to life. But this was another revelation of his time in Governors—he had no particular reason to cling. Closeness to friends, to family, to Sundra…none of these seemed good enough. He argued with himself in the dark, playing both sides, angel's and devil's advocate, and devil's usually had the edge. He encouraged death. It would be easier for all to just go away. But eternity, the angel cried, the vast nothingness, the negation of all you know. Don't rush there yet! Stay, remain! He sobbed that he would. He wiped his eyes, though they were usually phantom tears, the imagination of an outburst. His interrogators would return, slap him across the face, tell him to stop making noise. *Can't you be quiet?* Why was it so important to be quiet? He never figured that out. The place was so noisy anyway. The sounds he won't forget. The metallic clanging melded with the moans, the way an echo would stretch from cell to cell, reminding you of how fucked its occupant was. When he was sure it was easier to die, he would clench his fists and squish his eyes shut and try to physically crumble away, see himself as a creature willingly destroyed. He grew hoarse from asking why he was there. He knew no answer was coming. He was there because he was there, simple as that. He was there because he was commanded to be, and would go when they said so. Saying you didn't do anything was like saying you didn't go to the bathroom, you just absorbed piss and shit back into you. They didn't believe you and laughed. So when they were polite to him on the van ride home it meant a lot, he was grateful, and there was a part of him that would have offered to spend one more night in Governors to repay the favor of being driven to Queens and taking that new little bridge they connected to Brooklyn Bridge Park so he could press his nose to the window and see out to the harbor, the Statue of Liberty.

"Don't look so sad and mad, Rex. Let's go upstairs."

She led him up to her second-story apartment, an enlarged studio that could have been billed as a one-bedroom if you threw up a curtain around her bed. It was musty, with two windows facing a brick alley and the general feeling of being neglected. There were black and brown electronics swaddled in plastic packaging, unpacked cardboard boxes, and the smell of Styrofoam, though no Styrofoam seen. A green couch sagged near the window. Rex wanted to go home.

"Give me one sec in the bathroom Rex. I need to freshen up."

"Freshen up for what?"

"Tonight is an important tonight. The Plan unfolds in 48 hours."

"I didn't know..."

"Well, you plopped off the grid. Now you're back on. And I need you."

"I'm nervous, Sundra. I don't know about any of this. Can't we just go back to work tomorrow and the next day and do what we usually do? I don't know why we need some Plan."

"Because, Rex, we are slaves. Do you not understand?"

"No, I don't. I don't feel like a slave I don't think. I mean, I know it was upsetting to see your professor die like that. I was right there. It was bad. But I think, I dunno, whatever we need to do now..."

"Let me freshen up. You aren't afraid of hurting someone, right?"

"I am, well, yeah."

"*I am, well, yeah.* Maybe I can't trust you at all. Maybe I should tell you to leave. One person can do what I want to do well enough."

"Sundra, I mean, I'm not giving up."

"You're not? It sure sounds like it."

"No, no, no. I'm just worried."

"But I haven't even really told you what we're doing, so what's to worry about?"

"That's the point, I guess."

She shut the bathroom door. Poor dumb Rex. Every George needs a Lenny, right? Except Lenny only got in the way. Lenny killed puppies and broke necks.

George did a mercy killing of Lenny. She wasn't going to do anything like that. Life under Devora, life in the pit of slavery, had taught her at least to go after what she wanted and ignore everything else. There was an irony in the Age of Velez: it would ultimately reward someone like Sundra, who was seeking to undo it completely.

The pills, purple and blue, had of course been expensive. She was surprised she was even allowed to buy them, given the pricing that put them in Ent territory, and she considered whether all she was doing with this Plan was trying to establish the ability to consume freely. If that was the depth of it, she deserved to fail. In any system, consumption was a distraction, a misdirection for those with power to ensure the powerless weren't reminded of their original state of sin. ArteMs., she had to say, was fast-acting. Once she swallowed the two recommended pills she could feel a tingling between her legs, the flourishing of a warmth and desire she was unused to, at least so rapidly. There was a time when men only had the pleasure of a medically-enhanced libido. A backward age when sexual politics were inverted and perverted and the Devora Dimons of the world, no matter their cunning, served unworthy husbands. That at least was over. Her stomach shook. Rivers of blood rerouted themselves, a loose electricity rolling from her hips to her fingertips. She was sweating, itching. In the mirror, she was herself amplified, every morsel of Sundra simmering as it was meant to be, when existence was a simple game of potentiality, a proposition without consequence. She could love and kill. She saw how the emotions overlapped, one bleeding into the other. She lusted for action. Anything to fuck. To fuck a wall, a drainage pipe, Rex Umbra. The door creaked open and there he was, lumpen on her couch, gazing dully her way. What a thing to fuck.

"Rex, I am going to tell you everything. I want to tell you everything. We are going to change the world."

"You've said that before, but I don't know what it means."

She sat next to him, pulled him in, and attacked with a kiss. He tasted like mustard and bubblegum. She nibbled on his lower lip and slid her tongue inside his parting mouth, sweeping between a gap near his oversized molars. Shooting a hand down, she found his crotch and his soft penis squashed in his underwear. He was close to whimpering, or doing it already, and she closed her fingers around the shaft, forcing it erect. She stroked and tugged. He moaned, his cheeks pinkening. She wanted to do everything to him.

"We are going to change the world."

He understood he would have to do what she said. He had no alternative.

And anyway Sundra wasn't so bad to see without her clothes, panting on top of him. They fucked on the couch and floor, his back cracking from the thin cushions and floorboards, her breasts swishing ambitiously in his face. He didn't do this very often. She acted like she had, even if she hadn't, and Rex didn't know the difference. Sundra clawed the back of his head and shoved him down between her legs. From porn, he knew to swirl his tongue, but wished he could gaggle some tips for this part. One or two streams, just to get a rhythm…she had a coppery taste and he tried to like it. On top, she wished only for more, for his earthworm tongue to be bigger and longer, to slither into the womb if need be.

"Let's go Rex, c'mon Rex."

She saw then how Devora did it. It was so easy to live this way. Power comes naturally to those who want it. She wanted to devour Rex and find others, souls like him, to submit. It was the drug, one panel of her mind said, simply the drug. You will be "yourself" soon, whoever "yourself" is, given the chaos and fluidity of this infantile planet. Devora was an adult, at least. She gave up nothing she didn't have to. She killed because she could. She lived at the expense of lives. It was so easy. Why even go through the effort, why listen to Quentin Stellar, why follow through with a Plan that would deny her *this*, fucking the living daylights out of whatever she wanted?

But she saw too how this was one more shiny Velezian object dangled over her eyes, a way to subdue to her. Given the illusion Devora Dimon offered, wanton sex and accumulation of goods, it was tempting to lay her own guns aside, keep guzzling ArteMs., and stay home. Very tempting. Look at the mush beneath her, Rex's pliant husk. Oh how she wanted it. So easy to punish within the superstructure. Quite another to punish the superstructure itself. Gary Glassgarden wouldn't approve, either way.

"Sundra…I'm tired…please," he was huffing, begging, so red and sweat-stained he looked like he had been just pushed out of a vagina, newly-born. She felt something akin to pity, though not pity itself.

"You're not *done*."

"I, I am. I can't—I mean, I'm just drained."

"Almost there. Just give me a little more."

She tried his penis and it was floppy and shrunken. It mashed up against the outside of her vagina, rubbing like sandpaper. It would not go in anymore. She gripped and he whimpered. She gripped harder. His whimpering increased in proportion to the little thumb of crimson flesh in her damp hand. The release wouldn't come. She finally let him go and he sagged backwards against the couch, the shine of sweat or tears on his cheeks. She wouldn't look him in the eye.

"Go shower and we'll talk."

"Yeah, a shower. That's a good idea."

He went to the shower grateful. Sundra listened for the rush of water and went about collecting her clothes from various points on the floor. She wished he had made her come, but her body was glad at least to have been set off like that. Endorphins sang. Her heart thump-pumped. She was closer to the Plan than ever, thrilled to be on the brink of a true and lasting action. The beauty of undertaking such a significant act, by itself, was almost enough. She could withdraw, watch herself in the third person and admire the aesthetics of what she was about to do, as Devora might. She could get drunk this way. Was Devora ever sober in the real sense of the word? She existed in a state of perpetual and irredeemable ecstasy—not that redemption could ever be a concern for her. To be an Ent was to exist outside of the plastic morality erected by lesser men and women to keep the de facto ditch-diggers—Sundra included—in line. Sundra was already committing several acts of rebellion by having these thoughts and imagining a future outside of what a handful of corporate powers deemed acceptable.

President Octavio Velez, speaking in Osawatomie, Kansas, proclaimed that business must save America from itself. In business, big and small, there was the future. Within this blandness hid the kernel of what was to come: the slave economy i.e. the economy of gratitude. When Rex came back, she would begin there, in Osawatomie, where a Roosevelt and Obama made their own pitches for a national egalitarianism Velez would say was admirable but ill-suited for this century. What use was an increased minimum wage or an expanded social safety net offered by an increasingly frail government in a world where technology around us was changing so rapidly? By the time he finished this address, Velez thundered, a hundred American jobs would be lost to automation. Is this the world we want to live in? Is this a world we want to give to our children—one that constrains our best and brightest? Velez, as Sundra knew because she had watched the video dozens of times, said the government alone, in the traditional liberal sense, could not offer all the solutions, and this was the hard truth he must sell to a Democratic Party that he felt had its heart in the right place (he was a lifelong Democrat) and its head somewhere else. Republicans were mistaken too in believing an unfettered, unregulated market offered all easy answers, and he compared Smith's Invisible Hand to Casper, a terrifically dated reference that still drew its share of laughs. Rather, Velez said, we need to find *another way.*

Let's look to our entrepreneurs, the tech magnates who all but say human beings are a growing millstone around innovation's neck, with their inefficient processing power and around-the-clock needs. Let's partner with them in earnest. Let's find a solution.

Let's look, then, to our *Ents.*

He coined the term at Osawatomie in his first term, year two, but it was the Ents that began to speak of "premium" human labor, the need to ensure so-called "premiums" were provided for in the new economy, given that demand for human bodies, outside of a few select fields requiring ever more layers of education, was so low. Velez, with his oratorical gifts, brought the term to households. To employ premiums, Ents needed certain concessions, and thus the Velez administration's Department of Labor codified the contracting system, providing an avenue for stable, long-term employment for average Americans while bounding them, at their employer's discretion, to a company in perpetuity. Because capitalists, and not workers, of the world long ago united, there were quiet summits and more public meetings and soon Velez, for initially environmental concerns, was calling for an end to the cash-based economy, given both the threat to climate change the continued production of paper money created and, on second thought, how retrograde and analog the whole system was, considering the prevalence of digital currencies. Velez had rare bipartisan support in Congress—he was a Democrat who spoke Republican language when he needed to—and soon premiums found they had access to credit they never dreamed of in their years of unemployment, with a simple trade off: their generous employers now had much more say over where they lived and how they spent their credit. Fair enough, considering how much the so-called Ents were now doing for them. Look, Velez said, our business leaders could all fly off to China or a resurgent Africa tomorrow. They could pursue Mars colonization *for real.* Let's not give them excuses to leave, because they will. Let's make this a great country for *everyone.*

It was some version of this she told Rex, who was still dripping wet but no longer naked. Sundra was not horny for him. That reality now seemed quite distant. She spoke quicker than she would have liked and glossed over enough details for him to understand the sweep of the Velez vision, or attempt to. Their Gaggles were off to ensure no one could listen in. She explained the Plan.

"So, we're going to kill Octavio Velez? He's like retired now but I guess we could."

"We are killing him. But not in the way you imagine. Given the secret service protection former presidents retain, and the special scrutiny given to Velez, we would not be successful. That's a fact. Even if we were trained assassins, the odds would be against us. But Velez was not always so well taken care of."

"I think I understand."

"Do you? Tell me, what do you know about 1979?"

"It was the year Chase accidentally went back to. I know that."

"Well, we know the machine in the Trojan Tower can go there again. We know that in 1979, Octavio Velez was not yet born. We know that his mother was pregnant with him during that year. We know—well, *assume*—that she didn't have much in the way of protection. She worked mostly menial jobs, first in New York where Velez was born and then eventually they moved to California when he was in elementary school. So it's pretty simple. We knock off his mother, a woman named Lolita Velez, while she's pregnant with Octavio."

"We have to kill *both*?"

"The vagaries of time travel, dear Rex. 1979 is our destination. Octavio was born in 1980. *C'est la vie.*"

"I see. I guess I just wonder what will change, you know? Like, making sure Velez wasn't born—"

"The future will change. The present will change. Slavery will have lost its silver-tongued champion. No one could have succeeded at building this prison world except him. No one. I believe that more than anything."

"Okay."

"No one, Rex."

And he believed it because she believed it. The next step was for Rex to make the same surreptitious trip to Sheepshead Bay to have the dummy chip implanted. He didn't want to, but she would have her way. There was something dark in Sundra that equally attracted and repelled Rex. He was like a shard of space rock caught in a gravitational field, unsure of whether his home lay with his fellow cosmic detritus or the alien planet below. His default would always be Sundra, though, because what else was there? Other than work and the 4-D leagues he played in on his Gaggle, there wasn't a whole lot for him to do. Not very many people to see. Dead parents. Friends, unlike Sundra, not interested in overdoing IRL interactions. He would never use the word lonely to describe himself, even after the time spent in Governors. It was not something that belonged in his vocabulary. It was not a word anyone would admit to knowing intimately. It spoke to a failure not just of the individual but of society as a whole. What sort of country could let a person go lonely? Not *this* America.

Sundra told him he could spend the night. She took the bed, he took the couch.

18

Lolita

Last night was the only time I ever hit JoJo. I can't promise it won't be the last.

I was chopping mangoes for Devlin when he burst it. I knew he had something to tell me, because he was all cut up and was smiling too bright. He was sweating too, really soaked. I had an electric fan going from the kitchen counter but it just seemed to be blowing hot air all around. JoJo's black hair blew in the breeze, and I was staring at the split ends when he opened his mouth.

"You can stop wasting your time now," he said.

I kept looking, not saying anything.

"It's done, Lolita. Moving on starts now."

Lolita. When he used my full name, it meant he was more interested, at that moment, in being a brother than a revolutionary.

"You want a slice of mango or no?"

JoJo walked over, his smile fading away. He never looked so big to me. I realized how, in my tip toes, I could barely get to his chest. I saw him how others in the streets must see him: as a big bad motherfucker. In the overhead light, his scars, wriggling over his pores and acne leftovers, were shining.

"No. This is serious. You need to listen to me."

"Say it already, JoJo. It's snack time."

"You will not be seeing your friend anymore. You can stop hunting around. He's not coming for you and I made sure of that."

The way he said *your friend* made me feel angry and gigantically sick. The slight hesitation, the way he bit down hard on the "f" sound. Fucking pussy. I was shaking.

"You stay the hell out of my life," I said, barely above a whisper.

"You are my little sister living in my house. Your life is my business."

"I can live anywhere. I live here for you."

"For me?"

"Yeah..." I regret a bit what I said next. "For you. I don't give a shit whether I'm here alone or not, whether it's you or the new kid or some friend. I don't give a shit. You're the needy one, JoJo. You're the one who can't get over mom and dad ditching us so you need to play daddy to me, to be something you're not. You're fucking lonely and you think the revolution is gonna come and be your friend and I'll be there sucking my thumb, your little baby. No. I have a baby. I love it, and I love—"

"Don't you say it, you better not, you have no goddamn idea what the fuck you're talking about, *no idea* cause some degenerate gringo slipping his little cock in you, no idea—"

"What did you do to him?"

JoJo's smile crawled back.

"I gave him a message."

"What did you *do* to him?"

"He fought like the little white boy from Long Island that he is. He can't even take a headbutt."

I saw it then. Some dark alley in Brooklyn, Archie's fists and JoJo's fists, maybe Archie had the edge in the beginning and JoJo, as he always could do, took over. He had that way. JoJo never said outright he never lost a fight—he didn't brag as much as you think—but it was written all over him, in how he moved, in how *easy* he strutted through the city. You could get jumped anywhere really, even the Upper East Side, and all sorts of fucked up dudes roam around the burned out parts of the Bronx just looking for trouble, and you never know what's coming at you on the subway. JoJo wasn't bothered by any of it. The more the city spun out of control, the more JoJo seemed to thrive, coming closer than ever to the promised overthrowing of the white "plutocracy" or "murderocracy." Except I doubted he could overthrow it. Fighting a system is more than picking fights, and JoJo never seemed to get this.

"A headbutt..."

"He was just about knocked out cold. He can scrap a little. He's garbage, though. You deserve better."

"You don't know—"

"I know enough to see he knocked you up and abandoned you and someone has to explain that to you, in plain English."

"Stay out of my life."

"As long as he stays out of yours."

I turned back to the mangoes. I remembered Devlin was just sitting in the living room, staring at the gray screen of the broken TV. Who knew the last time it got reception. He looked like he was imagining his favorite show. Poor, lost kid. I wished I could get him *Gilligan's Island* or something, whatever they watched in his house, if it still existed. JoJo was still next to me, just looming, and I wanted to scream. He saw me as a child and I wasn't one. That's what happens when you live with someone for so long: you lose all perspective. At least for me, JoJo was always the older brother, so I could never not see him as some kind of adult, a pre-adult and then, after a bit, a full-fledged one.

He wasn't completely wrong and this probably burned me more. Archie hadn't come back. I didn't know where he was. He had slipped between the cracks of the city, an easy thing to do if you think about it, but surprising for me because I was used to finding whatever I wanted. The city was a puzzle I could solve, even at its darkest, its most fallen. *I am tired, I am weary I could sleep for thousand years.* Where had I heard that before? The song lyric was looping in my head as I sliced and sliced and finally missed the fruit altogether and cut the top of my ring finger.

"Shit, shit."

JoJo squinted.

"Lemme get you a towel. Put pressure on it."

"I know what to do."

I watched the white paper towel turn light red where I pressed. It stung and I felt, in my chest, a rising wave of rage. It was only made worse when I looked into JoJo's big, sad brown eyes and hated what I saw, the man who couldn't accept I wasn't a baby forever basking in the glow of Big Brother. The pain in my finger became the rage in my chest. They were twin channels feeding into my brain. Whatever JoJo meant—he meant well, he always did—it didn't matter. There was a person growing inside of me. Pressing hard on my finger, I thought about that: what could this person, boy or girl, really be? All I was ever going to be was Lolita Velez. All JoJo was ever going to be was JoJo. But here, inside me, I had the potential to have *anyone.* How many people on the Earth? Three billion? And how many of them amounted to anything? Maybe I have time to do something. What I liked about Archie was his *purpose.* I don't really believe in God anymore, I think people are on their own, alone, so you make your own reasoning for being alive. You build it yourself. I don't know if I built mine. It depends on the day. Archie knew. Like JoJo, he burned for justice. Unlike JoJo, he wasn't insecure about anything.

JoJo had a lot to be insecure about.

I mean, I got it too. Look at how angry JoJo is at white people. Archie is white. It's easy being white, so so easy. You don't even think about it. It's like a superpower you don't even know you have. JoJo's running around a city (me too) of superhumans, trying to get a taste of what it's like, and they of course never give it to him. He (like me) gets called a spic if he goes on the wrong side of 96th. He (much more than me) gets searched by police, beaten by police, told he better watch his step by police. He knew he wasn't getting hired in any of the downtown firms where the money was. He knew schools were an illusion, a way to keep us black and brown animals in the cage so we don't bite off the white master keeping us locked in, stepping down occasionally to pet us. I got it. JoJo seethed. He didn't know any other way. Archie seethed too, but for a very different reason.

It's hard to think about how much longer we can go on like this. Look at the city. All you hear every day, if you're one of these people to pick up the papers or watch the five o'clock news, is stuff about shootings and fires. Why were we born into this? I don't know if I really love this city. I thought I did for a while. I did, I think, when I rode around with Archie, when I was yo-yoing between up and downtown. But there was a darkness pulsing underneath that couldn't be ignored either. There was something making Archie be the way he was, stalking shadows, picking fights, hiding from me. There was something making JoJo trying to win those fights too. Driving them both. It couldn't be seen. Right now, pressing the drying blood, I feel it too. I feel the anger, the illusions peeling away, the way JoJo had talked to me, the way the city *made* him talk.

Everywhere you walked, talked, you tasted smoke. You could sink your teeth in it. The mangos were bright and cold on a white plate. It was almost October, and the heat was clinging to all of us.

"Stop standing over me."

"I'm not standing *over* you. I'm just standing here. In my kitchen."

"What do you think I owe you JoJo? What? I'm not killing my kid, my kid with his white slave master's blood. Is that what you think I owe you, as your sister?"

"I want what's best for you."

"You want what's best for the revolution in your head."

"I want..." when he got quiet, it meant the anger was just about volcanic, churning below the crust. It meant the city was winning. "...I want you to not be opening your legs for every fucking lowlife that slips—"

I curled my fingers and hit him straight in the mouth, doing it so fast it was half a slap, half a punch. He staggered back. It wasn't nearly enough to make him bleed. In that moment, I think I wanted blood, just to see that I had accomplished something with my time, my time that stretched endlessly out in all directions, past and future. Devlin was still there. He had turned from the couch and was watching. We all froze. JoJo's eyes were bigger than I had ever seen them. They were enormous, two deep punctures in his face. It was like when Papa, one time years ago, had hit him. JoJo was tough even when he was little and he didn't take any shit, but one day Papa lost it and smacked him on the cheek. He made a real loud *pop* on the skin and JoJo stood there, stunned, broken. I remembered JoJo didn't like getting hit. This was why he fought so well, why he kept his looks—he was always slipping attacks. The headbutt on Archie was an exception, dirtying his face to win a fight. He did it to make a point to me.

I would undo it. I would wind back time, use one of Space Boy's toys and tell myself *not* to do it. Because I would explain to myself, my past self, that this was not us fighting, me and JoJo, or JoJo and Archie, but the city fighting with all of us. Papa and Mami were telling us something by leaving. We were abandoned here because they wanted to save themselves and we had to stop lying to ourselves. We needed to face that fact. We were here on rotting ground. I am bringing a baby into this place. Me and Archie, wherever he is.

"You're nuts," JoJo finally managed, but I knew he didn't mean it. I could see the sadness in him. His eyes were saying *why do we bother, Lo? Why does anyone?* I didn't have an answer for him. I couldn't say how 1980 would be better than 1979, or if Space Boy held all the answers. I turned to the kid, met his eyes, and he just looked blankly back, like a stuffed animal. I wanted to help him then. Get him home. Get him to his real parents, not us. I wish I had words for him. A string of sentences to keep him from looking so lost. I swiveled back to JoJo. He wasn't holding his face anymore.

"You're nuts," he said again, heading over to the couch to try to fix the TV. We all wanted him to be successful.

19

21st Century

Firearms weren't allowed in the Trojan Tower unless you were authorized to use them. This presented an obvious quandary. They needed to enter the time machine properly armed to complete their mission.

Luckily, Rex had a casual friendship with one of the lower-level engineers who worked on Chase Dimon's ill-fated adventure to 1979. RuJay Starr, 43 and obese, liked to talk, and Rex was a good listener. After his time with Sundra in her apartment, he felt he needed to do good by her, especially since the sexual memory had lost its violent tinge and now seemed wholly erotic, an experience to be relived, except Sundra did not seem to want to take ArteMs. anymore and fuck. She was focused on the Plan. He had to be too, and return to her sexual good graces, smothering his entire face in the warm muff of her vagina like RuJay at a hypothetical pie-eating contest.

RuJay explained that the time traveling device emitted frequencies that could be rerouted and then captured remotely, opening a portal anywhere. Chase, for security and secrecy reasons, had chosen the Trojan Tower. "Temporal rifts," as RuJay called them, were accessible wherever the technology could be harnessed. The problem was that it was quite expensive to pay for the type of mobile devices capable of harnessing the time device's signal and also build, on the fly, the tech required to successfully open a rift. Since Chase's machine had last gone to 1979, the destination would be the same when they opened the rift remotely. They would also need to be equipped with transmitters and the means to open a rift from 1979 to return to the present. Also very expensive. RuJay explained they would need to deplete their savings to do an even quarter-decent job, and even then it was risky.

"I could front most of the credits myself," RuJay said. "But what would I get in return, of equal value?"

His small dark eyes didn't twinkle, though it was easy enough to imagine them doing so.

Thus began two solid months of fucking for Sundra and Rex. RuJay was gleefully bisexual and remarkably lonely, holed up most nights in a College Point studio. It began with Sundra boarding the Papa John's Line from Midtown and riding out to Flushing, the old Asian stronghold, and taking a bus along 15th Avenue to his two-story apartment "complex." For a high-earning premium, he either spent very little or squandered his credits on things other than a living situation. The single room was bathed in a brownish light and half the size of her own studio, which meant his unmade cot, reaching nearly from wall-to-wall, dominated the space. He had a corner for kitchenware and the smell, subtle but pungent enough, was on the spectrum of rotten eggs cooked on a malfunctioning burner.

The ArteMs. helped, though she couldn't undersell just how profoundly revolting a shirtless RuJay was. On her first visit, RuJay tried music—electrohop—to "set the mood," and Sundra quickly put an end to that. She told him this needed to be done in silence if he wanted it done right. RuJay agreed. The only way they could do it sufficiently was if Sundra mounted him, which she did, eyes closed. She imagined she was sitting atop a plush toy, a novelty-sized giant rabbit, and this made her feel better as the toy came to life and grabbed—not massaged—her breasts. To call RuJay gelatinous would be an understatement. He was like a gastropod, the vast oily expanse of chest, stomach, and breasts swallowing everything beneath them so the cot itself seemed imaginary. His skin was off-white, the color of eggshells left in the sun, and sprinkled with chocolate chip-sized moles. There were patches of redness, the body straining against itself, and hair that mostly congregated in the quivering hollow between his man-breasts and around his nipples, two pink buoys in a stale cream sea. It was unfortunate he was not a premature ejaculator. Their sessions could last an hour or more, RuJay grinding in her dried out and burning vagina, murmuring unsweet nothings from his chapped lips. She ached all over. A stipulation was that RuJay would not wear a condom. Sundra was obviously taking her birth control. When he came, it was like one of those fitful water guns letting out a final burst before the supply ran dry. He sighed, sweat rolling down his punching bag cheeks, and thanked her.

This was a time for Sundra to really focus on the future, the new future, once the Plan came to fruition. Rex was right that there was no guarantee, if they succeeded, that they would arrive in a liberated world. She had watched enough shows and movies about time travel to know about unintended consequences. Yet mounting and bobbing on RuJay, eyes squeezed shut, she knew there had to be a better world, an alternative quasi-utopia just beyond their reach—anything better than how the United States of America had evolved. There were so many sins to undo. Never, in a thousand trips back in time, could she fix everything, but she could start at the root with the man who Quentin Stellar said had locked the shackles in place. Never before in history had the means existed to literally undo sin. Sundra felt blessed.

Even as she excavated his balls beneath a wall of flab to do as he wanted next—suck suck suck.

Rex's trips to RuJay were no better. RuJay wanted three weeks with each, thrice weekly, due to some obsession with the number three he wouldn't explain to them. Sundra often found herself literally and metaphorically limping away from the College Point studio, teetering at a bus stop, praying for sleep. She imagined her body was covered in slime. She imagined a broomhandle had smashed her between the legs. *It was all worth it*, she thought continuously. *It all had to be worth it.* The bus would arrive 40 minutes or so after she got there, where she'd wait among stray cats, clapboard houses, and the warped smell of Flushing Creek. All the way home she would have an image of naked RuJay stuck in her brain, either the crust dappling one of the flaps below his neck or his geyser-sized belly button. Before she went to bed, she saw his shadowy outline behind her eyelids bearing down upon her.

Rex at first thought he had drawn the lucky straw because RuJay liked talking to him. He said he really wanted to be a poet, not an engineer, but poets are unemployable. He could never live in College Point as a poet. Rex nodded. RuJay talked and ate, slathering bagels with an unidentifiable chocolate cream cheese and biting off unreasonable chunks. Rex hoped he'd escape without doing any of the things Sundra told him to expect. 30 minutes in, RuJay made his move, bearhugging Rex and taking him to the mat. He held him tight and wouldn't let go. Rex was losing breath, moaning, and RuJay freed him to finally fuck him. RuJay wasn't experienced, so he mostly missed the asshole itself, jabbing around the rim and sparing Rex real pain. *Remember the Plan, remember the Plan.* He had to be strong for Sundra.

It was a fugue of murderous sex for them both. Sundra found her thoughts, along with speech, slurring along, dripping into crevices to be momentarily forgotten and recovered later, in the dead of night. She whispered *the Plan, the Plan*, enchanting herself, disappearing as far as she could into the language. They were so close.

Part two of the Plan, on their return, would be to murder RuJay. She decided that herself and didn't inform Rex. Not that he'd disagree.

During this time, she also went to work as she normally would. No one spoke about Chase anymore. Like Quentin Stellar, he was quickly airbrushed out of history. He was more searchable—Gaggle had no problem with obituaries and tribute streams—than Stellar was, but even details were selectively and mysteriously plucked out of cyberspace to make him, paradoxically, more mythic and forgettable. It was like trying to remember how many siblings Zeus had slept with. After Hera, you kind of just went blank.

No one discussed time travel either. This was silently agreed upon. What had killed their dear leader would not be dignified by lunchtime chatter. Sundra didn't feel like talking to anyone anyway, and she ignored messages from her father. Gary wanted to stream several times and Sundra pretended to be napping. These days before the day, when RuJay would be done with his engineering and they'd be able to depart, were days she wanted to bury immediately when she woke up in the morning. They were useless, fruitless. Dumb days, dumb time.

Rex and Sundra stopped talking about what RuJay did to them. It was understood. Each of them held the nightmare of the bulk in their mind's eye, the pain that would be his own pleasure. He told Rex he was never happier. He told Sundra he loved how she smelled, even though he was never a fan of a woman's smell. She didn't ask what she smelled like to him. She shut her eyes and took it. This is what you did for someone who would make your dream possible.

When the time had passed, they met in a scrapyard on the water across from LaGuardia Airport. RuJay had steak sauce in the corner of his lip. He held, in his flushed hands, what looked like a battery charger for an automobile. Sundra had never seen someone smile so serenely into a sunset.

"What a time this was," he said. "I've never felt more connected to people. I've never felt more gratified. Thank you to the both of you."

They each tried to say something, murmuring the approximation of a sentence RuJay could have taken as a sign of respect. Sundra held the case with the weaponry. She and Rex wore thin tactical vests beneath anodyne red and blue jackets, prepared for any potential shootout with the past. They carried mobile chargers for their Gaggles—currently turned on because Sundra didn't want to arouse suspicions over a Gaggle dropping midday from the grid—so the past wouldn't cheat them of their technology. Their dummy chips were blurring their signal if law enforcement caught on.

A tear came to RuJay's eye. He was laying down the wires, fastening rings and colorful machinery together, fine-tuning knobs and interlocking nodes. In minutes, they could see the air and dust around them flowing differently, as if they were caught in a gentle whirlpool. Was anyone watching? Sundra looked around and saw no one. This was a deserted lot beyond the reach of any houses. Rex was just staring at RuJay, the overgrown slug hard at work and sweating through his khakis. RuJay was fiddling with a keyboard, his tongue peeking out of the corner of his mouth.

"I can get you to an approximate point later in 1979 than Chase died. It's going to be New York City—"

"Chase wanted to go to the Jurassic Age and ended up in Chicago, 1979. How can you be that precise?" Sundra asked.

"Easy. Because I can see where they fucked up. They had lousy engineers on the project. They probably thought I was too fat to be a good engineer. Well, I showed 'em. You'll be coming in around September, it looks like, based on the vortices and tachyon readouts. When you return, as you'll see on the watches I gave you, you'll be back one minute later. For me, it'll be like you stepped into the weeds to take a piss. For you, it'll be something much more amazing."

Sundra looked directly at him.

"Aren't you afraid of what we're going to do? How we may change history? It's possible, through no fault of my own necessarily, you'll cease to exist."

"Oh, I don't worry. You've given me so much joy these past few months. I've hated my life anyway. I die, so what? Make me into a better person in the past. Change history so I don't have to go through my front door sideways."

"We'll do our best."

The light around them began to bend and whirl. The sky was as much the ground as sky and the waters rose up to meet them. Instead of drowning upside down, or whatever it was that could've happened, they simply stayed still. RuJay was a stream of light and gone. They saw nothing they understood, patterns and color streams that had no equivalent in the English language. Rex held her hand. She felt like she was going to die or fall asleep, her brain tugged down into her throat, when the world rapidly began to recompose itself.

She blinked, and there they were. Queens, New York, 1979.

20

1979

Sundra had done her research. In 1979, there was no internet. She needed to procure a physical book of phone numbers, which she did. There were 148 people with the last name Velez in New York, New York. 12 lived within the Harlem zip code where Lolita Velez, the now young mother of Octavio Velez, lived.

Much had changed, and enough hadn't. The subways were still shit. You saw graffiti, smelled piss, maybe took in more of a marijuana stench. There were more homeless. No one had mobile devices so they either stared at papers with news or stared at the wall. It disoriented her, at least briefly, to see so many people not immersed in technology. Such boredom. Such freedom.

Rex was more fascinated. He didn't understand why the subway hadn't sold its naming rights or why there were phone booths on the street. The Manhattan skyline was very different. Rex, not a student of history, knew little of the two large towers where the Trojan Tower now stood. Sundra said terrorists would soon knock them down. Rex was worried. "How *soon*?" "Like 20 years," she replied, not looking at him.

No one paid them much attention. Everyone in 1979 seemed a bit slower, sleepier, sadder. The city was ragged and sooty. Sundra imagined she'd be in awe of the past and gawk at all the ways time had changed New York, for better and worse. It would be like traveling to a theme park.

What she found instead was how quickly she assimilated to the reality, how air was still air and water was still water and people were mostly indifferent to other people. What had changed? She knew these were free people, not slaves, and they were not bound up in a neo-feudal system. They knew nothing of the future to come or how a young woman named Sundra Glassgarden would deliver them to freedom. Soon, soon. She touched her gun case, listening for a heartbeat. The guns would talk to her.

"So there's no SoFiDieBeca in 1979?" Rex asked as the train, dubbed the

Flushing line, pulled into Times Square.

"No. That neighborhood doesn't exist here."

"Huh, funny."

The trains were actually more prompt here than in her own time. They got out and studied a subway map on the wall of the station. The map, excepting the names of train lines, was virtually unchanged, and Sundra saw it was the Lexington Avenue line that would take them to East Harlem and young Lolita Velez, pregnant with the enemy. Rex groaned that he was hungry. Sundra preferred to do the deed as quickly as possible and return to their own time to eat. With so much shit to do, she had little time for the "quick bite" Rex begged for. She saw a shack thing, what they called a newsstand, and a lineup of candy.

"You want a Hershey bar?"

"I want real food."

"Eat the fucking Hershey bar. We have a lot to do, Rex. I'll buy you chocolate steak when we get back."

"You better."

He ate the bar on the Lexington line. They sat across from a black man in a hood who stared directly at them, grinning. Sundra wondered if he somehow sensed what they were up to. He was older, maybe 50, with the cockeyed twinkle of someone who knew more than he let on. There was no air-conditioning on the train and an overhead fan beat around hot hair. Sweat creeped down her armpits. The man kept grinning.

"Man, the past really smells."

"Stop referring to it as *the past*. You look suspicious, Rex."

"Suspicious of what?"

"Think about it."

"Okay."

"Was the Hershey bar good? Everything you ever wanted?"

"A little dry, actually."

"I'll try to procure you something, well, fresher next time."

"Hey, what do you think's gonna happen to RuJay?"

"I don't know. I don't care, frankly."

"He's a bad man, but he helped us."

"Put it this way—if his world hasn't changed when we get back, we can change it for him."

"I like the sound of that."

"I think he expects that, though. He's a man with a death wish. It'd be a shame if we just ended up granting his wish."

"Yeah, a shame."

"That fucking slob...."

But her mind was elsewhere, far from RuJay's phenomenal flab. She was going to kill someone. She was going to take a life. How many murderers were there in history? A thousand? A hundred thousand? How many people could be counted on to rise to the challenge? The military kills didn't impress her. They were anonymous, men in armor killing other men in armor or dropping bombs at dots on a landscape. Here, the kill would be personal. She would have to be ready for that.

They got out at 125th Street. She knew that in 1979, they were more enthralled with the idea of gun control i.e. keeping weapons out of the hands of law-abiding citizens. In her pocket she carried a piece of paper with the addresses of the Velezes in Harlem. It would've been easier to upload them to her Gaggle and do a direct thoughtstream so she wouldn't forget them, but she did not want to attract any suspicion. This was a pre-mobile world.

Since 1979, gentrification had cycled in and out of New York City. Her parents had the benefit of the glass condo kingdoms, the influx of affluent (and free) people who drove the city's economic growth and recolonized it long after the decade they were currently tiptoeing through. Her New York, in some ways, was like this one. Tilting not up but elsewhere, a little grimier and more unbearable with each passing year, like the way your train showed up less and less frequently. It was the once handsome man gone gray and paunchy, his blood pressure too high, his knees shaky. It was the city of the country that needed saving. Who knew what else Velez's death could bring about? She could be returning to a veritable renaissance.

They made a queer pair in East Harlem, two whites dressed in tight-fitting jackets, cases in their hands. Rex whistled until Sundra told him to stop. They tried a walk-up on East 116th, the buzzer broken. From her research, Sundra knew Octavio's mother had lived with her older brother and moved out shortly after his birth. The brother was a Joaquin Velez. He was set to die in 1987 after a confrontation with a police officer in the Bronx. The officer was never charged because Joaquin, nicknamed "JoJo," was said to have been carrying a firearm.

There were risks. She knew if Joaquin was around, he would defend his pregnant sister, and he was likely to put up a real fight, even with their superior weaponry. A quick draw with a handgun could undo them. It would also attract even more attention.

On the second door, a woman in a shawl answered, and said her husband was John Velez. "A good man. He is not here. He is in heaven. Now you may leave."

It was hot in their jackets. Sundra decided to rest for a minute, lean against a light post. It was more walking than she'd done in some time. Her thighs were too tight in the pants. The old hams, Gary would say.

She envied the people here. There were no chips to track them, no metrics to gauge their "progress," and no ways to network electronically. They had jobs or didn't have jobs. They all called themselves New Yorkers or Americans. The neighborhood may have been shit, but you had the freedom to live like shit. She wiped her brow. None of these people could suspect what was to come. The instability and fear. The emergence of a new and lasting order predicated on you struggling and dying for someone else, like Chase Dimon, to survive.

And then Sundra saw her. She had studied a few old photos in a Velez biography, the boy and his mother, and she knew. Sundra and Rex had wandered near a train overpass, a rancid stretch of abandoned motor vehicles, trash heaps, and homeless. Lolita Velez passed into the shade and passed out again. She was walking quickly, moving with a purpose she should not have had for just a 21-year-old mother-to-be with nowhere, in theory, to be. Sundra had to admit to herself she was beautiful. She was going to kill a beautiful person.

But what did beauty matter against the mission, the Plan? What were artificial constructs against freedom and slavery, future and past, the absolutes that lead us to live and die? Lolita would live beautifully or die beautifully and only the beautiful death would save the lives to come. The soldier kills for country, the greater good, the abstraction of nationalism. Sundra would be killing for something far greater and less abstract. She was going to be the world's greatest soldier.

"Hey Sundra—"

"Shut up. That's her. You see?"

"Uh, that girl…"

"Yes, her. We're tailing her. It's our luck. Our destiny. Follow and don't look too suspicious. Do you know how to do that?"

"Sure."

They followed her. Sundra had a feeling Lolita Velez knew exactly who they were and that they were after her. They kept a half block behind, never losing sight, never coming too close until Sundra decided to speed the hell up. They were going to catch her now. They wouldn't wait anymore. She had enough of waiting. They were so close. She checked the handheld transporters RuJay had equipped them with to jump them back into the time fissure once the deed was done. They wouldn't stay a moment longer than they had to.

Lolita was slowing. They were gaining. She wouldn't turn around. She was making it easy. She must know. The best understand the importance of sacrifice. Lives lost for lives to be gained, and existence shows us a net positive. We hope. Rex was begging her for cues. Poor boy. When they got back, she was going to fuck his brains out in celebration.

Lolita stopped. Sundra's case rattled against the sidewalk. Rex kept turning his head like a puppy dog.

"Lolita Velez," Sundra said at last.

What else was there to say?

21

Lolita

JoJo was gone for the day. It was warm, blue skies, so I decided to walk around the neighborhood and think. I had a feeling *he'd* be around.

Why? I don't know. There's no reason for feelings. You get a stirring in your gut and go. I wanted to get out, considering I'd avoided work for a while and was eating too much because that's what the baby demanded of me.

Can you imagine having a child? Actually pushing a living thing out of you, feeling that kind of pain? I wish men had to put up with it. Let Archie push. He's a tough guy but I'd bet he'd scream.

I went down underneath the train tracks for a while. It was a full-on bum encampment. I recognized a few of them, Benzino and Jose and Mandrake the Magician, guys who always hung around and tried to get free smokes from people walking by. I nodded my head and kept going. A few called out, one said nice ass, nice ass. I kept going. The shade of the train tracks was comforting. Why did I think Archie would be here?

It's hard to admit you were abandoned. You're taught the world is lonely and cruel and all that existential shit, what JoJo said and you believe because that's logic. You ever seen the face of God? Jesus? No. Logic, logic. But you don't really *want* to believe that. You know the world is terrible if you even half pay attention to the news—Vietnam when I was a kid and the brown babies getting blown up. It's obvious when you're in kindergarten. But there's the part of you that wants to think something else, that screams *no no* and bangs against the glass. The world must be better. I'm gonna be okay because…well, I'm *me*. That's as close to logic as you get. I was born me, with my arms and my legs, and I'm not gonna suffer like *other people*. I'm not gonna be another *madre soltera* from the ghetto. I'm gonna have a husband and raise a big healthy boy and he's not gonna smell like garbage and gas everywhere. He's not gonna be in a bum camp, even if all those bums were babies once, and their mamas maybe had high hopes for them. Sometime 50 years ago those bums were kids and they weren't going to end up like bums, they were gonna be playing for the Yankees or going up to the Moon. Benzino, Mandrake, all of them.

All that possibility. I suppose I got a lot myself.

I looked at my hands, clenched them into fists, unclenched them. Why couldn't I just hate him? It'd be so much easier. He fucked me and fled. JoJo's right. JoJo's always right.

As I headed back to JoJo's place, I saw something a little funny. A block behind me were a pair of chunky gringos in colored jackets. Shifty motherfuckers, if you really asked me. I kept on my path and they kept following. They stayed a block back until I started to slow down, and then they seemed to speed up. I decided not to turn around. I didn't want to give them that. Whoever they were, they weren't worth my time, and I was not going to call JoJo for help. I could handle myself, you know? I wasn't going to do the damsel in distress shit. I heard them getting faster behind me. A pitter patter on the sidewalk. A girl's voice. Then a guy's, whinier. Two of them, one of me. I forgot my blade. But c'mon, two white people jumping a spic in El Barrio? Really? I waited, breathed in, waited a beat, and spun.

"Lolita Velez," the girl said.

I kept my mouth shut. Let her wait.

"You're Lolita Velez," she tried again. While she was talking, the guy was bending down and opening his guitar case. I saw then. They were armed to the fucking teeth.

"Yeah, and so what?"

That was history, JoJo said. White people trying to kill brown people. The eternal cycle. The white capitalist devil lusting for blood. I dunno if I can believe that all the way because Archie sure as hell, for whatever it's worth, was not a white capitalist devil.

"We've been looking for you."

"Who are you? Vice squad?"

"No. We're here to make the world a better place. You should know that."

I knew immediately I should've been running sooner. A woman across the street was already screaming when the guns were out, and pointed at me, and I couldn't really believe it, because the scene barely had any dream logic, let alone logic. The woman across the street was continuing to scream and people up here don't really scream just from *seeing* a gun. You had to see it get fired at least. That was worth a scream.

This is bullshit, I thought. My lips were starting to move. *Bullshit.*

"We're very sorry, Lolita. You have to believe that."

22

1979

The mugger was giving him a rough time.

It was something about the punks. He had begun to study their subculture, the love of aggressive tuneless music, blind worship of anarchism, and the way they desecrated their bodies. Tattoos and safety pins through skin; hair dyed sick shades of purple and green; the leather and denim shredded for effect. He hated them all. If the city was to live again, the punks would eventually have to die.

But he had to hand it to these two punks, more skinheads really. They could scrap. In Riverside Park they tried to jump an old Negro couple and Vengeance was there, waiting. He punched them both out and the couple escaped, taking a winding path out of the park. One skinhead had a switchblade and came for him, cutting the flap of his coat, not flesh. It was going as it should. He got a second punch in, an elbow to the ribs, but the second skinhead, burlier than the first, was able to smash some type of rock into his upper back. The pain was savage and he saw Lolita, saw the outline of her, the ghost of someone real. He wanted to say her name. He must have said something because they were laughing, waving their fists like guns. He had tucked away a Saturday night special and he could've used it if he were the kind of person who ended fights that way. It seemed cheap to kill or be killed by a bullet. It was the bullet judging, not man and his fists. So Vengeance breathed, licked his lips, and sprung at the laughter, pinning one of them against a tree trunk. He got his knee in the skinhead's stomach and hammered away from there. It was always fun to turn a punk's weapon against him.

Vengeance spotted a switchblade tucked in a waistband, pried it loose, and stabbed the other guy trying to hit him from the rear. Once his friend saw blood, he scattered, and Vengeance had the strip of park to himself, cars off the Hudson gurgling in his ear. What a fucking place. He needed to live to see Lolita. He would make a world they deserved.

Inside Truncheon's apartment, chugging a glass of Ballantine, he talked more than usual. He could feel night through the walls, a sibilating presence he wanted to reach out, touch, and strangle. His muscles awaited further instruction. He was inside, on a chair, in a living room with a television, Truncheon sipping a glass of orange juice on his couch. The Mets played on the TV screen. Mets Dodgers.

He found himself forgetting. He was in Riverside Park because…he wanted to get here because…the Upper West Side is diagonal to Spanish Harlem, through the land of Harlem proper, where you better come walking with more than Saturday night special. Your fists plus a militia.

"This Locka feller," Truncheon said. "He's into the drug trade?"

"Drugs, extortion, hookers. You name it. The Candies must be crushed."

"I like the ring of that."

"It's not a game. It's not Steve Garvey, the faggot."

"Garvey. A fine player. Good fundamentals."

"Locka needs to die."

"You hardly know him."

"I know what he is. What the Candies are."

Truncheon creaked upward, trudging toward the kitchen. "I'm going to butter toast. You want some?"

"No."

"I'll say this." His voice was disembodied now behind the pale wall dividing living room from single-file kitchen. "You're an answer in search of questions. You need to go do what you got to do, and stop swimming in the swill. Bad for your heart."

"Focus on your baseball. Keep the fortune cookie shit out of here."

He heard munching. The idea of butter, toast, and Truncheon's mouth made him sick. He was looking straight at the TV when Truncheon returned, his footsteps set to the soundtrack of a Lee Mazzilli base hit to left.

"It's time we talk about what it is you want."

"Focus on your writing."

"Let's focus on you, eh? Luanne's coming in for the weekend."

"You want space. Ex-wife. Rekindling. I get it."

"No, not at all." He was back on the couch. "I can't ever be with her again. It's out of the question."

"I heard they're cancelling *Kotter*."

"That's a lie. Did Big Byrd say that?"

"No."

The Mets took a rare 3–0 lead on a Youngblood double.

"You're a father now, Archie."

"I am aware."

"You want to go up there soon?"

"I plan on it. I have to tend to a few things."

"What did I once write? I remember a line, it was good, I thought of it myself. 'The future, like a snake, will wrap around you.' I was very young when I thought of that. It made sense."

"It's not that smart."

"I think we should struggle less. You won't purge the world of sin, Archie. Go uptown."

"Shut up."

Dodgers coming up to bat. Commercial break.

"We're fated to never be gods. This is our human tragedy. To know of immortality, dream of it, approach it through some artistic and athletic pursuits, and never get there. Mickey Mantle was superhuman, no? And then his legs gave out. That's how it is."

"Another obvious point."

"You should stop struggling so much. Stop hunting. The conspiracy of human existence is a conspiracy you and I can't know."

"You're a fucking conspiracy theorist yourself."

"I ponder. I wonder. I write. I don't hunt. At least, not anymore."

Garvey was up. Strike one.

"Archie, we've been at this a long time. You have. You have a chance to escape this, escape me. Go uptown. Go see her. That's all that matters. Reproduction, keeping the species alive. That's all that's been really asked of us. The rest we make up. Justice, we make up. I kill you, you kill me. The fiscal crisis, Elvis, Carter, Garvey. We make it up. We make up a system, build the prison, and lock the door ourselves."

Garvey singled to right. Archie grunted.

"The Upper West Side. Who says it's up? What's up? What's down? Guttural sounds transmogrified into language to punish us. Go to your girl."

Archie stood up.

"I'm going out."

"Taking my advice?"

"Going out, Trunch."

He fastened his coat and donned his hat. For a long second, he considered how hot he was, why he was sweating so madly, why it mattered. The TV looked thimble-sized. The apartment could be a crumb at the side of his mouth.

"You shouldn't come back for a while. I say this as your oldest friend. There isn't a point. You'll just keep struggling."

Archie shut the door without answering, taking the stairs down to the lobby. The echo made him sound like two or three people, the past and future selves linking arms for the descent. He would find Lolita. Then what? Play house? For how long? The selves were ambling and bickering, telling him to stay and go, find her and run, dive deeper into the dark to eradicate evil. Ras Locka. He didn't even know what he looked like. No one did. He never appeared before the Candies. Like a God, his message was delivered through surrogates, loyal deputies who never betrayed secrets. Lolita's brother could be one of those deputies, he suspected. JoJo moved like someone proud of the knowledge he held over other people.

Archie could find JoJo in El Barrio and pay him back. That's what this night would be for. After enough bruising, he would talk. They all do. The path to Locka runs through JoJo. This was immediately decided and solidified into fact. The lobby was swollen in beige light, the doorman Sternweiss dreamily waving as Archie pushed into the night. He was going to walk across town and take the Lexington Avenue up there. If that fucker JoJo was waiting…

Archie's body was practically crackling. He didn't like to smoke but decided to get a pack at a newsstand on Amsterdam Avenue. It was a warm night and he didn't have any interest in cutting across the park. He'd go north to 110th and take that over to the neighborhood. Easy enough.

The pack of Marlboros rattled in his pocket. He smoked one to take some kind of edge off, even though he wasn't the type of person who needed edges taken off. In fact, he preferred them. There were alternatives to this life. He could spend his nights in one of the Bay Ridge Irish bars or the pool halls, bull-shitting with the likes of Big Byrd, swapping cop memories. Watch the game on the TV. Eat sandwiches. Go back into private investigating, take it seriously enough to pay the rent, get the sink fixed, and kill the roaches for good. Hmm. The Candies would fester. He and Lolita would—what?—get a place some-where, calm like Riverdale, Jews in black coats and potbellies all around. He'd join a reform Democratic club. Lolita could settle into some easy gig in the city, steady pay, secretarial work if she wanted it. Or nothing at all. She could do nothing. That'd be fine with him. He could win bread for her and the kid. To get out his frustrations, he could take up boxing.

Meanwhile, like any good gringo, he could feel the Upper West Side warping into Harlem, the desperation gradually swallowing the attainment. The flagstones showed cracks, scuffs. Burger wrappers floated off overflowing, long ignored corner cans. The last white faces flashed on 90th street, then gave way to black. The Jew from Long Island in him was wary, even if Archie suffocated him long ago. He was afraid of nothing, not even JoJo with a gun to his head. JoJo could be beat.

Everyone could.

He was done with the cigarette and stamped it out. He flicked a dime at a bum listing from a shattered bench near 110th. The bum's eyes swam up and down, missing the silver coin at his feet. Archie did not look to see if it was pocketed. Getting rid of the money was enough. He had so little regard for currency. If he could, he'd buy the bum his house.

The moon was patchy and enormous, an ill shade of milk-orange over northern Manhattan. A ghetto blaster played a disco song he didn't know from the park. Reefer stink curled around him. It made him want to sleep. Up ahead, a kid was fucking with a fire hydrant, trying to get it to spray around. He was laughing in that caterwauling way only the people with nothing else to give the world laugh. The water wouldn't spew. Archie should've told him to cut it out, but he didn't really have the energy. He was more tired than he expected. The city heaved, slowed, asked him to stop. He was 25 blocks away from the apartment. He had never been inside, never known where she and JoJo retreated at night. Any minute, he guessed, he'd be slipping out of the dark and they'd continue where they left off. It was foregone, foretold. He just had to wait. There were empty benches on 110th and 5th Avenue, around the circle. Defying the brain that told him to keep walking, get up there already, he sat down and felt his consciousness collapse.

He saw it was 1955 and they needed him. Podres was sick. Couldn't pitch. Could young Archie London take the mound on such short notice? Game 7 of the World SERIES against the Yankees, in Yankee Stadium, where the Dodgers never win. Archie was going to do it. He was pitching a shutout when in stepped Lolita Velez, holding a bat the size of a goalpost. She said to pitch the fucking ball. When he did, he was falling, oozing, drip drip drip as rain down on gray old New York. They were singing "So Long, Frank Lloyd Wright." He was dripping. JoJo found him on his shoetops, wiped him down, flushed him away. He was years into the future, old and dying, where had the world gone, he asked. Where? *Where?* A bullet was caught in his heart. He could see it. He could see himself losing life. Up above was a man in a chair. He was floating, watching. Archie was angry he got to watch. He wanted to switch, to be in the chair, to never die. *Are you an angel?*, he asked. *No, I'm nothing like that.* The chair ascended. *I am here to watch you die, and that is all. You can ask nothing else.* The man was Truncheon. He was traveling eternally, enjoying the rebirth and destruction of the universe. Archie looked up at the tree canopies. Heaven? Hell? Lolita homered to right, the Yankees won, the Dodgers stayed in Brooklyn, they had to keep avenging and avenging losses. Archie was taking the bullet out. *I'm here, give me the chair.* The chair would not come back. Even with the bullet out, he would die. He held it between his fingers, squeezed, and saw the blood rolling, his life in miniature. *All the nights we'd harmonize till dawn, I never laughed so long.* The ballgame was over.

Eyes open, mouth dry, he saw he was on a bench, by a park, in the same year he fell asleep. Night had turned to day. Harlem. He figured it out soon enough: it was morning, and he had slept all night. No one had apparently tried to mug him. Talk about a miracle. He stood up, returning to himself. His back throbbed from where the rock had hit him earlier. He was damn tired. The dreams weighed heavily on him. Steps uncertain, breaths slow. Pigeons wheeled overhead, bright in kaleidoscopic sunlight. He remembered uptown. The word was dribbling from his lips. If they came for him now, in this moment, he'd be dead. No time to reach for his blade or gun. Too slow. He was still looking for chairs and bullets, godheads in the clouds. Truncheon was probably asleep after watching TV all night. He saw a truck run a red light, nearly kill four Latin kids, and he could only blink, one eyelid at a time.

At a bodega he bought a black coffee, even though he hated coffee, and slugged it down. The guy behind the counter was smoking a cigar and reading the *Post*.

"You know any Velez?" Archie found himself asking.

"Yeah, so?"

"I'm looking."

"Well, if they wanna find you, they'll find you."

They. He hated thinking of them as a unit. There was Lolita and her scum brother. Impressive scum, but scum nonetheless. He would have to be taken care of. This was not in doubt. He would find Lolita and get her out of here. Then, when she and the baby were in a safe place, maybe upstate, he'd come back for JoJo. There was no other way. It was the opposite of a Truncheon novel, where the threads never tied together and drowning in enigma and paranoia was the point, what gave the Ivy League critics their modest hard-ons. There would be a showdown. He told the guy thanks anyway and headed back out on the street.

It was warming up. The blocks melted away, one after the other, rotors in his brain spinning. Why had he been hiding from her at all? His strength was trickling back. This wasn't so hard. He would need time to kill the Candies, kill Locka. This she would need to understand. When the time was right, when it was safe for their child, he would stop. Purge sin first. The problem was the police. You defeat the gangs, then there's the NYPD, the ultimate degenerate paramilitary. He would have to force them to stand down. She told him JoJo dreamed of a world without police and this Archie could agree with, though for very different reasons, not to usher in a deluded anarchist utopia, where the mutts and scum would own the streets, JoJo their pied piper. The police just needed to go because they were as fat with sin as the gangs. For the city to have life again, to be a place for humanity, they needed to go. Easy enough. He had time. Give him a decade and it'd be done. He believed all of this.

For a mile, he was the only white face. It was something he had grown used to in his travels across the changing city. He'd bust a skull of any skin color. What was the point of race? There was good and evil, light and shit.

The shit was in the soil.

One problem, at least, was that he found himself no closer to Locka. No clues had turned up. He could be hiding anywhere, nowhere. There were rumors of temporary refuge in Venezuela or Cuba. He was a friend of the Castros. Or no, he went to the South to kick a bad heroin addiction. He could be dead already, with stand-ins conducting his business, a class of thugs uniting to make the whole Locka. He did not know what Locka looked like. He had to come back to this irrefutable point—if Locka walked down Park Avenue right now, naked with his dick swinging between legs, Archie wouldn't know.

Yet JoJo would. He believed wholeheartedly in JoJo. A kid with answers, at home with terror. Was Lolita right? Was he good, somehow? Lolita was blood. Blood always has a way of clouding logic.

He smelled the reefer. A church storefront had been smashed in, plywood and bible pages and triangles of glass twinkling on the pavement. There was a man in a wheelchair, bandana over his eyes, giggling. The reefer mingled with the scent of fresh dog shit. He saw a yellowed "Re-Elect Rangel, Our Congressman" sign pasted over the window of a bodega. Still, the sky was deeply and heartfelt blue. He was hot in his coat, even if it was autumn. Indian summer. When he was a kid, they played the World Series in weather just like this. This was the only weather for baseball, for anything. He passed a row of out of order parking meters. There was ample space for vehicles.

His heart began to speed up. Lolita's place—JoJo's place—was only five blocks north. He had forgotten what it was to be nervous. It was a common biological reaction to the fear of death. Or change. Death and change, two heads of the same hydra. We are all transitioned from life to death, making that transition as we speak, think, hope. Who transitions first, who goes last? Conga lines to infinity. He needed a drink. Another bodega thankfully came into view, ELROY TOBACCO CORP, and he went in for a Coke. He felt the need to consume substances.

Typically, his body cycled through various stages of rejection, turning down sustenance for more time spent alone, tensing for the next clash. There were always more. Now, with a conclusion in sight, he was feeling the disadvantages of his humanity. Fear, thirst, hunger. Anticipation. Boredom. Love. A dog, chained to a fire hydrant, barked apologetically. He stepped into the sun, the Coke can crushed underfoot. Three blocks now.

He walked faster, resisting the jog, the full on sprint. As a boy he sprinted around imaginary bases, stretching doubles into triples. The ball would hit the gap and the announcer, usually a rube from the South, would assume Archie London was going to stop at two, but no, he was *still running*, dashing for third like a madman, and here came the throw in from, let's say, Musial, and Archie slid spikes up like his father said Ty Cobb used to, monsoon of dust swallowing his jersey. The umpire roared safe and the crowd, his crowd, surged, the applause like 50,000 kisses to every pore of his body.

He was happiest at that time imagining crowds.

The gunshots and the screaming were alien before they were real. You heard a lot of them in the city and didn't believe them because, invariably, they had little to do with you. Harlem, Coney Island, wherever—erupting with disconnected screams. The full spinning wheel of human emotion. He turned on Lenox toward the female sound. There were no sirens accompanying it because the cops, budget-slashed, didn't go up there unless they had to.

He started to run. By the time he was sprinting and the screaming had stopped, he knew whom the sound belonged to. There was the option, in the final seconds before he arrived, to not believe it, to turn back and return to simple darkness. Beating thugs. Putting Candies in comas. There was a world there.

All he needed to do was stop running.

"Archie," Lolita said to him, the blood running from her stomach. "Archie."

By the time he drew his gun to kill the people who had done this, they were vanishing in a cloud of smoke, like the comic book wizards of his lost youth.

23

21st Century

"I shut my eyes and imagine I'm dying."

"There's an opening line for your book."

"I close them tight and try to lose myself in the blackness. I go back to my childhood. New York City then was a city of death. You felt it everywhere."

"It's different now. Death is concealed."

"Yes, Devora. It was an honest city then. Now we tuck the slime way. It's all below the surface, slipping through the soil of premium neighborhoods. Back then, we just said ghettos."

It was night now and Ulivia was tired. She was pouring wine, another glass for each, and begging in her mind to be let go. Tonight she would sleep in the quarters attached to the estate, making it three weeks since she had last seen her family. She was lucky to be here, however, and would not dream of complaining. There was another batch of truffles to serve.

"Dishonest, honest. Who cares? Don't answer that. I know you do."

"Tell me, why do you think people want to kill me?"

"You're pretty."

"And?"

"You made another mode of life possible, as you said. You saved the country."

She was smirking at him. He drank, rather than sipped, his wine.

"What do you *think* of me, Devora? Really?"

"Oh, I just adore you. We all do."

"Cut the bullcrap for once. Drop the mask. Let's be honest."

"But why? Why must we? For your benefit?"

"For a better world, a better nation. Extinguish the democratic lie once and—"

"Let the titans lead, squash the pygmies."

"Not quite. I want to lift everyone up, ultimately. But I don't want to just continually dangle myths in front of people."

"You would like to be a god, wouldn't you?"

"What do you mean?" He was back to sipping.

"I mean, you are no longer a young man. Out of office, out of power. You see this indignity of mortality, these limitations imposed upon you. You see a system devised that didn't go nearly far enough. You think, *how unfair. Must I decay like everyone else?* There are scientists who are sure we will be able to upload our consciousness to a cloud and then download it into a fresh body. How wonderful that would be. We could forever elude death."

"I don't know where you're going with this."

"What I am trying to say is don't fret so much for immortality." She took a hard bite into a truffle, treating it like bone. "Because you can't have it. No one can. No memoir will save you. No economic system will save you. No presidency will save you."

"I never would've thought Devora Dimon could lapse into such faux profundities. *We're all gonna die.* I get it. I really do. You've helped me plenty here but I really should get going. It's so nice to see old friends, though."

"I was always fascinated by you because—I used to even tell my dim-witted husband this—you were so good at playing different roles. Life is little more than playacting, whether we pretend to be friends, lovers, enemies, mothers. Most of us can only do one or two at a time. I chose to do one or two and then, one day, none. But you, Octavio…you were special. You were a convincing statesman, friend, father, husband, son. I can see you as a one-year-old sucking your mother's breast. I can see you at six clutching her, asking about this strange land called California. I can see you alone in the White House, dying to know what your future will be. It would be so much easier if we could know. We can travel back in time, why not forward?"

"It has something to do with tachyons and dark matter, not exceeding the point of origin, I dunno. We had physicists who knew well enough."

"A god gazes into the future. A man does what? Squints in the dark?"

"I'm going to go. We'll do this again."

"Don't you want me to write you a check? Isn't there some conscience-soothing foundation I'm supposed to underwrite with my husband's money?"

"The Velez Foundation is doing fine."

"I love the logo by the way. The sweeping blue V. It reminds me of the first campaign."

"V for Victory."

"I do love the letter V. You have two points, apart, and they later converge in such pretty symmetry. The most attractive letter. I sometimes think we live in nothing more than a series of convergences. Me here, you there, and *poof*, our destinies intertwined. How did it happen? How can we know? Not even our time travel machines can tell us."

"Maybe they can."

"Oh I don't know. Sometimes I think, why not put you out of your misery? So terrified of one of the aggrieved rising up and killing you. It would be better, I think, if I could do it myself, at least to alleviate your stress. Our age of terror has taught us to fear the random assassin, the suicide bomber, the lone gunman, so much that we fear everyone and everything. The virus of fear eats away. If I confirmed the fear at least, I would remove the uncertainty…"

Octavio stood up. His hands were hard at his sides, like he was looking to punch something but couldn't.

"I don't know what the hell your problem is."

"*My problem?* I'm as happy as a clam. You know that."

"If it weren't for your money, people wouldn't give you the time of day. They'd call you deranged and keep walking."

"There you go again, submerging yourself in hypotheticals. Why not just *do* it already? Whatever it is you wish to do. End our pseudo-democracy. Kill me. Siphon a billion from the Velez Foundation. That's the problem with fear— it leads to so much bluster, so much incapacitation and moral constipation. Let's have another *war* to stop it, the terror. Better yet, let's turn the clock back and make a better world. Did you ever consider that, Octavio? My husband went back to another century to give our son an unforgettable pre-bar mitzvah present. You could've actually changed something."

Octavio was still standing, frozen.

"I consider everything, Devora."

"Then you're simply a coward."

"I came here to discuss my memoir, and here you are insulting me."

"I think you impose too much meaning on things. You know God is dead, so you wish to frame reality on your terms. You don't have the courage to be God, but as the world's best playactor, you will play it long enough. I just want to know when you'll stop playing."

Octavio was walking toward the French doors. Ulivia was hastily opening them.

"I'll be seeing you," he said.

Still seated, Devora was smiling. Beyond the doors she could see a pair of secret service emerge to take their boy away. He looked so slight next to them. She gently shook her head.

Poor, poor boy. He came so close.

"Oh Octavio, please let me at least make a check out for the foundation. Otherwise, we've just wasted the hours, haven't we?"

He turned around. "Right. What value is time if we're not monetizing it?"

"Let me get my finance people on it. What is it you'll need? Anything at all."

"I don't need anything. You know that."

The two agents were circling, motioning to leave. They were deeply uncomfortable here, even with their weaponry and training.

"Tell your men to not be so skittish. I didn't make a real threat. You'd know it if I did."

"They know we're old friends. Blood is thicker than water, and friendship trumps blood."

"There's our Octavio. Tell Nivea I say hello."

He was nearing the stairwell, not looking back. Hearing his wife's name from her lips unnerved him, though they all had met many times.

"I will."

It was only at the bottom of the stairwell, with the front entrance in sight, that Octavio Velez felt less of himself. First it was a thought—*I am lighter*—and then the thought trailed off like an echo. He saw his feet, his hands, and then they were gone. He saw and thought nothing. The agents wavered, trying to bring hands to firearms, but found there were no hands and no guns. Devora, walking over to the stairwell, saw her gargantuan atrium was empty.

"Someone beat you to the punch, Octavio. That was always your real fear. You were right to be scared."

Ulivia ran up behind her.

"Miss Devora, what's the matter?" she asked.

"Everything or nothing. I don't know yet."

Devora gazed at the spot where Octavio and his agents had been.

"Where did they go?"

"Go?" She had to chuckle. "They never *were*."

24

1979

His great-grandfather and great-grandmother looked so young. They were, barely 40, and set to raise a new boy who shared their blood.

"Call me mom," great-grandmother Georgine said. "Call me dad," great-grandfather Paul said.

Both were dead before Devlin was born, so he still thought of them as ghosts, even as they were showing him his room in the Forest Hills co-op he would have to call home. They were each lawyers. He barely understood what lawyers were for. That kind of knowledge was always left to dad.

"Oh, with Charlie off to college, it's no trouble at all, you staying here. We have plenty of space."

Grandpa Charlie. Off to college. He died when Devlin was nine. Heart attack. Maybe he should tell Georgine and Paul. Maybe not.

"You like chicken pot pie, sport? No one in America whips up a pie like Georgine."

This was his land, it had to be. There was no other land. He would be an orphan eternally.

The one person in this time he felt he could talk to was actually dead. She was not even a living ghost, like his great-grandmother and great-grandfather, winking that he could try a *little* white wine when they watched the ball drop for New Year's. A Dimon tradition.

"Our family tree is so marvelous. We didn't even know Paul had a cousin Chase. Second cousin, third cousin?"

"I don't know," Devlin would say repeatedly, losing interest.

"Well, that's okay. You'll just love Charlie. Do you like football?"

"No."

"That's okay."

The sunny, sad people. He wanted to know where they had buried Lolita. He didn't know how to find out. There were a lot of cemeteries in Queens.

Apparently Queens was the land of the dead. Could be she ended up there. Anything was possible.

He stopped caring about his Gaggle. Since it didn't work, and never would again, it was just another appendage in his life he didn't need. One day, he walked out on Austin Street and threw it into traffic. Watching a truck crush it to bits gave him fleeting joy.

In the winter, they were going to enroll him in school. No one could find his transcripts from his old school anywhere and Cousin Chase was of no help because he died, orphaning poor cousin Devlin Dimon. Paul thought he was a smart kid and should try to take the test for Stuyvesant when it came up in the fall. Georgine argued he should just go to school right away, get to know the nice neighborhood boys at Forest Hills High. Devlin offered no opinion.

He deliberately ensured he would make no friends because they were living ghosts too, likely dead or trending toward death (well, everyone is, technically) in his old world, the real world of the present that, to Paul and Georgine, must have been an unfathomable future. Why bother? He went to the park sometimes and watched pick-up basketball games, Jew on Jew, brown skin on brown skin, everyone sticking to their cliques. There were no cliques for him. That was simple enough to understand. They were ghosts. He was alive.

"I miss her," he found himself saying out loud one day, running his fingers along a fence outside the park. "Why did she have to die?"

It was almost dinnertime. Georgine couldn't text him because Gaggles didn't exist. There were so many ways to remember you weren't from here.

But he would live. He would adjust. The light and air and language were the same. Three dimensions. Pain as pain. He took a deep breath. Look around. Something told him to take a step forward. One more. The future would come. He would arrive, however it came, as himself. The snake would take hold. It would crush him tighter and tighter and it would be up to his own animal instinct to resist. To thrive.

There was a world in front of him to conquer. He walked toward the basketball court, flexing his fingers, ready to score.

25

21st Century

Rex was bleeding from his left pectoral and thigh. Sundra could tell they were nonfatal wounds but the way he bellowed out for help made her wonder if he finally understood something she didn't.

When they returned, Rex's blood-soaked hand clenched to his blood-soaked chest, RuJay was gone. Her watch said they had only come back three minutes after they left, yet there wasn't a trace of that piece of shit. Thank God. That made up for Rex's cheap tactical vest failing.

"We'll get you to a hospital," she said, firing up her Gaggle to check for the nearest medical facilities. She knew Queens to be particularly barren. Rex deserved to get help and live—he had done the job.

History would show Sundra orchestrated the Plan to liberate the future and fired what could have been, in theory, the death shot. She knew that wasn't really true. Rex had his assault rifle up before her and fired first, riddling the Velez womb with more than enough bullets to end it all. The mother was going to die. Sundra was momentarily stunned. She wasn't pulling the trigger. Rex had been unafraid. And then the peculiar man in the trench coat emerged, the mysterious ugly duckling who could've been Joaquin except he was white and clearly not anywhere near his 20's. He reached into his jacket and pulled a gun. Sundra activated the device to get them out of there. It took several seconds for a fissure to open and for their disappearance to be complete. That was enough time for Sundra to fire her own single round, to mostly spray the sidewalk, and for two bullets to strike Rex. One missed his heart but came close enough. The other was a flesh wound around the thigh. They were gone before a third bullet could hit him.

College Point, RuJay's neighborhood, looked the same. It was quaint and ragged and no one was outside. Sundra turned on her Gaggle, also unchanged, and hunted for her cab app. If she did a thoughtsync, she could just think of a cab and summon one, but that was not important right now. Staunching Rex's bleeding—and finding out just how free she was—mattered most. She swiped for a cab. The nearest, according to her Gaggle, was a Surge cab. Velocity never signed a deal with Surge so in her past life she could only ride with Mecha, another company. Now, though...now she was free. Free to purchase. Free to choose whatever to call herself.

"Sundra, it hurts."

"We'll get you to a hospital soon, honey."

"Am I gonna die?"

"No."

"Good, good."

Good, good...the Gaggle was telling her that due to her employment contract with Velocity Ventures, she was only permitted to hail cabs from Mecha. The Surge cab would not pick her up. She stared at the screen. Rex was asking what was going on and she could barely hear him. The words on the screen were taking on their own reality—as light, laughter, rage, anything. She could not focus.

Due to your employment contract...due to your employment contract...

"Hey Sundra," He was peering dumbly over her shoulder. "What's wrong?"

Due to your employment...

"We could probably get a Mecha soon, they come around Queens sometimes, we just gotta..."

Due to your employment...

She did hear the sirens. They slashed open the lukewarm afternoon and bled it out. She was standing still, or walking, when the first squad car pulled up. When the second arrived, the first officer was out, taking hold of Rex. He was asking what the hell happened here but Sundra wasn't listening. "What is this, we saw something funky on our scanners and...and..."

Can you drown outside of water? Can you kill yourself by force of will alone?

"....We saw, miss, you and your wounded friend here, miss, excuse me, that we weren't picking up any employment chip inside of you even though our scanners told us you are Sundra Glassgarden, correct, contracted to Velocity Ventures, very impressive granted, but you've somehow deactivated your chip and we're going to have to take you down to the precinct, miss, and don't worry, we will get your friend medical attention..."

How can this be? How, how, how, how, how, how, how, how, how, how, how...

"Miss, excuse me, just come over here, Officer Tryon here will, miss, are you alright, what are you trying to…”

How how how how how how how how how how how how how…

“…a class B felony if we found you knowingly deactivated your employment chip or implanted a dummy, but that's something we can sort out down at the precinct if you'd just come….”

She was outside, and suddenly she was here. She was sitting in the back of the squad car next to a bandaged Rex. They whirred through College Point to downtown Flushing.

“Quite a haul of weapons you two had,” the officer driving said. “All legal, we checked it out. But what in hell were you folks up to?”

Up to. A game, a lark, a prank. All of her life given to this. She took life to come back here and find it wouldn't have mattered if she never woke up this morning.

“Where do I work?” she asked, of all people and things, her fucking Gaggle. It was expedient.

“Hey Sundra, you are a quality assurance technician at Velocity Ventures, LLC, of course.”

“And who is my boss?”

“Hey Sundra, the chief executive officer and founding partner of Velocity Ventures, LLC, is Devlin Dimon, of course. Date of birth July 12, 1966, eye color hazel, blood type O positive—”

The kid. That kid.

“Alright quiet that thing down back there. We're gonna have to do a sweep of your metadata when we get inside the precinct. Just protocol, miss.”

There's no Chase, but there's Devlin. No Chase, but Devlin.

“Sundra, what's wrong?”

She was sick and already dead, alive on a technicality. Soon she would be dead. They all would. No matter what, there was an end. Kill all the pregnant women you want, and still find the future right in its place, bearing down upon you, or you rushing blindly into it, the maelstrom of profundities and plots and pieties amounting to the lonely death, always your own.

“Why are you laughing?”

She had another question.

“Officer, tell me about our greatest president, Octavio Velez.”

“Uh, who?”

“Velez. The Age of Velez. Tell me about him.”

“I don't know who…”

"Tell me."

Before they forcefully removed her Gaggle in the station and locked her in an interrogation cell, she performed a final search. She asked for a certain president of the United States of America credited with restoring order and dignity to the United States of America. She offered the years he might have served. The Gaggle answered. The Gaggle always had an answer.

"Sundra, the president of the United States was Joaquin London. President London is credited with advancing a system of—"

"That's all I need. Thank you for your assistance, as always."

Sundra thought the precinct looked nice, for a precinct at least.

"My little people," she said to no one in particular, offering her wrists for the handcuffs. They locked as tight as they should.

Rex kept asking why she was laughing and she just wouldn't tell him. He wanted to know the joke too.

26

1979

Ronald Truncheon started reading the newspapers again. The murder rate had spiked over the past week, the *Post* and *News* dutifully noted. They were mostly gang affiliated kills, so less to worry about, as opposed to a psychopath stalking young lovers in the midst of a make-out sesh. The police so far had no leads. Among the dead was Joaquin Velez, 24, who was the brother of Lolita Velez, 21, also dead. Archie's Lolita. They found Joaquin bloated and blue in the East River.

He had an idea, a good idea, of who did it. He hadn't seen Archie in a week until, two minutes ago, there was a knock on his door. And like that, his high school pal was back in his living room in the usual costume.

He looked worse. Haggard, owl-eyed, smelling subtly like the meat and cheese aisle of a Key Food. But he hadn't been eating. He had been smoking.

They both knew what happened, and they let that hang fat between them. Archie scratched at his face and went to chug ginger ale straight from the bottle. When he was finished, he sat in Truncheon's TV chair, and Truncheon took the sofa. Against all odds, Archie spoke first.

"I had them both. I could've killed them."

"Yes, there is always an alternative to what was done. That's the hellishness of being alive."

"I heard her screaming. I ran. There were two of them. The guy had shot her. The girl was shooting, rubbing it in. I had a kill shot on the guy and missed his heart by an inch."

"What happened to them?"

"They vanished. They were real or weren't real. They were demons, but I know they weren't. Of this world, and not. I was eventually shooting through the air. People saw. They killed her and disappeared completely."

He saw that Archie was shaking. His hands were clenched on his knees and the veins flared beneath his skin. He was staring into the carpet, looking for the murderers there. If Truncheon were the type of person to do this, he would go over to Archie and put his arm around his shoulder, like Pee Wee supposedly did for Jackie. It would be one of those moments. But he wasn't that type of person.

"They were gone."

"Archie, this doesn't mean anything, I know, but I'm sorry."

"Sorry…what can you be sorry for…you did nothing. You were in this fucking apartment."

"I know. It's just a customary word. I'm sorry for that, too."

"She was alive when she saw me. I held her. Her eyes had little tear drops in them. The blood was pouring out of her. I wanted to shove it all back in. I held her."

"Archie…"

"I held…" He was about to stand up, but decided against it. "When she was gone and our kid was gone, when I knew there were only things to be gone, and nothing to come into this irredeemable shitstain planet, I ran. If I stopped, I was going to kill someone. I ran to the water."

"The instinct when someone has taken something is to take it back. I wish you got to bring justice to those who did this. I don't know what it'll mean, ultimately, because the dead are dead, but we can want what is not rational. That's only fair."

Truncheon stood up to bring him some more ginger ale. It seemed like a thing to do. He handed it to Archie and he knocked the glass to the carpet. They left it there, watching the soda turning the carpet dark brown. Truncheon only felt sorrier for him, though he wouldn't articulate this. The most important things are left unsaid. That's why these books are a great waste.

"Her brother blamed me. I understood. I was by the East River, walking through an empty warehouse by the pier. You always find people in this city, diseased city, and he found me."

"Joaquin Velez?"

"He was going to kill me. I was going to let him. I even asked him to. He came at me, no weapons, just his fists. Strong fucking kid. I kept pace for a bit but he knocked me straight through the side of a wall, this flimsy sheet metal shit. No pigs nearby, just me and him."

"Jesus, Archie."

"He was beating me to death. I stopped blocking. The punches all rolled together into a wave and I was getting taken down. If I went down far enough into the deep, I would see Lolita again. I was going to choke on my own blood."

"You're here."

"We were by the pier, by the water. It was starting to rain and the wind was blowing hard off the river. He was having a hard time keeping his hands on me. Something inside me didn't want to die. I wanted to die, but something else didn't. It just told me to continue. Persist."

"You listened."

"JoJo was screaming at me, said I had done it, killed his sister, that I was a rapist and a colonist murderer and he was going to put me in hell and keep me there. He wanted to lock the gates of hell on me. I believed him. I respected his hatred."

"You respected the intensity."

"The belief. We live in a weak world without belief. No convictions. JoJo was good. He believed until the end."

Archie breathed in.

"It was all over. I was at the edge of the pier. I was ready to fall back into the water. One or two more kicks and I was ready. I wanted to lose my breath. I was resisting what was telling me to persist. I was going to win over it."

"I'm glad you're here."

"JoJo was barely visible in the rain. I heard him, saw his shadow move closer. It was dark and the blood and rain were swirling in my mouth. I accepted the taste. I accepted all of it. This is what I am."

"And then you lived."

"The pier gave way. The wood was old, rotting and soaked. JoJo must have gotten the worst fucking plank. His leg shot right through. The rest collapsed with it and you had a hole. There was a bang I barely heard, wet bone on bad wood, and the splash. He must've hit his head on a beam down below. I went over and called out to him. He needed to live."

"Shit luck," Truncheon said.

"He went right down. I saw the waves and he was gone. No hand reaching up. He shot down into the river. I was going to go with him, see what he found. We could both learn about death. But the fucking voice. *Persist, persist.* My section of the pier was shifting. I sprung up, sidestepped the hole, and ran for land. I threw up on South Street. I threw up everything I had, Coke and scrambled eggs."

"You needed to cleanse."

"I didn't eat for a while. I needed to see what came next. What the purpose of this was."

"An immortal couldn't figure that out, Archie."

"I thought about it. I went home. I even paid my rent to the fucking Greek. I sat in my room and thought about it."

"The Greek must be happy."

"I thought about Lolita and JoJo. I thought about a world that didn't deserve them."

"Does the world deserve any of us?"

"I thought about the baby. A boy. It was going to be a boy."

"I didn't know this."

"She never told me what she was going to name him."

"You didn't ask."

He looked away.

"I would have named him Joaquin."

"You're thinking, someday, of trying for another then."

He still hadn't turned back to look at Truncheon.

"Redemption this way," Archie said, softly.

"Redemption."

They fell quiet for a moment. Truncheon considered the depths of the word, its greatness and its horror.

"Why? Fatherhood…it won't change anything. Nothing will change. We will die and nothing will change."

Archie stood up, looking toward the door. He felt hungry for the first time in days.

"I'm going out," he said.